THE SWIMMING POOL

THE SWIMMING POOL

Frances Paige

This first world edition published in Great Britain 1999 by
SEVERN HOUSE PUBLISHERS LTD of
9–15 High Street, Sutton, Surrey SM1 1DF.
This first world edition published in the U.S.A. 1999 by
SEVERN HOUSE PUBLISHERS INC of
595 Madison Avenue, New York, N.Y. 10022.

British Library Cataloguing in Publication Data

Paige,   Frances
          The swimming pool
          I.   Title
          823.9'14 [F]

          ISBN 0-7278-2271-3

Typeset by Hewer Text Ltd
Edinburgh, Scotland.
Printed and bound in Great Britain by
MPG Books Ltd, Bodmin, Cornwall.

Prologue

I came off the train into the warm night, into the station yard lit by lamps which hung like moons in the darkness. In the shadows beyond I could see the name of the hotel necklaced by coloured lights, '*La Bonne Étape*'. How often, long ago, it seemed, the four of us had dined there when Chloë and Rick had met Ben and myself off the same train.

I looked around. The forecourt seemed deserted, and because of the high lamps and the straight lines of fencing round the square bulk of the station, it had the look of an Edward Hopper painting. Two figures were emerging from the shadows. One, a woman, had her arms outstretched towards me. I started forward, calling, "Chloë! Oh, Chloë . . .!" I swayed, felt dizzy and sick, and then I knew I was enveloped by strong arms and that Rick's voice was in my ears.

"Miranda! Hey! Did I startle you? You're shaking!"

I released myself, putting my hand to my face, trying to smile. "I must be tired. It's been a long journey, and then for a second I thought . . . never mind. How are you bearing up, Rick?" I looked into his dark face – he would be tanned, of course. I couldn't expect him to look pale.

"Well, you can imagine, all the arrangements for the funeral, and the terrible loss – you've been through it too. Come along, it's over here." He took my case, put his arm round my shoulders as he guided me to the far corner of the forecourt where his car was parked. I was still trembling. His arm tightened as if to support me.

"I couldn't believe it," I said. "Someone like Chloë . . . so alive . . . so much to give . . ." He didn't speak as he helped me in.

1

When he had stowed away my luggage and was sitting beside me, he turned, his dark face came close. "I need someone like you, Miranda. It's good of you to come."

"I wanted to. I was desolated when I heard the news. And I had a month's leave due in any case. I thought if there was anything I could do . . ."

"Your presence is enough." He leant forward and kissed me briefly, a thank you kiss. "Knowing that you were coming has been my mainstay." He drew away and put his key into the ignition. "You're sure you want to stay in your house alone? I made arrangements as you asked, but . . ."

"Oh, yes, I'm used to that in London." I was beginning to dismiss that strange moment when I thought I'd seen Chloë coming towards me. It had been the long journey, the sad news, memories . . .

He started up the engine and we glided past the hotel with its glittering sign. So it had been often for the four of us . . .

One

We met Chloë and Rick when we first arrived in France in the spring of 1993. Ben, my husband, had been appointed Research Engineer in an aeronautical firm in Toulouse, and Rick, who was a house agent, had found us a house near their own in the little village of Meloir twenty miles or so north of the city. We became friends immediately.

They were both English but had lived in France for years. Chloë had a French mother, and her fair hair, brown skin and slanted brown eyes, her smile, were very French. How to describe a French smile except that it was enchanting, one-sided, sophisticated, not the toothpaste smile of so many of her English counterparts. Seductive . . .

We had a lot in common. We were of an age, and both our husbands were ambitious and personable. There was no poaching. I was researching on the crusading families of the Duchy of Aquitaine, and while Quercy at the beginning of the twelfth century was inclined to think of the antics of French and English kings as irrelevant, there was always Raymond IV, Count of Toulouse to contend with, a powerful and persuasive man. I was in my element, absorbing and collating, and Chloë helped me with translations of medieval French in the books I bought, or borrowed from the Cahors or Toulouse libraries.

Our house hadn't a pool, and the Gillams said we could use theirs any time we liked. In that hot summer three years ago we often finished our day swimming there, and dining at either of our houses or in the local restaurant, *Le Repos*, which put on a good meal – rich country soups and cassoulets, chicken, duck, omelettes dotted with *cèpes*, a satisfying if rough *vin du pays*.

Happy days. Those warm evenings – French evening air seems like velvet on one's skin, the fireflies glancing over the pool, the sound of the cicadas. It's all been said before, and warm summer evenings in England are equally enchanting, except that they lack that . . . foreignness. We talked endlessly, we laughed, we were carefree, no problems beyond trivial anxieties about work – Chloë helped Rick in his office at Cahors – and no children as yet. We were, the four of us, on the right side of thirty, too young to have problems about ageing parents.

It was an idyllic life. Occasionally I drove to Toulouse with Ben, but as my research deepened and my enthusiasm grew, I found Cahors further north to be a better centre – a walled town with the hint of South in its old bones, its wide Gambetta Square, its graceful bridge across the Lot. Sometimes Chloë would take a day off, and in my sturdy little Deux Chevaux we would drive around what I began to think of as part of my territory. Ever since we had spent family holidays in this region I had felt a rapport with it. I had only to cross the Channel to remember the old Vauxhall, the excitement of Customs, the drive off at Dieppe, to feel the magic once again. I remember one conversation Chloë and I had as we sat above the ruins of the château, ancient property of the Cardaillac family.

"It's a real medieval landscape," I said. "It's easy to picture it peopled with knights in armour, the red cross on a white tabard over their chain-mail, their ladies weeping as they bade them goodbye. And yet," I was babbling on, "strange to think that an ancient place like Saint Cirque Lapopie was the haunt of the Surrealists – André Breton and that lot." I stopped talking and looked at her. The cheek turned to me was pale. "Are you all right, Chloë?"

She didn't turn round. "You seem such an ideal couple. You steeped in your research, Ben in his. And he's so equable."

"Ben? Yes, he is. He's been good for me. I've found it a waste of time to lose my temper with him. But, isn't Rick?" I knew he was more volatile than Ben, and perhaps his job as an estate agent made him more consciously charming, but he seemed sincere enough.

4

Chloë turned towards me. I saw dark shadows under her brown eyes, repeating their colour. "What do *you* think?" she said.

"Well, of course, he's a charmer." And lightly, to counteract her seriousness, "I bet you have to keep an eye on him in the office."

"It doesn't worry me, that part." She turned away from my questioning stare. "Tell me more about Raymond IV."

As I talked, and answered her questions – she had a quick, lively mind and a feeling like mine for this old part of France – my mind strayed to Rick: his undoubted charm, his eyes which sometimes seemed to hold mine a fraction longer than necessary, questioning eyes . . . was it a question, or an invitation? But it was an old masculine trick that one, and it might have been imagination on my part, accustomed as I was to Ben's utter reliability. 'What do *you* think?' Chloë had said. I could trust my life with Ben. Was it that slight doubt about Rick which gave him his charm?

I dismissed the idea because I was so happy with Ben. We loved our life together in Meloir. Our minds were fully occupied, we played together, loved together, saw the Gillams, and although we made other friends through Ben's work, Rick and Chloë remained our closest.

We had had a particularly happy evening with them – Ben had to go back to London for a week and we had eaten in the village, a special meal the Carvels at *Le Repos* cooked to speed his return, quail stuffed with prunes soaked in brandy, local *chèvre*, a *tarte des mirabelles* to finish.

We got back to our house about midnight. When we were undressing, Ben said, "Are you 'sure you won't come with me, Andy?" This was his name for me; he said that 'Miranda' made him think of a dark, blowsy, Hilaire Beloc kind of woman.

"No. I've spoken to Mother on the phone." I pulled my dress over my head. "I don't fancy the flight."

"You're feeling all right?" He came over to me, naked, and stood behind me, his hands cupping my breasts.

"Fine." I turned in his arms, put mine round his neck.

"Nothing that time won't mend." I met his eyes and pulled a face at him, then buried my face in his neck. "I feel a fool. It's such a hackneyed situation." My voice was muffled. "You're supposed to say, 'You don't mean . . . ?' And I've to look at you all bashful-like and say . . ." His hand came under my chin so that I had to look at him.

"You're pregnant," he said. He had a look on his face like a little boy who'd hit a boundary at his school cricket match. "And I thought you meant you didn't want to come because it was too hot . . ." It had been oppressive all week, no wind. We guffawed together like a pair of fools.

"Someone should have told you the facts of life," I said, and then we were in bed together and he was saying all the things I wanted to hear.

When I saw him off in the morning it seemed that we were both still shaking with happiness. I walked with him to the car. "I'll get back as soon as I can," he said. In the open car as he drove off he looked like a fresh-faced schoolboy, too young to be a father. Women seem to become maternal as soon as they are pregnant.

That was the last time I saw him. Some fool crashed into him on a blind corner on the way to Toulouse. They were both killed.

My mother and father flew over as soon as they heard the news. I think either Chloë or Rick had rung them. And Ben's parents were being contacted. They were in South Africa. I was like someone who'd had a stroke, unable to think, to act, to talk. Everyone was very patient with me, and the Gillams were especially kind, driving my parents to Lafont, our nearest market town, for shopping; calling every day, helping with formalities.

Ben was buried in the village churchyard. My parents didn't gainsay me. It wasn't what I wanted, but then I didn't know what I wanted except that I wanted him back, and knew I couldn't have him. The one advantage was that it was a quiet ceremony with only a few local friends and the Gillams, and Ben's director from Toulouse, a Frenchman who told me that the company "would take care of everything". There were no friends from England. It is a strange fact that people will fly to France for weddings, but not for funerals.

6

The Swimming Pool

My father flew back, his business needed him, as did Ben's father and mother, who had arrived a day after the funeral and were stricken by the death of a dearly loved only son. My mother stayed on, patiently, waiting for me to break out of my misery.

"You have this great consolation, Miranda," she said, "the coming baby. You may not think so now, but you will. You will still have Ben." I didn't believe her.

The beautiful countryside, the rolling landscape, the old villages with their rose-pink roofs, their *bastides*, meant nothing to me now. The Duchy of Aquitaine ceased to exist. Everything reminded me of Ben: the stone-flagged kitchen where we had sat in the early mornings before he drove to Toulouse; his collection of old cooking utensils on the scrubbed dresser; my Delft pots of scarlet geraniums spilling over the window-sill. He'd had green fingers. Mine were better in a mixing bowl; I was a budding Elizabeth David.

"I think I'll have to go back," Mother said one morning. "Dad pines." That broke my heart, only momentarily, with envy. He was alive to pine, twice Ben's age. "Will you come with me, darling? We could lock up the house."

"No," I said, "I've made up my mind. I'm going to sell it. I shall have to be here to show people around."

I went through hell after mother had gone back to Kent. The one pinprick of light at the end of the day was Chloë's visit. She drove from the office to see me before she went home, bringing French goodies, roulades and apple jellies from the delicatessen in Cahors, small tubs of delectable salads, vegetables in mayonnaise, bottles of walnut oil for the lettuces which were growing into pyramids in the garden. They too missed Ben.

I had told her I was pregnant and she cosseted me. She arranged for Luc Devreux, her gardener, a young lad who had just left school, to come along. She fixed up a woman in the village, Colette Jourdan, to come in each morning and do the necessary chores. Previously I had taken pleasure in running the house myself. I was a charwoman at heart, liking above all to scrub. Colette was understanding, not a gossip. She performed her duties and left, didn't want to sit down with cups of tea and sympathy which would have crucified me. Sometimes Chloë took me back with her to their house for supper, but I generally resisted this. We had been a foursome, and although Rick was understanding, I felt uneasy, looking for Ben all the time. I wanted him, all the time I wanted him.

One evening when I was there, Rick said to me, "A client of mine is interested in your house, Miranda. He's offered a good price for it. I think it's the location he's interested in."

I, who had said to my mother I was going to sell it, at that moment felt anger, the first emotion except grief I had felt since Ben's death. I couldn't contemplate anyone else living in our house where we had been so happy. "I've decided not to sell," I said. "We might want it later." And that was a new emotion too. I was carrying Ben's child. I had to think of what it might want.

"I thought the money might be tempting," he said.

"I don't need it." This was true. Ben's insurance from the firm had been exceptionally generous. The Director had been as good as his word, and I had some money of my own. It had never been my problem.

"Miranda's made up her mind, Rick," Chloë said. She smiled her French smile at me, and again I noticed the dark smudges under her eyes as she put a consoling hand on my wrist.

A week later when I was pushing a barrow full of garden rubbish (I had discovered manual labour was the best antidote for grief), it ran away from me and I fell heavily on my stomach. I was only winded, and my knees were bruised, but that night when I woke about three in the morning I found myself swimming in blood. I waited until morning before I called out the local doctor. My misery was too great.

He came immediately, a young man with an old man's goatee beard and a robin's bright eye. He had gentle fingers. "Well, I do not have to tell you, poor Madame Stanstead, you have lost your baby," he said. "But you are young yet. Plenty of time . . ."

"But I have lost my husband as well," I said, and burst into tears. He sat down at my bedside and talked in the way French people often do, as if they had a direct line to Descartes. "What you say is true, dear Madame, but you must take the larger view. Everything is part of the Divine Purpose. The unexamined life is not livable by man. You are a young beautiful woman." It was not a personal remark. I knew by his eyes. "I understand you are an art historian, cultivated, you have an entrée into the minds of all the great men, your own Ruskin, for example."

"*C'est ça.*" I was forced to agree.

"You are living in the most beautiful country in the world and you have loving parents in England and good friends here. I would say," he said, cocking his head, "you are not bereft."

"No," I said. "I am not bereft." Perhaps what he had said was better than a prescription.

Two

W hen I went back to London I was lucky in getting a job in the British Museum where I had worked before, and I managed to find a flat near Great Russell Street. To begin with, I spent each weekend with my parents in Kent, but after a time I got in touch with old friends and I began to stay up in town for theatres and concerts.

René Bonnard's philosophy was beginning to work. I thought, there can't be a worse deprivation than losing a husband and child in one year. Surely the worst cards stacked up against me have been dealt and anything else will seem trivial. Now I shall have to get on with building a new life. It will never be as good as it might have been with Ben and our child, I'll never know that shaking happiness again, but there are different kinds of happiness, and it's life, of a kind.

And there was Chris. It seems odd to introduce another man into my story, but I didn't think of his gender – just that he worked beside me, sometimes we lunched together, and we had a mutual interest in music. We both liked the Barbican because of its wide comfortable seating, and I sometimes accepted a lift from him because one car was better than two for parking.

He was divorced. He had a son and daughter who were with his wife – he missed them more than her, he said – but he had limited access. 'Like a National Park,' he said wryly. I never met them. He kept that side of his life apart.

As a matter of fact we didn't confide in each other. We had both been deeply hurt, buffeted, you might say, and we had a fear of whingeing. History helps you here. You take a broader view of life, feeling yourself part of a process rather than a victim of fate.

11

It was what you might call an intellectual friendship. I don't know what he did for sex, although at thirty-six he must have natural cravings. For myself, I was still missing Ben too badly to think of any other man.

I couldn't face going back to Meloir even to visit, although I stubbornly held on to the house. It meant France to me, a composite of sights and sounds and feelings. I could think of the evening procession of the *troupeau* passing our house, the jangle of their bells, the caressing quality of the evening air when we sat in the garden. I could hear Ben's voice, his laugh, taste the aniseed on my tongue from my nightly Ricard. I lent the house to various friends who wanted a holiday, and corresponded with Chloë who gave me the low-down on how it was being treated, and how one family had let their children run riot causing minor damage. I didn't care much. All I knew was that in spite of Ben's death and the loss of the baby, I wasn't ready to sell.

I think Chris Balfour was my instigator there. "Property in France is a good investment, although I don't think you're money conscious. No, the important thing is you're a born researcher. You have a gut feeling for France, and sooner or later you'll want to get embroiled again. And you'll have to go back for the hands-on stuff, the occasional jolt, the thrill, like sitting down on a cat!"

I laughed, knowing he was right. The 'hands-on' stuff was like discovering how much the Templars influenced the Crusades until the end of the twelfth century, and having to change my notes, and the 'cat' stuff was like the occasional nugget one turned up, such as Richard having an army of washerwomen following his battles to wash, comb and delouse his knights. Old women welcomed. No delectable camp followers. Too distracting . . . yes, I had to go back. Quercy was exercising its old magic.

Winter set in, my first winter without Ben. There were no more tenants in my house in Meloir, and I wrote to Chloë to ask if she would arrange for Colette Jourdan to continue to go in occasionally. 'I'm so grateful to you, Chloë,' I wrote. 'You've given me such practical help always. I'm settled in a decent flat in Bloomsbury. Couldn't you think of having a week off and

spending it with me? There's lots to do in London, cinemas, theatres, concerts. I want to repay you for all your kindness'
I got no reply.
After Christmas, which I spent in Kent, I wrote again. 'Perhaps my letter went astray, Chloë, or you were too busy to answer. My offer is still open, and I'd love to see you, hear all your news of the village.' I had an idea that, if she came and we talked together, I might confide in her, how much I missed Ben, still grieved for the loss of the baby in spite of René Bonnard's philosophy, how the memory of those happy days in Meloir could still reduce me to tears. She would understand.
But when I thought of it, I realised that the confidences had been one-sided. There had been a reserve about her. I remembered that conversation we'd had about our husbands when she had said, meaning Rick, 'What do *you* think?'
Thinking about her, I remembered that, unlike Rick, she had never been gregarious. We met a few couples at their house – I remembered in particular an American girl called Ellen Lerner – but there always seemed to be a reserve about Chloë. Between us there had been a natural affinity, but she had never been demonstrative.
I waited patiently. Spring came, and because Chris and I were researching an article on the Marquis de la Fayette who fought in the American War of Independence, we went to New York for a week. We slept together in the Algonquin. We both said it was a mutual need, and I rather liked it. It seemed to restore my femininity, but I didn't love him. I told him this and he said it didn't matter, liking was far better. When I got back there was a letter with a French postmark waiting for me. The address was typewritten, but I thought Chloë might have typed it in the office during a slack period. And it meant she was working. I'd been worried. It was from Rick, a long letter.

'Dear Miranda,
    You will be surprised to hear from me. I usually left keeping in touch to Chloë. I missed you very much when you left. Ben and you meant a lot to me, and I often thought

13

of you in London, struggling to come to terms with life without him. I thought of, and still think of your gaiety, your forthrightness, your sweet face always so full of laughter, and then after Ben's dreadful death, so pale with grief. I felt your pain.

Chloë hasn't been well for some time. She still drives to Cahors daily, but she shuts herself off from me. I must be honest with you. She has wanted a child for a long time, but was unable to have one. She wouldn't see a doctor, although I implored her to do so. When she knew you were pregnant – I wonder if you realised how much that upset her? She wouldn't tell you, of course. She was envious, eaten up with envy. When she told me you had miscarried I was looking at her. I saw her hide a smile . . .

I shouldn't be telling you this, but I wanted you to understand her better, and to see her state of mind. She has given in to my wishes and seen the doctor who has given her the usual pills and advised her to take a holiday. I'm terribly busy with the approach of summer – house prices are soaring in this area – and I couldn't possibly get away. But she knows that I'd be happy for her to go anywhere she fancied.

She still looks after your house, I believe she checks on Colette Jourdan, and often I'm back from the office before she turns up. She makes supper and goes off to bed early, and I get on with some work. Such is our life. Not much fun, but I look back with great joy to those happy days and evenings we spent together. I hear your laugh, how your eyes danced when you were being ridiculous, I remember how you went into the pool like an arrow, how you shook your head like a puppy when you came out. Happy days!

Please don't write to Chloë. She would guess I had written to you, and she would be annoyed. I have to watch what I do or say. But if you want to write to me, send it poste restante. I should hate to upset her, but would love to know how you're getting on.'

The letter surprised me, even shook me. I was upset to hear about Chloë's illness, and sorry she hadn't been able to confide in me. And a little self-righteous that I'd managed to cope with so much more; but that was only momentary. She had always been reserved, and I had thought sometimes that loyalty to Rick had kept her silent. I had respected that. But Rick's letter changed my mind about him. I had always been aware of his charm, indeed been a little wary of it, but now I saw him as a husband who was seriously perturbed about his wife and had to tell me, as her friend.

Why, I thought, hadn't she told him of my invitation? That would have been an ideal holiday for her, a fillip, something different from rural France. It was very odd, but to envy me my coming baby and then be glad when I miscarried . . . that was hard to believe. Should I believe it? Had I been tactless perhaps?

My mind went back to one afternoon when the two of us had sat in the stone-flagged kitchen of our house – it had been too hot to go into the garden. I had mixed a jug of Cassis, and we sat on either side of my scrubbed wooden table, frosted glasses in our hands. There had been a bee buzzing drowsily on the window-pane, a summer, heady buzz in the coolness.

"You have an added sparkle today," Chloë said to me. Her skin was brown – she always tanned beautifully. If the smudges under her eyes were there, they were concealed. Her hair was pale gold against the brownness. "Have you come into a fortune?"

"In a way," I said, and the cool intimacy of the kitchen, and the Cassis, perhaps, made me carry on – "I'm pregnant. I haven't told Ben yet." I had been to the doctor only that morning.

"I'm so glad for you," she said, and then because the table was broad between us, she picked up my hand lying on it, and kissed it. Her smile was warm, her eyes full. Surely that had been genuine? But now Rick was telling me something completely different. Who was I to believe?

"It'll be you and Rick next," I smiled back at her, feeling touched by the gesture.

"Not a chance." She looked sad. I was on the point of saying something comforting, I didn't know quite what, but she had turned away as if the subject was closed. "Which *brocanteur* did you find that hand-churn in?" Her interest seemed false. "Look at those wooden paddles!"

"It was Ben," I said. "More work. Now I have to scrub it every day!" We both laughed. She knew about my love affair with a scrubbing brush.

My recollection of that episode was of two young women who had shared a genuine rapport, not of one who had been eaten up with envy. What you should do now is telephone her, I thought, say that you've been wondering how she is; but I hesitated. Rick hadn't thought that was wise. The last thing anyone should do was get in the way of a married couple. If she bore me some kind of grudge, there was no point in upsetting her further. But what if she were ill?

Ben would have advised me, I thought. I knew that sense of loss, not the searing grief after his death, but a dull ache. I could have told Chris about Rick's letter, but I didn't want his opinion. Besides, we had never, either of us, harped back to the past. All I knew about his children were their names, Sophie and Jon, not even the name of his wife. I imagine he felt some of the same sense of loss that I did for Ben, like biting on an aching tooth.

I remembered that at the beginning of my friendship with Chris, I couldn't mention Ben, or the baby, without weeping. After one attempt, when he looked at me level-eyed, making no effort to comfort me, I had understood. There was to be no comparing notes. It was easier that way. An uncomplicated friendship. No fag ends.

Three

I have always been what Chris calls an 'up front' person. What you see is what you get. Once he said to me, 'You're good at your work because you have a clear mind. You can follow a trail without deviating, and that makes you a good researcher. You don't know the meaning of subterfuge.'

This conversation occurred between us when he made the suggestion that we might move in together. "We're two lonely people," he said, or rather sang, putting on a woebegone face across the table from me.

We had got into the habit of eating several times each week in an Italian restaurant near the BM, probably because we both disliked the thought of eating alone in our respective flats. At least I know I did. I'm an optimistic sort of person, up front, as he said, and I was happy in my work, happy with the people I worked with. It was when I was back in my flat, especially when the evenings were lengthening and the sun was flooding in, that I felt lonely.

I still missed Ben badly at those times. Often I would go out and walk about the streets around Russell Square, but I stopped this after I'd been approached by men several times. "I'll think about it, Chris," I said, "You see, I'm not in love with you."

He put on a stricken face, clasping his heart. " 'I am dying, Egypt, dying,' " he was having one of his daft fits. "Okay, but we have a solid basis of friendship, we like the same things, we don't repel each other when we're in the altogether, do we?" Actually I quite admired his body, taller and heavier than Ben had been, good shoulders. "That's pretty good to be going on with, isn't it?"

"Not bad," I said, "but you don't *shake* me." I thought of that night after I had told Ben that I was pregnant, and how the love between us had been frightening in its intensity. I had sometimes wondered if it had been ordained, so that I should have something to remember, so that it would set a standard for me, and nothing less would do.

Chris, all right, had gentleness, passion when required, a quick sense of humour. Also he had an especially fine-shaped nose – I had a penchant for finely shaped noses – and the rest of his face wasn't bad either. His temperament, that essential soundness, wasn't too far removed from Ben's; but as I had told him, he didn't shake me.

"All right," I said again, "I'll think about it. Look, if we don't drink up we're going to be late for the concert and you know how hard I've been working on Mahler." I didn't as yet share his enthusiasm.

That night, as I was in bed alone – I'd said I was tired with a woman's tiredness, which was true – I thought of his saying that I was without subterfuge. He was wrong. Since I had received Rick's letter I had been carrying on a correspondence with him. It was a strange departure for me as I had always been a devotee of Mr Bell's invention, and never wrote letters if a telephone call would do. I liked to talk. I generally expressed myself better that way, but strangely enough that hadn't been the case with Rick. We never telephoned, and I found a new secretive pleasure in sitting at my desk and writing to him. It was a bit like self-analysis. I explored my psyche, found myself revealing thoughts and feelings which could never have been expressed otherwise. These letters, flying between London and the poste restante at Meloir were forming a bond between us.

I opened my heart to him. I told him how much I missed Ben and our life in France. I painted a pen picture of my life in London, and in return he did the same for Meloir, reminding me of the old lanes round the village where I had often walked, of the glow-worms which lit the path to the copse behind the church. He talked about our mutual acquaintances – Monsieur Fecamb, the *boulanger*, and Chantal and Alain Carvel, owners of *Le*

Repos – and how they often enquired about me. The picture he painted was often false, most obviously when he mentioned the other inhabitants: Monsieur Fecamb hardly ever exchanged a word with me – he was a gloomy individual – and the Carvels, while always polite, had never been intimate. He said he never swam in the pool without thinking of me, and that might have been true.

And he told me about Chloë. She had gone to her sister's house in Angers for over a month but had come back when he implored her. 'She has given up working for me,' he wrote, 'she helps the Carvels, shops for Chantal in Lafont, and each day she spends some time in your house. I do everything I can to please her, but she lives in a world of her own. I've spoken to René Bonnard about her, just as a friend – she sees a doctor in Cahors now – but he says to be patient. You can imagine how I feel, Miranda. Only your letters keep me sane. How I wish you would come back, and yet I know it would be the wrong thing. She has turned against you. She won't hear your name mentioned.'

When I wrote in return and asked him if I should try telephoning Chloë, he said, no, it would upset her too much. 'You have no idea what her temper is like these days. She threatened to slash her wrists if I mentioned your name again.'

For some reason, I hadn't told Chris about this correspondence. I can't understand why, except that deep down I recognised it as some kind of addiction, something foreign to my character and to his conception of me. Perhaps Rick was the link between those happy days in Meloir with Ben. I felt their memory every time I saw the French postmark. As summer came round and London grew stuffy and overcrowded with tourists, I longed to go back.

Rick's letters changed. Subtly they had become almost like love letters. Mine had changed too; a tenderness had crept into them which I recognised, but left. It was almost as if he was taking the place of Ben in that part of me which Chris didn't touch.

Perhaps it was because of this development that I didn't move in altogether with Chris. I felt that if I kept my flat I kept my privacy – to write those letters, to have my own place to think of Ben and my life in France with him. Rick was part of this. Rick, France and Ben, it was a composite thing. I didn't recognise it as a kind of retrograde step, a reluctance to let go of the past. Had I thought about it, I might have seen it for what it was – a falsification of the past. I had never been part of the village life in Meloir. Ben and I were too wrapped up in each other, too wrapped up in our work. We had accepted that French villages take a long time wholly to accept you. We had been in no hurry.

But Chris and I didn't have any hard or fast rules. Sometimes he stayed in my flat in Great Russell Street, sometimes in his in Holborn. It depended what we were doing and what was most convenient. He was my present. We shared a fondness for each other. He could be fanned into passion at a moment's notice, he said, and sometimes I was glad to assist in the fanning. I missed Ben terribly at times. In my saner moments, I knew Rick and Chris were substitutes. Chris understood. 'Use me,' he once said, holding me closely in his arms. I was near to loving him then. He was what I called a fine-tuned man. You couldn't imagine him being petty, mean or malicious.

One weekend when we were walking along the stony shore at Aldeburgh – we were going to the Maltings that evening – he said, "When are you going to go back and fix up things in France?"

"What do you mean?" I was surprised at the question.

"Well, you never speak of it, which is unlike you, and there's your research. You had done a lot of work. You told me about it when we first met."

I looked at the cold greyness of the North Sea and compared it in my mind's eye with the green Lot and its slow gracious curves, the red roofs of Meloir climbing the hill, that rolling, golden landscape. I remembered the enthusiasm I'd had for writing about that ancient region, and how the chapters had begun to form in my mind: The Cathars, The Templars, The Crusading Knights of Quercy, Witchcraft in Medieval Times, Guillemette – that young girl who was burned alive on the castle hill at Gourdon. My mind filled with images . . . Chloë and I sitting

20

talking on the green slope at St Cirque Lapopie . . . 'What do *you* think?' she had said. And then I felt the illicit thrill I got from Rick's letters and closed my eyes for a second before saying, gaily, "Oh, I've dropped all that."

"I don't believe you," Chris said. He tucked his hand in my arm, "I know you. You're like a terrier worrying a rat when you get your teeth into something."

"Charming." I looked down my nose at him.

"It's true. You did a lot of work, you showed it to me, and you're due a month's leave. It would seem a good idea to take it up again – you have a house to stay in – and," he stole a glance at me, "I thought I might come along as dogsbody. I can cook, clean, drive, use a laptop, I'm invaluable to lady researchers."

I shook my head. "No, it wouldn't work." I was serious, unlike him. "I'm sorry."

I looked at him as we walked. His face had lost its brightness. He looked strange for him, discomfited, even sad. I felt I had to explain. "You see, there's someone there . . ."

"A man?"

"Yes. He deals with the house . . ."

"Deals with it?"

"Well, he could sell it for me. He's an estate agent. He's asked me often, he's had good offers for it. And then there's his wife . . ."

"Oh, he's married?" His tone was level.

"Yes, but she's taken against me, as they say. We used to be such good friends, and she was taking care of it . . ."

"Has she told you why she's taken against you, as they say?" He mimicked me.

"No, Rick's told me. He says it would upset her terribly if I wrote or telephoned. Actually he's having a pretty bad time with her. He's spoken to his friend, the local doctor, about her."

"This is what *your* friend, Rick, says?"

"Yes, he's been worried about her for some time. He's done everything he can think of."

"Like what?"

"Well, he doesn't expect her to work in the firm now. She helps in the village restaurant where the four of us used to go, and she goes to my house a lot, comes back to theirs late, goes to bed early, doesn't speak to him . . ."

"This is what he tells you?"

I looked at him again. There was no vestige of a smile on his face. I was angry with him, angrier with myself.

"I don't like your tone," I said. "Why should I doubt a friend whom I can trust, who was so kind to Ben and me when we were there?"

"And she wasn't?"

"Oh, yes, Chloë and I were good friends. She was reserved, but she was partly French. I've noticed that trait in French girls. They don't open up."

"I haven't noticed that, but then I haven't had much experience with French girls, or partly French ones." It was as near to a sneer as someone like Chris could go. "I find Italian ones more . . . open."

"Oh, let's drop this conversation," I said, exasperated with him, "I don't know how it started."

"It started by me suggesting you might go to France on leave and take up your research again, and I offered my services, but you turned them down. Well, leave me out of it, but I can't see why you don't go there and find out why this Chloë, who was a good friend, has taken against you, as her husband says." There was heavy emphasis on 'husband', and it made me seethe.

"I know why," I said. "He told me she was envious of me becoming pregnant."

He stopped walking and turned to me, his face registering astonishment.

"But you *lost* your baby!"

"So what?" We were close to shouting at each other now.

"Well, it seems logical to me that that would cancel out envy in your friend, that any friend would only have sympathy for you in your loss."

"But she's deranged!"

"So her husband says. Rick, isn't it?"

"Never mind what it is. Let's drop it now. I'm going to walk back to the hotel and get ready for tonight. I'll see you in the lounge at six."

"Hey, hey!" He put his hand on my arm. "Is this a quarrel?"

"It looks like it to me," I said. "And in future keep your nose out of my affairs, will you?"

He was as angry as I was. "I should think you could do with my nose *in* your affairs. Or anybody sensible. You don't sound like yourself. You sound like someone who's been bewitched, you who have such a good mind, who can weigh evidence for and against and usually come up with the right answer. You sound like a gullible child, like my daughter, Sophie, when she falls for a boy at school."

"Shut up!" I said, shaking his hand off my arm, "Will you just shut up!" I turned on my heel and marched away, or rather hobbled away over the stones which had been rounded by the North Sea.

I didn't enjoy the concert. I shivered in my evening dress, Britten's jolly sailor didn't make *me* want to dance the hornpipe, and I scarcely spoke to Chris. We were sharing a bed, but he knew better than to touch me. He made no effort to apologise. I rolled to the edge and spent a sleepless and uncomfortable night.

In the morning we decided to drive home that day instead of staying on at Aldeburgh for the rest of the weekend. I wanted Chris to apologise, which he didn't do; I knew it was because he thought he was in the right. I had come across his stubbornness before. This, I thought, was typical. When he dropped me at my flat I had my speech ready.

"We have to work together, and you won't find me difficult. But I've deeply resented your behaviour this weekend and I think I would like some time on my own. I'll be going to Kent this coming weekend, and possibly for the next few."

"As you wish," he said. And drove away, face stern, mouth closed.

If I had told my mother or father about our quarrel I'm sure they would have given me a different slant on it. They had met Chris, they liked him, and I knew they had secret hopes that given time we would marry. Mother, I knew, wanted grandchildren, although she had never said. She had grieved deeply for Ben and then for my losing the baby.

When they had visited us in France, Father had particularly liked Chloë. She seemed to open up with him, and they had long, companionable talks. Mother and I teased him about it, but he bristled and said she was a fine young woman, with character.

He had never expressed an opinion about Rick. Mother, on the other hand, thought he was charming. "It's the touch of French in him," she had said. "You know his surname is derived from 'Guillaume'? He was telling me about his French forebears. He went to Toulouse University, and that's where he met Chloë. He hasn't said anything much, but I gather she's, well, difficult."

"She's far from that!" Father said stoutly. I had noticed that as they grew older they contradicted each other more. "And you don't get her casting aspersions at him! She's utterly loyal, but sometimes there's something, well, sad, in her eyes."

"And you're a sentimental old fool," Mother said, laughing at him. "It's her French *je ne sais quoi* which has turned you on."

"Stop it you two," I said, laughing at them and, as daughters do, failing to give them credit for their astuteness. Dad was probably right about the sadness. Chloë had wanted a baby.

The correspondence with Rick continued. I had asked him in a letter of mine why Chloë seemed to have turned against me, and his reply surprised me.

'Well, I'll tell you,' he wrote, 'something I've kept to myself all these years. When we met in Toulouse she told me quite early on in our friendship that she was pregnant. I knew the child couldn't possibly be mine. The man responsible had decamped. I had fallen in love with her, and I offered to marry her, but I soon discovered that it had been a ruse. She hadn't been pregnant after all. It spoiled any love I had for her.'

To say that I was astounded was to put it mildly. Yet this explained so much – her reserve, the fact that she now found herself in a loveless marriage with no one but herself to blame.

But why had she been so desperate to marry Rick? Because she was in love with him and thought he wouldn't want to marry her while he was studying? Or a wish on her part to get away from home? But why? my logical mind asked, and then, inevitably, Why don't you ask *her*? Because I would be betraying Rick's confidence? Because I felt guilty? I longed to ask Chris what *he* thought, but I had told him at Aldeburgh not to meddle in my affairs. He wouldn't have forgotten that.

And then, looking at it from Rick's angle, was it Chloë's deception which had made him bitter? Had he wanted the child that Chloë had said she was having? Or did it seem to him at the time that it was the only way of having her? But it had showed Rick's magnanimity. He hadn't hesitated to offer to give the mythical baby a name. In my reply to him I said I now understood why their marriage had gone awry.

And yet, and yet . . . my logical mind wasn't entirely happy. I was still puzzled about why Chloë should want to *marry* Rick. There was abortion, unless, being a Catholic, she couldn't entertain that, or . . . I remembered she had worried because her father was facing bankruptcy. Had she thought that Rick came from a rich family, and there would be money available to help her father? There was only one solution. Get Chloë's side of the story, and that I felt I couldn't do.

I missed Chris popping in, taking me to dinner, staying overnight. We were both adult enough to maintain an amicable working relationship since we were still engrossed in *La Fayette*, and we even established a *modus vivendi* to the extent of having an occasional meal together if we had stayed late at the BM. But France, my house, and my research there were never mentioned.

I tried going out with women friends, even accepted invitations to parties, but I disliked them. I preferred to have a relationship with a man. I suppose it was my way of missing Ben, but as well as that I had never enjoyed women's shopping expeditions, or their tittle-tattle (perhaps that was why I had liked Chloë's reticence), or the company of what my father called 'blue stockings'. I liked humour with my culture, and that tended to be in short supply in the academic world.

And that was perhaps why I kept on writing to Rick, and why

my letters reflected my state of mind, a need for comfort because of the quarrel with Chris and the constant ache for Ben – or had I fallen in love? I looked forward more than ever to his letters, I would tear open the envelope eagerly to read them, to bask in his affection. 'You are rarely out of my mind, Miranda', 'Chloë and I are like strangers' 'When I think of you in comparison with her, your joyousness of spirit, your smile . . . there's no comparison'.

'She has taken to having a dip in the pool every evening, naked. I see her bathrobe swinging open as she passes my door. Tonight she stopped. "You monopolise the pool every morning," she said, "this is *my* time." I resented her attitude, her cutting me out of her life. It was a sultry evening. Tomorrow, I made up my mind, I'll go in naked as she does, when she's there – after all, it's my pool – give her the fright of her life . . .'

I thought of them as we had known them three years ago. It was true Chloë had always been quiet, but not noticeably so, perhaps because Ben, Rick and I were chatterboxes. And when I was with Chloë alone, surely there had been a rapport? But every couple had a public face, it was said, although Ben and I hadn't been long enough together to acquire, or indeed need one. I could only feel sad for them both.

One morning, I was feeling mildly disturbed because Rick's usual letter hadn't arrived, when the telephone rang on my desk. I heard the operator say in my ear, "Will you take a call from Mr Gillam?" My heart leapt. Was he in London? His voice was hardly recognisable, harsher, strangled. "Is that you Miranda? I have terrible news for you. Chloë has drowned herself in our pool."

Four

"I can't believe this!" I said. My heart was hammering. "Are you saying that Chloë . . ." I couldn't go on.

"Yes." His voice was still hoarse. "I know it's a terrible shock to you."

"Shock?" I felt breathless. "Yes, it's a terrible shock. But you, Rick . . . it must be hard to believe . . ."

"I'm just beginning to . . ."

"Tell me how it happened."

"Luc found her. You know, the gardener. In the morning. Yesterday morning. I had last seen her about nine o'clock the night before. All day was a nightmare. Doctors . . . she was taken to the hospital. I stayed there last night . . . in Lafont."

"Terrible." I was beginning to take hold of myself. "Did she seem all right the night before, when you saw her?"

"She didn't speak. I was working in my study. I saw her passing. The door was open. She went straight up to bed. I've told you . . ."

"Yes, I remember. And the next morning Luc . . . ?"

"Yes, at seven. He comes in at seven. His first job is to clean the pool of leaves. He knows I often take an early swim . . ." His voice broke. "I had to let you know. I must go. René Bonnard is coming to help me. There are arrangements . . ."

"Of course. It was good of you to take the time to phone. I'm so sorry for you, Rick, so sorry . . ."

"I had to tell you as soon as I could. We had become close those last few months. You understand . . . I must go, Miranda. Think of me . . ." There was a click at the other end of the line. I had stood up when I heard his voice, now I sat down again because my legs were unable to support me. I looked at my watch. Ten o'clock. There was a committee meeting at twelve. Somehow I must get through the day and then when I was home think of what was best to do. I'd ring him again, ask him how I could help, if he would like me to come.

My secretary was in the room, bright-faced, mini-skirted, wafting her distinctive Miss Dior all over the place. I was pretty sure she would be whisked out of the British Museum before long to gladden the heart of some equally smart young man in wedded bliss. She smiled brightly.

"Morning, Miranda. Oh, you do look poorly!"

"Who wouldn't on a Monday morning?" I managed a poor quip.

"Heavy weekend?" She had a lovely smile which got her off with murder.

"No cheek." I pulled myself together. "What was the plan for today, Caroline?"

"You wanted to go through the American files while I took notes."

"So I did." I was surprised at my calmness after the terrible news. Maybe I wasn't easily bowled over nowadays. Graduate from a hard school.

I telephoned my mother at lunchtime and told her, just to have someone to share the news with. I was still shocked.

"You'll be able to sympathise, Miranda . . ."

"Yes," I agreed. There wasn't much to choose between – a fatal car collision or drowning in ten feet of water. But Chloë had been a strong swimmer.

"He'll be devastated, poor soul."

"Yes." One runs out of words to express shock.

I met Chris in the corridor outside my room when I was scurrying towards the elevator at five o'clock.

"You look woebegone," he said. "Are you missing me very badly?"

"That happens to be in poor taste." I didn't smile. "My friend, Chloë, in France, has been found drowned in their pool."

"Oh, God, I'm sorry!" He put his hand on my arm. "I'm a

28

clumsy fool. And the husband . . . poor chap. Are you thinking of going there?"

"I haven't decided." I warmed to his sympathy. "I don't know the date of the funeral yet. I'll have to think."

"Don't tear yourself apart over this, Miranda." His hand had slipped to cover mine. "You've had enough."

"It makes it easier to sympathise with Rick, know what he's going through."

"Right." He took his hand away. "You'll go. Remember, I'm around to do anything to help. Just ask me."

"Thanks." I sped on, reflecting that I should have quite liked to talk to him over a drink. Although I dearly loved my parents, I had grown away from them with marriage. Their style of life suited them. I was a disturbing presence, and I had reached the age when I didn't want to offload my problems on to them.

I telephoned Rick when I got back to my flat. I was calm, I felt responsible, I had made up my mind. "Rick," I said, "I've been thinking. I can take time off work and come to Meloir if I can be of any help to you. I haven't forgotten how kind you and Chloë were to me when Ben died."

He sounded touched. "It's so good of you, Miranda. To have you near would mean a lot to me. Chloë's parents are both dead, and although Chloë's sister is bound to come to the funeral, she shan't be able to stay on. She works, and there are two children. Besides, there never was any rapport between us."

"That's settled, then."

"I still feel Chloë's presence so strongly, although there had been . . . difficulties. But you know I tried hard, and René Bonnard has assured me that I couldn't have done more than I did."

"Everyone feels guilt," I said, "it's part of bereavement." I hadn't. Only resentment at Ben being taken away from me, which had now turned to sorrow, a kind of healing sorrow. I knew I had to thank Chris for that. We had talked together about death, or the loss in any way of one's partner, and how one must sooner or later adopt some policy towards living. He was more introspective than Ben had been, more profound in his thinking. I had enjoyed these talks.

29

And I had enjoyed our lovemaking. At first it had been a substitute for Ben's love, but there were differences, pleasant differences. It was more mature, less intense, but still passionate. And fun, too. We could laugh ourselves silly, and that had been good for me.

My feeling for Rick was different. Originally founded on personal contact when the four of us were together, there was no doubt I had been aware of his charm then, but I had always been too much in love with Ben to give it more than a moment's thought. Our correspondence had brought us closer, and I had begun to see him as a sensitive, unhappy man who needed a friend to confide in. That friendship had grown into something warmer, and now added to it there was the pity I felt for his terrible loss, in its own way as tragic as mine had been. He needed help.

When I had arranged my time off from the BM, made all my arrangements, I asked Chris if he would have a drink with me after work.

"Sure," he said. "Funds would stretch to lasagne and a bottle of Chianti, if you like."

"Well, thanks," I said. "I'm having a month off and going to France. I'll tell you why when I see you. I'd like to part on good terms. That quarrelling was stupid."

"It was my nosiness."

"Let's call it concern for my welfare. See you, then, at the usual place, at the usual time."

He was understanding when I talked about Chloë's death. He listened sympathetically to what I knew, and I found myself slipping into our old companionable state. Perhaps the Chianti helped. I told him about the whole background, our happy foursome with the Gillams, and how sad I'd been to hear of Chloë's illness, and what sounded like her depression. How I had invited her to visit me.

"I might have been able to help," I said.

"Don't have regrets." He looked thoughtful. "I'm surprised she couldn't swim."

"Of course she swam. The four of us did. Rick and I were

30

possibly better, very much at home in the water. 'You went in like an arrow,' he had said. But she was perfectly capable."

"It's odd to choose drowning if you can swim. They're presuming suicide?"

"What else?" I looked at him. "I haven't discussed anything like that with Rick."

"Of course not. Did they have any other friends besides you?"

"Yes, but not so close. Rick had quite a few from Cahors, probably Chloë had too. That was where his office was. We met them occasionally."

"Can you remember their names? It might be helpful."

"Let me see. There were the Machins, Lenore and Guy, and Yvette and Raymond Lavange. And Chloë had an American friend in Cahors whom she talked about." I racked my brains for her name. "Ellen . . . yes, Ellen Lerner."

"If you get round to it I should get in touch with them. It might give you a better picture. After all, you've been away for three years."

'Yes, I probably shall. But I'm really going to see if I can help Rick cope.'

"That's noble of you."

I looked at him, but his gaze was level. "He's a special friend."

"Quite. Maybe you'll be able to decide about your house when you're there?"

"Yes, that's a thought. Rick always says I'd get a good price for it. I could see how I feel about things while I'm there, have a look at my life from a different perspective."

"True."

"It depends on a lot of things."

"True again." He smiled warmly at me. "Remember I'm your father confessor. Just let me know how you're getting on, if I can be of any help."

"Thanks, Chris." I liked him a lot then. "You helped me through a bad patch. I think I'm standing on my own feet now."

"I'm still here."

Afterwards I wondered if I had been too dismissive. I decided that after Chloë's funeral was over I'd invite him to stay with me, take him around the district to see the châteaux I was interested in. We might take a look at the archives in the Toulouse library. He had been very knowledgeable about Raymond IV, and the Crusades. 'History would have been much poorer without that pageant,' he had said. Yes, Chris and I would enjoy delving together . . .

But my mind soon veered off to Rick and to Chloë's tragic death. What a shock! And poor Luc, that young lad who was far from outgoing, a failure at school with a dominant mother. Chloë had taken an interest in him, offered him a job. Was Rick presuming it was suicide, or had he been told? Chris had said it was difficult to drown if you could swim. But not difficult if you wanted to die. I could imagine how Rick felt at this moment. Utterly desolated. I was glad I had decided to go.

Five

That strange apparition in the station yard of Chloë with outstretched arms was still there as I sat beside Rick in his BMW. The hood was down, and the air was different, French, that peculiar mixture of warm grass, dust, garlic, an earthy, countryside odour.

"Was it a tiring journey, Miranda?" Rick asked. He was slowing down at the junction of the road to Lafont.

"Not really. I left Heathrow this morning, caught a train from Toulouse soon after I arrived . . . *me voici!*" My laugh was shaky, unsure. We hadn't met for three years, and who would have guessed it would have been under such circumstances. "I feel so sad for you, Rick," I said.

"You've been through it too. You know how I feel." He put out his hand and touched mine, briefly. "It's been such a comfort to me to know you had decided to come."

"You need friends. I discovered that."

Silence fell between us. We were now going through Lafont where Ben and I had shopped so often. I remembered how we used to speed home so that we could sit in the garden for our evening drink. There would be a cantaloup moon and the smell of stocks . . . nostalgia overwhelmed me. I would go indoors afterwards to cook the evening meal, and from the kitchen window the fields beyond the stone wall at the foot of the garden would be pale gold, the trees black silhouettes at their periphery.

Chloë . . . my mind was back with her, my reason for being here.

"You have some in London?"

"Some what?" I had forgotten what I had said.

"Friends?"

"Oh, yes. Not many. Mostly at work. There's someone . . ."

"Man or woman?"

"Oh, man. Chris Balfour. We're often on the same projects."
And because I felt it a strange question I said, bending forward,
"There's Madame Lacouche's shop. I remember Chloë buying
me her tiny quiches to cheer me up."

I went on talking because I was afraid of silence falling
between us. "It's all so French to me, having been away so long.
Those narrow streets and the tall buildings leaning against each
other, and the narrow alleys. Medieval. There's La Voie Bertrand. Ben and I used to go up it to the ramparts where the fish
market came, every Friday, I think. Richard the Lionheart took
the castle from Fortanier and gave it to the Count of Toulouse, I
remember. Here I go again. And Bertrand, Fortanier's son is
supposed to have been the man who mortally wounded Richard
at Chalus, revenge for his father . . ."

I stopped, but Rick didn't speak. It didn't matter. My mind
was full of memories, climbing up to the top of the castle to see
Lafont, another cantaloup moon, and Ben saying, 'Spooky, isn't
it? As if someone's ghost was hovering, a girl,' and I had told him
of Guillemette, the young girl who was burned up there as a
witch. I shook myself. Rick was slowing down for a car in front.

"I see the Café Bar's still the same," I said. Martin, the
moustachioed waiter with the long apron was hovering over
the tables. He had kept photographs of his numerous children in
his waistcoat pocket.

"And the same people sitting there, I expect." I was glad Rick
had spoken.

"That looked like Madame Lacouche's son, the one with the
yellow hair . . ."

And then we had left the town behind and we were speeding
along the road leading to Meloir, dark, tree-lined, passing the
gentilhommerie which we had always envied because of its many
turrets and the shimmer of its blue pool through the cypresses.

"Would you like to stop at the Carvels and have something to
eat?" he asked.

34

"No, thank you, if you don't mind." I was suddenly dog-tired, possibly emotionally. "I've been nibbling all day, the way one does, when travelling. I'll go straight to my house. Have you the key?"

"Colette left it in the door. And she's aired the bed, I have to tell you, and left some food. I could make you some coffee, or give you a drink, if you'd like to come back with me."

"It's very kind, Rick." I felt ungracious, "but, no thanks. I'll fall into bed and meet you tomorrow. And perhaps we could go to Carvels in the evening."

"Yes, but I'm back at the office during the day. It's better for me. The house is . . . unbearable at times. By the way, I could still sell *your* house at a substantial profit."

I was surprised at the remark, or the timing. We reached my house as he spoke, and he stopped and got out my two cases. I was beside him as he turned the key of the front door. My legs were trembling.

"You're sure you're all right here, Miranda?" His voice was kind. 'You could still change your mind. I know how you must feel . . .'

I shook my head. I was full of memories at the sight of the house, and afraid to speak in case I would burst into tears. I had to remind myself that it was Rick who was the bereaved one now.

"Truly. Do forgive me, Rick." I turned to him and put my arms round his shoulders, kissed him on the cheek. "I'm so very sorry about Chloë." I bit my lip, willing away the tears. "You go home and have a good rest. We'll meet tomorrow." He stood for a second or two within the circle of my arms then released himself.

"I'll put your cases in the hall." He walked in and put them down. Colette had left the lamp on, and filled a green bowl with zinnias which glowed in the soft light. He put his hand on my shoulder at the door and I saw the strain and sadness in his face. "*Bonne nuit. À demain.*" He took a deep breath. "We shan't go to the Carvels tomorrow evening if you don't mind. It's . . . we'll go further afield." I understood. He possibly dreaded meeting people he knew. "I'll call for you at seven." He walked down the path to the gate, got into his car and was gone.

35

There was a smell of lavender as I went slowly up to the bedroom. The stairs creaked in the same places. I stopped at the landing window and looked out, or tried to, but it was pitch black. The moon must have gone behind a cloud. In the bedroom I stripped to my bra and pants without bothering to open my cases and crept between the sheets. The loss of Ben was as searing for a few moments as it had been three years ago and I wept for a time before I stopped, telling myself it was self-pity. Rick was the one now who needed help. That was why I had come. I realised that part of my awkwardness with him was the thought of those letters we had exchanged. How did he feel, or had the thought of them disappeared with his grief over Chloë?

I remembered Ben once saying to me, 'Who do you like better, Chloë or Rick?' One of those silly questions people who are intimate ask each other. 'Chloë,' I had said, without a moment's hesitation. Had it been that being aware of Rick's charm I didn't want Ben to guess? How did I *now* feel about Rick, I asked myself.

With the thought of Chloë, her apparition again swam before me, beseeching. I began to tremble. There was a scuttling noise in the bedroom and my heart gave a leap of fear and subsided as quickly. 'Our neighbourhood mouse,' Ben had called it. I heard his voice in my ears, 'Don't think, Andy. You're tired.' I imagined I was in his arms as I fell asleep.

In the morning I felt refreshed, almost my usual self. I walked to the village bakery and bought some croissants from Monsieur Fecamp. "And your usual two baguettes, Madame Stanstead?" he said, as if I had been in his shop yesterday. An affectless man. Ben used to say that all that flour had clouded his brain. Floury Fecamp.

The autumn sun was warm, and I ate my croissants and apricot jam with coffee on the patch of grass in front of the house so that I could admire it. We had always sat there for breakfast because it got the morning sun, and because we had been naturally nosy and liked to see who was passing by. The house was built of Querçyois stone, that mellow golden colour, and interspersed with the occasional grey of slate and green of lichen. It was 300 years old and not overly restored, and it wasn't true to say we would rather have had the *gentilhommerie*. We had loved our house. I loved it at this moment.

The previous owners had been an elderly English couple who had become anxious to get home and shelter under the umbrella of the National Health Service. Rick had been the agent and it had been an easy transaction. We wanted it. We agreed immediately to the owner's price. I remembered Ben's wry smile when Rick had reminded him of the 'bargain' he had got for him. Perhaps this had weighed in the balance when we were deciding who we liked more, Chloë or him. Or had Ben been a little suspicious of the effect of Rick's charm on me?

Above all, it was a welcoming house with a friendly face like that of an old peasant: the racemes of wisteria, now withered, round the windows, resembled bushy eyebrows; the door was wide, like a smile. It was at one with the countryside, as if it had grown there, deep in the south-west of France and tucked between its two lazy rivers, the Lot and the Dordogne. The muted colours of the pantiled roof could have been the old peasant's cap.

Peace flowed through me. I forgot my sadness about Chloë for a few minutes as I washed up my breakfast dishes in the stone-flagged kitchen, admiring how Colette had scrubbed Ben's hand-churn so that the wooden paddles inside the glass jar shone white. The smell of lavender everywhere soothed me. I could think of Ben with calmness, and of his early death without bitterness. Now I had to brace myself to be of some help to Rick.

I tidied up and went downstairs, full of purpose. I would call on the Carvels, and perhaps they would be able to tell me about Chloë since she had been in the habit of helping them occasionally before she died. Perhaps they too had noticed the change in her that Rick had spoken about in his letters.

I set out through the village, bowing politely to the ladies with their shopping baskets, and noticing that Vivienne's chairs were already occupied by her rollered clients having their weekly coiffure. Perhaps there was a *fête champêtre* on in the evening. It was only the elderly people nowadays who liked them with their accordion bands playing waltzes and polkas. The young preferred the disco in Lafont. I liked Meloir, its atmosphere; Ben and I had always said it would take ten years at least before we were accepted, but I was happy to be back.

Six

Our pub near the British Museum, I mean the one Chris and I frequented, had an owner who welcomed you jovially, as did the other regulars. But Alain and Chantal Carvel in Meloir were different, as the French are different. Whenever you entered a French bar there was always a slight air of suspicion; or at least you thought of it as that until you realised that English people are recognised as being English even before they open their mouths, and they have to be regarded carefully before they are accepted. After all, there was the Hundred Years War. Ben thought they were like a colony of woodland creatures, wary of any intruders.

And this process naturally takes longer in a small village buried in the south-west of France. Alain and Chantal were always courteous but self-contained, although Chantal had begun to relax with Ben because his friendliness was so difficult to resist. Still, they always addressed us as 'monsieur and madame.'

However, when I went in that morning I found a change in them. I had established myself three years ago. I had been bereaved, and now I was back, and welcome. They shook hands, offered me coffee, and both joined me at my table after having asked my permission.

"We wanted to write," Alain said, "but thought it might be an intrusion." We spoke French together, and this may have been partly the cause of their reticence, because although I was fluent enough – having been educated partly at a Lycée and having spent a year in France for my degree – I didn't have to hand the colloquialisms of what I called 'Secret France' where the argot still flourished.

"And now Chloë," Chantal said, shaking her head. "So very sad."

"Terrible."

"They say it is suicide. The post-mortem has taken place, I believe. The funeral will be in three days' time. Everyone is so sorry for Rick."

"Yes. I hadn't liked to ask him. He met me at the station when I arrived last night."

"How kind. He has asked us to prepare a meal after the funeral for his friends."

"His sister will be coming from Angers?"

"Yes. She and her husband, I believe. How are they called, Alain?"

"Monsieur and Madame Knocke. His other friends come from Cahors, his solicitor and banker. Chloë had an American friend also, Mademoiselle Lerner. She spoke highly of her."

"It would be good if you could see Mademoiselle Lerner." Chantal's eyes were warm with sympathy as they met mine.

"I'm hoping to do that."

"Mutual sorrow brings one closer. *Bonne idée.*" This to Alain who had gone to the bar and brought back three cognacs on a tray.

"*Merci, Alain.*" I smiled and took the proffered glass. "*Bonne idée.*" Our friendship seemed to be progressing because of Chloë's death.

We were talking together when René Bonnard came in, doctor's bag in hand, a hat perched on his head. I imagined that being bald on top he would have to guard his head from the sun. His goatee beard was neatly trimmed, his eyes were still brightly brown.

"Ah, Madame Stanstead," he said, doffing the hat to greet me, "I am not surprised to find you here. I knew you would be deeply distressed to hear of your friend's death."

"I arrived last night," I told him. "I felt I had to come when Rick telephoned me. Even now I can scarcely believe it."

"Nor I. Nor the cause. A healthy young woman. And a good swimmer. You can imagine Rick's distress." His bright eyes were on me.

"Yes, indeed."

"And a shock for you too, madame, when you were no doubt managing to put your own life together again in London. How is London?"

40

"*Il va bien.*"

I remembered how kind he had been to me after Ben's death, calling every day to see me, gradually leading the conversation into happier channels, telling me about his twin interests of speleology and music. 'These are my solaces,' he had said once, 'for a rather lonely life. But I like solitude. My mind is well stocked. That is the secret of happiness.'

He had been pedantic but comforting, and in a way had been instrumental in my deciding to write a book about the Knights of Quercy. His remarks were true. When I was researching my mind was fully occupied. And in between, I could, so to speak, select a book from this library I had built up there. It had proved to be the best cure for grief.

When I rose to go, so did René Bonnard. "Permit me to drop you at your house. I'm going that way in any case."

"Thank you." I said to the Carvels: "I'll have to hire a car at Cahors to get around. I didn't want to drive all the way from London, but I'll need a car here. I've taken a month off work."

"We'll see you at the funeral, then, if not before," Chantal said. They both shook hands with me.

"I'll probably look in before that. Thank you for the coffee, and the drink."

"It was our pleasure," Alain said. He bowed, and I wondered when we'd be able to relax with each other completely.

"They're very pleasant," I said when I was sitting beside René Bonnard in his car. "At first we found them, well, rather formal."

"The death of their son from meningitis before you came changed them."

"I didn't know." I felt guilty that I had prejudged them.

"They prefer not to talk about it, especially Chantal. It has coloured her view of the village, shall we say. But before their son's death they were much lighter in temperament. Then their parents died in quick succession, then your husband. I think Chantal began to feel there was no happiness to be found in Meloir. And now Chloë . . ."

"I can understand that."

"I think she's on an even keel now, at least I hope so, and

41

Alain's been a wonderful support to her. She's stopped talking about the curse of Meloir."

"The curse?" I felt distinctly uneasy. So many deaths in such a small village . . . I shook myself. 'Negative thinking,' Chris had said to me once, 'destroys your soul.' "It's pure coincidence," I said. One shouldn't let it spoil a lovely village. Ben and I loved it the moment we saw it."

He spoke, looking straight ahead. We were passing the farm which had a duck pond at the side of the road and the inhabitants of it were likely to take a stroll across with a retinue of tiny siblings. "You have the great gift, Madame Stanstead, if you will permit me to say so, of a sanguine temperament. I have observed you. And Chloë had the same; not so volatile as you, but not the type to give up . . ." He kept his eyes straight ahead.

"I agree." My eyes were travelling idly over the landscape, the ground sloping up beyond the farm to the high causse where the grass was short and springy and pricked with thyme. I knew because when Ben and I had lain on it one summer's afternoon the smell had filled our nostrils. You had to watch where you lay. The rocks stuck through like shards. The rivers disappeared underground there – now you see me, now you don't – we had been fascinated with the terrain, as René Bonnard was, and with what lay underneath. We had meant to explore Les Eyzies and read up on prehistory, we had meant to do so many things . . . tears filled my eyes. Then I remembered René Bonnard's remark about my sanguine temperament, and turned them off.

"I never found Chloë depressive," I said. "Sad, but that was different."

"Did she ever confide in you?"

"No. She was . . . self-contained. Now Rick—" I said, and stopped. I was remembering his letters.

We had reached my house and he drew up at the rough grass in front. We had never trimmed it like an English bowling green, knowing it would look out of place.

"Your grass is baked brown," René said. "I must tell you about my Aunt Leonie." He laughed. "She brought me up, a typical French spinster, *une célibataire*, kind but quaint. That is why I am quaint. The front grass was her place for bleaching the linen – it's an old country habit – and my job was to shoo the hens off it because you know . . ." I met his eyes, twinkling like a robin's.

"I understand," I said, "but you know, it's a way of feeding the grass. Bleaching greens are . . . green! There are compensations for everything." We laughed together. "Thank you for the lift."

"*De rien.* I was going to ask you . . . you will think this impertinent . . . when you said Chloë didn't confide in you – did her husband?"

I looked at him. Yes, his aunt had made him quaint. What was his reason for asking me?

"I've offended you." He looked mortified.

"No, no. I was just wondering if I should confide in *you.*"

"It isn't idle curiosity, I assure you. I'm a researcher like you, every doctor is. If I told you that I found Chloë a deeply unhappy woman but never a depressive one, and I was anxious to find out why she was so sad, would that satisfy you?"

I met his eyes. They seemed to be honest. "Yes, it does. I was puzzled too about her sadness." I hesitated. "Well, I'll be honest. Rick and I have become friends since I left Meloir. Only by correspondence. His letters showed me a different man from the cheerful, charming one I knew before. He was deeply disturbed by Chloë's state of mind. She cut herself off from him completely and he couldn't understand why. He opened his heart to me, perhaps because I was truly sympathetic. Our friendship deepened, and . . . well, that's enough." It was probably too much.

"Please, Madame Stanstead." He held up his hand. "I've been guilty of extreme rudeness in prying. It's because of my anxiety . . ." But there was no further need for anxiety, I thought – Chloë was dead. "I'm puzzled, frankly," he went on. "Rick is a charming man, well-thought-of around here, a good business head. He and I are friends. We shared the same interests. Please excuse me. I was trying to see the problem from a different angle."

"Is there a problem?"

He hesitated for a second, as if he had been caught on the wrong foot, then smiled. "Nothing that can't be solved. "I'll say

43

au revoir." He took my hand and kissed it. He must have seen my look. "Blame Aunt Leonie. 'You must always be the little gentleman, René, where ladies are concerned.' Alas, what she didn't know was that ladies don't prefer little gentlemen." He laughed and opened his door, went round to mine and helped me out, quite the little gentleman.

I stood with him, looking at my house. "I'm glad I came back," I said, "in spite of the Jinx."

"Jinx?"

I racked the French side of my brain. "*Encorcelé?*"

"Ah, yes. Well, it's the right region for that."

"We hanged witches in England too." I looked again at my house. "It's welcoming, don't you think?"

"It's the gem of the village. A *pigeonnier* and a *bolet.* Such largesse." He gestured to the outside stair which led to the roofed terrace. "I'm sure Rick must be giving himself several kicks for having disposed of it so reasonably."

"It was really a case of the owners being anxious to sell. Now Rick tells me I could re-sell at a good profit."

"Would you?" I thought he looked interested.

"No. It's part of Ben and me. We loved it together. And there's so much to do. That wild garden at the back's crying for attention. And did you know there's a little *gariotte?*" He didn't answer. "I shall make a feature of it . . . oh, I have great ideas! I plan at nights when I can't sleep. I have a friend in London who is a keen gardener. His window-boxes are a credit to him." I laughed. René Bonnard didn't seem to see the joke.

"You have a capacity for making friends," he said. "I expect you have many in London. Even suitors?"

"Oh, hundreds," I said, laughing again. "I notice you're not applying for the post?"

"Alas, no. I'm wedded to my work and my speleology. I must go. *Au revoir.*"

I thought of him when I was going about the cool flagged kitchen making a sandwich with a baguette, some tomatoes and *chèvre.* Odd customer, I decided.

Seven

I spent the afternoon familiarising myself with the house again, and realising that to live here was no longer the painful experience I had imagined, but a solace. Memories of Ben permeated it, but it was a different Miranda with him, more carefree than the present one. I was thirty-two. Ben's death had taken away my girlishness. I could flatter myself that I had reached the state to which my mother had long ago promoted me when I told her I'd had my first period. 'You're a woman now.' That had been premature, but I thought the title could be fairly applied now. I still felt full of vigour, but more sensible, I might say, even more mature. Those two young people who had romped here no longer existed.

And I loved the garden. It was as if part of the terrain had been enclosed by the stone boundary wall. I was full of plans. Where the rocks pushed through could be the nucleus of a Japanese garden, and where there was a preponderance of wild flowers under the south-facing wall could become my meadow garden. I would sprinkle poppy seeds amongst the harebells, vetches and large white daisies, and the honeysuckle and wild sweet peas could be induced to clamber over the stone.

And there was the *cabane à pierre sèche* in a far corner, a relic from the time before our house existed. Ben had found out in the Cahors library its country name, *une gariotte*, intended as a shelter for a shepherd. Perhaps it could be used for an ice house as they did in Victorian times, although it was too low to enter without difficulty, and it would be sacrilege to alter it, or take off the extra roof of rosemary and thyme which had grown over the years.

*   *   *

I came near to complete happiness that sunny afternoon as I stood at the foot of the garden and looked towards the high causse with the purple mountains of the Pyrenees behind, the only sound the singing of the cicadas (I preferred to call it singing rather than the noise of their legs scraping together).

I was dressed and ready and sitting at my desk in the *pigeon-nier*, the tower adjoining the cottage at the back, when I heard what I thought must be Rick's BMW stopping outside.

I ran down the steep stair, then down the main one and opened the door. I saw he had another passenger, a large dog in the back seat. "Stay!" he said sharply to it, as he banged the car door and came towards me.

He looked freshly groomed, but drawn. Everything was dark about him except the white open-necked shirt. His dark hair was so thick that it rose steeply from the side parting, his dark glasses, even his skin was dark.

"I didn't know you had a dog, Rick," I said, kissing him on the cheek.

"Yes, for some time. When Chloë . . . withdrew from me, I bought Leo for company. He's a good friend. Very obedient."

"Not any more." The wolfhound had leaped over the car door and streaked past me to the back garden.

"Leo!" he called. He sounded angry. "Come back here at once!"

I laughed. "He seemed in a great hurry to go round the back."

"I'll get him." He was curt. "Are you ready? It's time we were on our way."

"An aperitif first?"

"No, thanks. I've already had one. I have to watch it. It's too easy to take refuge in the bottle." I noticed again how drawn and sad he looked.

"You're right, of course. Well, I'm ready. I'll just get my bag and lock up."

From the kitchen window I saw him striding down the garden, and I joined him there when I had locked up. "This damned dog!" he said. "Look at him!" All I could see of Leo was his rear end and a waving tail protruding from the mouth of the *gariotte*.

46

"What's he after?" I asked.

"God knows! Leo!" he shouted. Get out of that!"

"Perhaps he's found a hedgehog?"

"I'll flay him alive! Leo. Here! At once!" His face was flushed, his voice even more strident, more than the occasion warranted, I thought. The dog emerged, albeit reluctantly, and joined us, looking crestfallen. "He's trading on the fact that you're here!" He aimed a flying kick at Leo and the dog cowered at his side. I was upset.

"It was probably only a hedgehog," I said again and was surprised to see Rick's face change.

"Was that it, Leo, old thing, a hedgehog?" He bent down and stroked the dog's head. "Shall we go, then?" he said, smiling round at me. Leo followed us sedately to the car and jumped into the back seat without being told. The volte-face on Rick's part silenced me.

When we were driving through the village he said, "I must apologise for losing my temper. And taking it out on old Leo. He was only being nosy. But you know what it's like, feeling the bottom's dropped out of your world and having so many arrangements to make, and people calling. Have you had a miserable day like me, Andy?"

I winced. Only Ben had used that name. I felt he had taken it with him when he died.

"What's wrong?" He had noticed.

"I'm never called that now. It was Ben's." I couldn't have been so blunt three years ago.

"Sorry, sorry. This is not my day."

"Forget it. Actually, I've had a lovely day, Rick, falling in love all over again with the house. It's like coming back to a friend."

"You're seeing it in good weather, of course."

"No, it's more than that. And I saw the Carvels, and René Bonnard. He called in when I was there. They're devastated about Chloë's death. As we all are."

He had stopped at the junction to the N20. "It gets worse," he said. "There's talk of making a slip road further up. This is on a blind bend here. Dangerous, but they'll never get permission to cut through. Too many properties around here are *musée clas-sée.*"

"I seem to remember ours isn't. It's just outside the bound-ary."

"Yes, you're right. But don't raise your hopes. Even if the local council have no jurisdiction over it, the Government might."

"I wouldn't part with it. There's your gap," I said, seeing a lull in the traffic.

We crossed and drove through the village of Meyrac on the other side. I could see its Norman church steeple from my garden. "Glorious views from here," I said. "It's so high. Ben and I used to drive over to the *point de vue*. We were always struck by that wide panorama. You could stretch your eyes . . ."

"Gorgeous, yes." He scattered a few hens who were pecking round the village green then drove down the hill into the wooded banks of the river, so dark with the dense foliage that he had to switch on his lights.

"Have you ever fished here?" I asked.

"No, I'm not a country boy at heart, really, although we chose to live in Meloir. Well, Chloë did. My idea of bliss was to drive back from Cahors in time for a drink and a swim before dinner. Well, you know, Miranda. In winter we dined out or had friends in. Latterly, as I told you, Chloë became difficult. She said she didn't like to socialise." I met his glance. His eyes were full of suffering.

I put my hand on his. "You'll grieve, Rick," I said, "that nothing lasts, and then you'll reach the stage I'm at, a new kind of life, perhaps without the sweetness of those early days, but with its own compensations. You may meet someone else." I felt Leo moving behind me, breathing on my neck. Did he think I was laying it on too thick?

"I have," he said. I looked at his face in the dusk. It was set, grim. "But you seem to have forgotten."

"No, it's not that." I felt uncomfortable. "I just feel it's not the time to discuss anything personal."

"You're right, of course."

I took my hand away. Leo lay down on the seat behind me as if

48

the danger was over for the time being. I changed the subject. "I wonder what really interested Leo in my *gariotte*?"

"You'd be right. A hedgehog. Dogs are curious creatures, Leo particularly." He smiled. "His antics amuse me."

As we climbed up again and the gloom faded, the last of the sunshine enveloped us briefly, that stray shaft one gets at the end of a hot August day and which seems to give a golden edge to the landscape, the occasional house, even the sheep grazing acquire a blurry halo.

"Ben once saw a snake when we were driving along here," I said. "*Un serpent*. Sounds more sinister in French, doesn't it? We stopped and got out to look at it, bigger than a grass snake, coiled at the foot of the hedge, barred with gold. It was quite beautiful. It uncurled itself and I thought of the words, 'sinuous as a snake'." Rick sighed, it sounded like an impatient sigh. Was I boring him, tiring him with my reminiscences? Keep off the subject of Ben. Chloë had usurped him in the land of the dead. "Here's the village of the barking dogs," I said. I didn't mention that is was Ben who had called it that. "What do you bet they'll start now?"

"Let's see." He revved his engine as he drove and there was an immediate cacophony of sound from the farms we passed. Two villagers were standing talking at a gate and they glared angrily at us.

"They object to us disturbing their peace."

"What about their barking dogs?" Rick gave the men a casual wave.

"Now they've set Leo off." He had sat up, lifted his mournful head and begun to bay. I held my ears, laughing. "How to shatter the peace of the countryside," I said, but when I looked at Rick he wasn't smiling.

We reached the village on the high road where the restaurant was, and found it busy with chatter and music. They had set tables and chairs round the war memorial in the little *place*, but I thought we would have been better with the quieter charms of the Carvel's hotel.

We talked desultorily, peculiarly ill-at-ease with each other.

49

The expedition was a mistake. He should have stayed at home with his sadness and memories; I should have been pottering about my own house. I didn't want to make him sadder by mentioning Chloë, and I couldn't think of any other topic of mutual interest. I wanted to say that it had been different when we were writing to each other, but now that seemed detrimental to Chloë's memory. Neither of us seemed to have any appetite, and we drank too much, Rick more than me.

"Would you like me to drive?" I said when we were back in the car. Leo was asleep in the back and only lifted his head when he saw us.

"Don't you think me capable?"

"It isn't that. Just that you are under a strain."

He laughed. "Not to worry. The one and only policeman will be in his bed now." I didn't pursue it.

"I was going to ask you if you would give me a lift to Cahors tomorrow, if you're going to your office. I want to rent a car."

"Certainly. And don't worry about me, Miranda." He seemed to emphasise my name. "I'm noted for my good driving and I'm quite capable. Look how confident Leo is, lying in the back there. Aren't you, Leo?" He stretched an arm behind him to pat the dog, "Confident of your old man's capacity?"

My heart jumped about a bit as we drove back to Meloir at a speed far in excess of safety, considering the narrow roads and their frequent bends; but even though he was drunk, there was no doubt about his expertise. The only advantage of the speed was that we were back in Meloir in much less time than we had taken to go.

When we reached my house Leo sat up and made to jump out of the car but Rick put a firm hand on his back. "Down! Down!" His voice was stern. It must be a very seductive hedgehog, I thought, but then dogs do have to be obedient. And as for Rick's flare up of temper, grief did strange things to people. I had been unapproachable for days.

"I'll see you tomorrow, Rick," I said. "Thanks for a lovely evening. I hope it took your mind off your grief for a little. I'd ask you in, but I don't think either of us are very good company." I met his eyes and in the darkness I thought they glistened with tears. "Poor you," I said. Once you get through the funeral it won't be so bad. And you'll have Chloë's sister and brother-in-law. Family." He sat silent, then turning round suddenly, took me in his arms.

They were strong. One slipped down to my waist, seemed to be going further. He was breathing quickly. "Comfort me, Miranda," he said. He kissed me, his mouth travelling over my face. Desire and pity were mingled in me for a second before I pushed him away.

"That won't help," I said. "Go home now and get to bed." He muttered something about letters, and knowing what he meant I thought that the woman who had written them and the one now sitting beside him were two different people. The letter-writer had been the transitional one, this was the thirty-two-year-old who had begun to understand what made her tick. But how could you say that to a man who had just lost his wife in the cruellest of ways?

I got out of the car. "Thanks for the meal," I said again. "Good-night."

Leo sat up and seemed to want to follow me but Rick pushed him back. He subsided, and I crossed the rough sward, fumbling for my key. Supposing Rick follows me, I thought. The village was in darkness, and ours was not a barking village.

Anything could happen. Had happened. Chloë had drowned herself, Chloë who could swim. I lifted my hand in farewell without turning as I opened the door. I heard Leo baying sadly, and looked up. Yes, there was a moon. I went in and shut and locked the door, putting on the stout chain, surprised at the sense of security it gave me. I went straight upstairs to bed.

Eight

It was a sad and dreary little retinue which followed Chloë's coffin from the village church down the lane to the cemetery. Ben was buried in the far corner with its view across the fields to the Pyrenees in the distance. I hadn't felt able to visit his grave when I left for London. This time I would . . . but not yet.

Chloë's parents were both dead, and Rick's were not in evidence, nor any of his brothers or sisters. This was not commented upon, and to me seemed somehow in keeping with his persona.

The weather was funereal also. A molten sun hung low in the sky, sometimes disappearing altogether behind thick pewter-coloured clouds. The guests, sombre and mostly silent, drifted slowly back to Rick's house where the Carvels had laid out inappropriate festive fare, cold salmon decorated with cucumber slices and frothy chervil, flanked by jugs of mayonnaise, pâtés, salads and several *tartes de mireilles,* a local favourite. There was a separate table with wines in abundance. They helped themselves, and bearing plates and glasses, stood about the salon or the patio. They all avoided the pool.

Not surprising, I thought, finding myself beside René Bonnard. "One couldn't imagine swimming there now," I said to him.

"I agree. Especially if one has a vivid imagination." And then he said, surprising me, "Have you spoken to Luc Devreux yet?"

"The gardener? No. I met his mother in the village yesterday and asked her to tell him I could do with some help if he felt like it."

"Rick told you of the circumstances?"

53

"Yes, by letter, but I felt I couldn't bring it up. I had dinner with him last night at Terailles. He had hoped, I think, that going there would be easier than somewhere local, but it wasn't a success."

"I'm not surprised. Sudden death is bad enough, but under such circumstances . . ." He looked across the room. "That's Chloë's sister he's talking to. Have you met her?"

"Briefly, at the church. She's a striking woman." I watched her, thinking she gave the impression of suppressed anger rather than sadness. Her eyes looked cold. There was a family resemblance to Chloë in the colouring, but there was none of her feminine sweetness.

"She and Rick have never got on well. I doubt if they'll see much of each other after today, if at all. Her husband is quite different, self-effacing, *accommodant?*"

"*Compliant. D'accord.*"

My eyes were drawn against my wishes to the pool, and I noticed Leo, the wolfhound, lying with his head between his paws close to the edge, the picture of grief. René had followed my glance.

"A strange dog, that," he said. "It had never budged from there since we came back to the house. Possibly before that. Every time I've visited Rick it's been in the same position."

"It came with him last night. Yes, it's an odd dog. Do you know the *gariotte* in my garden?" He nodded. "When Rick called for me it streaked round to it and he couldn't get it to come out." I smiled. "Maybe there's a ghost there." Surprisingly, I saw René's face change, a watchful look come into his eyes. He spoke after a second or two, as if he had been searching for a comment.

"Let us see. Neanderthal man? His remains?" His smile seemed forced.

"No such luck," I said. "Perhaps an aura of some sort. You get that in some places, as if a previous happening had imbued—" Suddenly I heard Thérèse Knocke's voice rising above the subdued conversation. I saw Rick lay a placating hand on her arm and then look round apologetically. She shook it off angrily. I looked at René, eyebrows raised. "Trouble?"

"I hope nothing happens. Everyone's nerves are, shall we say, overstrung." We both looked again. Rick was talking quietly, and, by his attitude, placatingly to his sister-in-law, but she looked far from happy. Her head was turning in an agitated fashion.

René Bonnard looked about the room and turned to me. "Come and I'll introduce you to Madame Bovier if you haven't already met." He led me towards a tall, thin woman whom I had noticed in church, principally because of her elegance; *Parisienne*, I had thought. "Allow me to present Madame Stanstead to you, Madame Bovier," he said to her, bowing.

"*Enchantée*," we both murmured.

"I saw you in church," I said. Her black suit, impeccably tailored, emphasised her gauntness. Frenchwomen are often gaunt rather than slender.

"Madame Bovier is just back from Antibes, but she has a family home here," René offered.

"You're in the charming house just outside Meloir?" Madame Bovier said. "How clever of you to have bought it."

"I'm glad we did. It gives me a base in France."

She nodded. "I was so sorry to hear about your husband's death a few years ago."

"Three years now. We were friendly with the Gillams, Ben and I – they gave us the free run of their pool . . ." That was an ill-advised remark, I thought, today. "When I heard about Chloë's death I felt I had to come and offer my sympathy, and help. I've been thinking for some time of perhaps dividing my time between here and London."

"A foot in two camps. I hear you're a historian?" She seemed to be well informed.

"Yes, I was researching into the medieval knights of Quercy when Ben was stationed in Toulouse. I've always been fascinated by the Crusades."

"*Vraiment?* If you care to come to my home I could let you see our library. There might be something of interest to you there. Since my husband's death I spend most of my time in Antibes because of *la bronchite*, but I can arrange for you to be given access at any time."

"That's exceedingly kind of you." My former enthusiasm

rushed back. "I'm hoping to come to some arrangement with the British Museum where I work. I've only taken a month's leave at the moment but I love it here. The pace is much slower than London, and I'd forgotten how friendly and welcoming the house is."

"I can see you like it." She tapped my wrist. "Take my advice and don't spend too much time supporting Monsieur Gillam. He'll have to do as others do, get on with living. Ah. René." She put a hand on his arm. He was hovering beside us, casting occasional glances towards Rick and his sister-in-law. "You knew my Yves. Such a beautiful man! I can forget about him only in Antibes . . . he preferred it here. 'You go, Adèle,' he would say, 'and fry the skin. I'll remain with the—' " Her voice was drowned by a harsh shriek. It was Thérèse Knocke. Everyone turned.

"*Non! Non!*" she was screaming, "I shall not be quiet, Fabrice!" A quiet-looking man, presumably her husband, was patting her arm, at the same time looking around apprehensively. "He made life miserable for my sister!" She screamed again. "I want everyone to know!" There was no sign of Rick. Her husband was attempting to lead her away when I saw René Bonnard had quickly joined them.

"René will calm her," Madame Bovier said. She lit a cigarette in a long black holder with a silver lighter. "She's been imbibing too heavily, of course. And then the strain . . . they were good friends, the sisters, but in Angers she was too far away to come here often. There, René is leading her away. It's his forte. Keeping the peace and speleology. If that husband of hers has any sense, he'll get her into their car and start for home *tout de suite.*"

The interruption had been like a signal to break up the gathering. People were shaking hands, bowing, going into the house. Perhaps Rick was there. I decided I would go home as well.

"I'll take my leave," I said to Madame Bovier. "I hope we meet again. I'm sure we would have lots to talk about."

"Have you a car?"

"Yes, I rented one in Cahors. Rick dropped me off when he was going to his office."

"If you aren't doing anything this evening, why not drive to my house and have dinner with me? I shall be on my own."

"It's very kind of you but I thought of calling on Rick."

"I imagine René will be there. A trying day, especially with Madame Knocke's outburst. He may give him a sedative."

"Perhaps you're right." Still, she was rather managing. "Thank you. I'd like very much to have dinner with you, and perhaps have a glimpse of your library."

"*D'accord.* And Marie, my housekeeper, is also a very good cook." Her smile was mischievous. "An enticement, perhaps?"

I smiled. "How shall I find your house?"

"It's three miles from Meloir. Nearer the river, a hamlet called Le Petit Ouisselac. Our house takes its name from it. Anyone will direct you to the Manoir. We'll chat together and you will give me your opinion of Marie's cooking. She adopts the Provençal method from time to time. Seven-thirty? Women can dine earlier. *À tout à l'heure.*" We shook hands.

I had to pass the pool on my way to the gate. Leo was still there, moaning softly under his breath, if that's possible for dogs. The sad sound was at least apposite to the day and the occasion. I was glad when I got back to my kitchen with its cheerful geraniums on the window-sill and to put on the kettle for a good English cup of tea.

I looked forward to meeting Madame Bovier again. She was local, and intelligent, and would be able to fill me in about Meloir and its inhabitants – some womanly gossip, in fact.

I set off that evening for her manoir, refreshed after my several cups of Earl Grey, my pottering about the garden, my shower. I had looked inside the *gariotte*, but the ground was overgrown with a thick tangle of prickly brambles, and I didn't fancy tearing the skin on my arms and legs.

It had cleared up towards evening, and there was a glorious sun setting as I drove along. At Les Trois Lapins (why three?), I turned left for Le Petit Ouisselac and found myself in a lonely road bordered by fields of maize and tobacco with an occasional isolated farmhouse. It was a remote place. I could understand Madame Bovier preferring Antibes. She was probably a bridge player. She had a competent air. As a member of a non card-playing family, I generally steered clear of competent card-playing women if I met them in hotels. People who devoured books as I did could rarely spare the time for bridge.

In ten minutes I had run into the hamlet which had a cluster of small cottages built of the same golden limestone as a high wall which ran beside them and into which was set an arched gate of wrought iron. It was open. The Manoir de l'Ouisselac, I presumed, and drove through and up the short drive leading to a low, rambling house much to my taste but far beyond my means. It had mullioned windows and a stone balustrade, and there was a stone griffin on either side of the steps which led to a heavy oak door, iron-hinged. A late middle-aged man opened it when I pulled the bell, and behind him stood Madame Bovier in immaculate trousers and silk shirt. I had worn a long summer evening dress, thinking I ought to dress formally, and she was plainly discomfited.

"Oh, dear!" she said, drawing me in as we shook hands, "you have taken this trouble while I . . ." she indicated her own outfit, "as you see am in *le style anglais*. But, welcome! Jean will show you to the *salon* while I go and change."

"Oh, please don't!" I smiled, shaking my head. "I love your outfit. It's just that I thought . . ."

"And it's just that I thought," she said. "No, I insist. Jean will pour your wine and I'll be downstairs in two shakes of the tail of a lamb." She laughed. "I have an English friend in Antibes and he teaches me those phrases. Is it correct?"

"That, or 'two ticks'. " I laughed too. I followed the man into the *salon*, long and low with an unnecessary fire on this humid evening. Possibly *le style anglais* as well, I thought, but I was wrong.

"This room becomes damp while madame is in the south," he informed me. "She returned only two days ago and we have strict orders to light the fire in the evenings. Is that to your liking, Madame?" He had given me a crystal goblet of golden wine.

I sipped. "*Parfait*," I said. I had noticed that his hands, although scrubbed clean were rough and work-worn. Gardener as well, I thought. I wondered if he knew Luc Devreux.

Madame Bovier burst into the room wearing a long black dress with sparkling drop earrings, diamonds, I felt sure. She waved a hand towards herself. "Better?" She coughed, her hand to her mouth. "Pardon." I had noticed she coughed rather a lot. Perhaps it was the change of weather from Antibes.

"*Très soignée*," I said, smiling.

"Dinner in half an hour, Jean," she said as he handed her a glass of wine. When he had shut the door behind him she sat down near me, leaning forward confidentially. "I am blessed with Jean and Marie. Jean is . . . *indispensable*. Is there an English word for that?"

I thought. "Head cook and bottle washer?"

"Ah, *bon*, but not quite accurate. He is the gardener and butler" – I should have said 'general factotum' – "and Marie as well as being the cook is a fine seamstress. She keeps the house and linen in impeccable order. I dread the day when I shall have to pension them off. They'll both be sixty quite soon."

"They are married, presumably?"

"No, they are twins. They have worked in this house since they were sixteen. Isn't that remarkable? Since my parents' days. The only time they are parted is when Marie has her annual holiday with me in Antibes. She likes to copy the Provençal cooking. But Jean won't budge. He worries too much about the garden."

"You're very lucky. I don't need much help as my house is small in comparison with yours – Colette Jourdan kept an eye on it when I lived in London – but the garden is large. Chloë had arranged for Luc Devreux, a young man in the village, to look after it for the past three years."

"Ah, yes, Luc Devreux. His mother took him away from school to work. She does rough cleaning here for Marie. He's a nervous lad, I think. I believe he's been very distressed since Madame Gillam's death, not surprisingly since he found her in the pool."

"Yes, that was dreadful for him. I've asked his mother to tell him to come and see me when he feels all right, but so far he hasn't turned up."

"Alice Devreux, that is his mother, tells Marie he is having nightmares. Well, you can imagine, a young boy—"

There was a knock at the door and a plump woman appeared. She had a bright pink complexion, and with her build and manner gave the impression of a mature woman who because of her air of innocence was an odd mixture of both child and woman. Her twin, I thought, had the same air of unworldliness.

"*Servi, Madame.* You said Provençal, but then I thought, madame here might prefer some of our local dishes. I have made a *confit de canard*, there is some ripe *cabecou* and to follow, *pastis* with apples, soaked in *eau de vie, naturellement.*"

"*D'accord*, Marie," Madame Bovier said with a smile and raised eyebrows. And to me, with what could only be called a Gallic shrug, "*Que voulez-vous?*"

"It sounds marvellous," I assured her.

The food was delicious, although I noticed Madame Bovier only toyed with hers. I nearly made a pig of myself with the *confit*, but I left room for the *pastis* where Marie had certainly not spared the cognac.

We kept off the subject of the funeral and the incident with Chloë's sister, and talked almost exclusively of my research. She drew me out to talk about the stage I had reached in my work, and was a mine of information about the knights, principally the Bertrands, who were local, and the struggle they'd had to recoup their losses after Richard had usurped them.

"Property in those days, or their standing as knights, was more important than lives," she said. "You know the phrase, 'nasty, brutish, short'? But that isn't quite right either. 'Honour' was the important word. They lived by the sword, died by the sword."

"And the one who kept his head, as always, was the entrepreneur, Jacques de Coeur?"

"A man of culture nevertheless. Eleanor visited him from time to time when she wanted silk for her gowns." She spoke as if the Queen of Aquitaine was a next-door neighbour. "Shall we go outside for our coffee? It's such a beautiful evening."

I felt she had satisfied herself that I was worthy of letting loose in her library. I said that I should like that, having been enchanted by the food, and incidentally, the barrel-vaulted ceiling, and she said she always used the dining-room even when alone for the pleasure of looking at it.

The terrace where we sat overlooked the garden, dark except for the occasional bone-like gleam of a statue or that of the urns at the rectangular pool. The water-lilies showed pale against the dark water.

Her face behind the glow from the candelabra on the wrought-iron table was luminous with memories. "We have a fox which slips in and out. My dear Yves and I sat here for hours waiting for it to appear. Perhaps not the same one, but we called it our fox. It was . . . magical."

She told me about her husband and his property business in Paris, and how she had inherited this house when her parents died, and I told her about Ben and how much I had loved him, but that I had recently come to believe that love like that isn't wasted. "And that the world is still beautiful, like tonight," I said to her. "It was coming back to our house in Meloir which made me realise it, although it was for a sad reason. That's why I've decided not to sell it."

"Shall you continue to work with the British Museum?" she asked me.

"If I can come to a satisfactory arrangement about my own project," I said. "I think I can."

"Tell them you have a library at your disposal," she said. And then, "If you will forgive my curiosity, is there any other attraction in London? You are a lovely young woman."

"Who wouldn't confide when they are paid compliments like that?" I laughed. "Yes, I have a friend – a lover." The wine had loosened my tongue. She didn't turn a hair.

"How satisfactory," she said. "Every woman up to the age of ninety needs a lover. I have one in Antibes. An Englishman. He understands he will never compare with my Yves, but then I understand I will never compare with his Joan, and so we are both happy." Her delicate yawn made me look at my watch.

"Goodness!" I said, "it's nearly midnight."

"That is when the fox appears. And see," she said, pointing, "You are in luck." I looked towards the pool and saw the slim shape sitting in the moonlight beside a patch of water-lilies. The sight was unreal, like a painting, a poem, like a dream.

"*Charmant.* It licks its chops, and then it goes. It was worth waiting for. But I understand. You have had a busy day and so have I. We must get our beauty sleep."

"And I haven't seen your library. I have talked too much."

"No, it was I. It is a rare treat for me. But perhaps the omission was deliberate on my part. You shall have to come again."

"I would enjoy that. It was a rare treat for me too. Thank you. And the meal, being local fare, was . . . *parfait*. Please tell Marie."

"I shall. And I shall telephone you in a day or so."

We walked through the dining-room and into the hall. Jean was sitting in a chair, seemingly asleep, but he rose to his feet when we appeared.

"Now you can lock up, Jean," Adèle Bovier said. "But first I shall walk with Madame Stanstead to her car."

I thanked her again as we stood outside in the balmy evening. We had enjoyed each other's company, I thought. I hoped so, because it had been a lovely evening for me. "Tomorrow I'll get busy," I said. "I'll call and see Rick but when I go through the village I'll see if I can find Luc Devreux at home. He would be better working."

"I think you may find him still distressed; it was a shocking experience for him."

"Finding Chloë's body in the pool . . . shocking." I felt suddenly cold.

"Tragic."

"She was naked, I've been told."

"Oh." I didn't find that shocking. Chloë and I had sometimes swum in the nude. Water on bare skin is one of the most seductive things, we had agreed. "Still, he was a mere country boy."

"Not only that." She hesitated, looked away, looked at me. "You know . . . she had long hair?"

62

"Yes. Gorgeous hair." I could see it, flowing in the water. Ophelia . . .

"Some of it was missing." Her voice was low.

"Missing?" I looked at her.

"On the left side. It was as if someone had . . . gripped her hair and pulled, pulled very hard . . ."

"My God!" Now I was really shocked. "How did you know?"

"It came out at the inquest. I belong here. I have friends." She looked anguished, her eyes large in her white face. She even wrung her thin hands. "Forgive me, Madame, that was ill advised. I had kept it from you all evening, and now I blurt it out like a silly schoolgirl. And you a stranger, going home to a quiet house . . ."

"Please don't apologise." I patted her hands and got into the car. I spoke to her through the open window. "It was a shock, of course, but I would have been told in time. And it doesn't alter the fact that Chloë is no longer with us. That is the sad thing. Nor that poor Luc is having nightmares."

"How true. Thank you for being so gracious. I shall ring you. Drive safely."

I did, and slowly, while I tried to think calmly and rationally. But it was difficult.

Nine

I t had been an eventful day, but when I got home I found I wasn't sleepy. My conversation with Adèle Bovier and my mention of Chris made me think of him and, for the first time since I came to Meloir, really miss him. There just hadn't been time. I had telephoned when I arrived, but the line had been bad, and I had said I would ring again.

I looked at my watch. Twelve-thirty. He would still be awake and probably not even in bed. That had been one of the differences between us. I am generally an early bedder, preferring to do my reading there; he seemed to get a burst of energy around ten p.m., and start on tasks which could occupy him until one or two in the morning. I rang his number, and his voice came through, clear as a bell.

"Miranda! I was just thinking of you. I've tried once or twice but you've always been out."

"Yes, I've been quite busy. How are you?"

"Missing you like hell. It's a good test."

"Of what?"

"Love."

My heart warmed. "I've been missing you too, but there was the settling in, and then the funeral, and tonight I had dinner with a woman I met there . . . and there have been several disturbing things happening . . ."

"Like what?"

"It's chiefly the atmosphere. And the circumstances surrounding Chloë's death."

"Like, did she fall or was she pushed?"

"Goodness no. The post-mortem result was suicide, of course, but there's one peculiar circumstance which this woman I had dinner with told me about – she's called Adèle Bovier – part of Chloë's hair was missing on the left side."

"Missing?" I heard the astonishment in Chris' voice.

"Missing. That's just how I reacted. It's weird."

"Was she *dragged* to the pool?"

"Or did someone try to drag her out of it?"

"Phew!" There was a pause, then, "There's bound to be a logical explanation." He was reassuring. "Has it put you off staying on for the month?"

"I'm not allowing it to. I love it here. I imagined the thought of Ben would make me feel sad, but it doesn't somehow. As if he had put his blessing on the house, saying, 'Be happy'. I can't quite describe it."

"As long as you feel it. You think he wouldn't regard me as an interloper?"

"I don't think so."

"Because I'm planning to come in a week or so, if you'd let me. I have a paper to read at Chichester, but after that I'd really like to see you. Should I book in at a local hotel?"

I laughed. "I've already told Adèle Bovier that I have a lover, so you'd better live up to your reputation. We became quite matey." I suddenly thought of Rick. Would he be surprised? There were the letters we had exchanged. But somehow, since I'd met him, the rapport we had established in writing had evaporated. There was something about him that was . . . different. Well, of course there was, I told myself – he's grieving for his wife. Remember how you felt in a similar situation.

"You haven't mentioned the bereaved husband," Chris said. It was as if he had been reading my thoughts. "That was your chief reason for going, wasn't it, to comfort him?"

"It was, actually. I've had dinner with him once, but he's gone back to his office in Cahors, he's busy, and . . ."

"And what?" Was Chris psychic tonight? I didn't know quite what to say.

"And nothing. Yes, I'd love you to come. I could do with your company. We might spend some time at Les Eyzies. I've always wanted to do that, and the doctor here might give us some tips. He's an amateur speleologist . . ." I felt a slight ache in the middle of my forehead. Images were going through my mind: the funeral; Thérèse Knocke's outburst; Leo, the dog with its head between its paws at the side of the pool; my visit to Adèle Bovier's manoir and what she had told me . . . "It's been a strange day, Chris. I'm suddenly tired. Funerals are like weddings. They turn into a kind of cocktail party, and yet behind there is all the tension and the sadness . . ."

"That's very true. I'll just have them scatter my ashes in the Thames. No fuss. Get off to bed, darling, and think of me instead."

"Not a bad idea." The warm feeling was back. Chris was a comforter. He would be quite nice to grow old with.

I telephoned Rick in the morning and asked him if he would like to come for coffee and he said he would. His voice sounded strained, and when he drove up and I greeted him, I saw how his appearance matched it. There *was* something different. We kissed, and he held me, putting his cheek against mine.

'You're very good for me," he said. I couldn't deny him that bit of comfort, but all feeling for him had gone, at least of the kind which I had expressed in letters. The Rick I had conjured up was a different person from this grim-faced man who, although he was tanned, still looked pale round the eyes, haunted. I drew myself away.

"Come and have coffee," I said. He followed me into the kitchen. "Well, it's behind you now, the funeral." I put out cups on the table. "That's always an ordeal."

"Yes. But that woman had to shout her head off!" His eyes sparked. "I suppose you heard her. Everyone did."

"She was overwrought. She and Chloë were probably very close."

"I don't know what tales Chloë carried to her. Not in my favour, you may be sure." I decided to ignore that.

"Did she go right away?"

"Yes. René Bonnard gave her something to calm her nerves,

and then that poor sod of a husband persuaded her to get into the car. Of course it was malicious nonsense. She's always had her knife in me."

"I should put it out of my mind, if I were you. What are your plans for today?"

"I'm going to the office after lunch." He brightened. "I had a telephone call this morning from one of my clerks. Something has blown up. Sales are increasing daily. I've several clients who would jump at your house, you know."

"Yes," I said, "You told me, but I intend to keep it on. I've discovered since I've been back, in spite of the sad reason for coming, the house has an extra dimension for me because of Ben. I hope you'll find the same kind of comfort from yours in time. You'll forget the little differences you had with Chloë, think of the good times, of her sweetness . . ." His eyes were flat, as if he were waiting for me to stop.

"I doubt it." The window framed the *gariotte* at the foot of the garden, and I imagined he was looking at it. I remembered how Leo had made straight for it. He hadn't brought him today. I thought of saying that maybe if he used the pool again it would help, but then decided against it. If he should invite me to join him there I should have to refuse. I still had the picture of that naked girl, hair floating behind her, *some* of her hair.

"I tell you what," I said. "I've had an idea. When you've finished your coffee, let me give you lunch in Cahors. I have some essential shopping to do. I want to stock up with wines, get some English papers, and some books on prehistory, and maybe have a walk round the old quarter."

"All right. We can go in my car. I have plenty of room for your shopping." He smiled at me over his cup.

"No, thanks, I'll take my own. I'll have to drive around to different shops, and I'll try to park near each one."

"Okay," he said, "but only if you let me give you dinner pretty soon."

"I've invited a friend of mine to stay – Chris Balfour. Perhaps we could have dinner together?" His face seemed to close up, as if a blind had been pulled down.

"I didn't think you were going to make a holiday out of your stay. I thought . . ." He didn't look at me.

"What did you think?"

"You led me to think in your letters that you and I . . ."

"I got carried away in my letters, Rick. I was sad about Ben, and you were sad about Chloë's behaviour. We found solace in confiding in each other. It can happen you know."

"Can it?" He raised his head. His eyes were dark with anger. "The truth is you were leading me on!"

"What a stupid thing to say!" I was as angry as he was. "Surely you know me better than that."

"Oh, I can see it!" It was as if he hadn't heard me. "It was all right until this man turned up in your life. The one who's following you here!"

My temper flared, but I had to remember that Chloë's funeral had occurred only yesterday.

"Let's drop the subject, Rick," I said. "You've had a harrowing time. My regard for you hasn't diminished . . ." That wasn't strictly true. "But there's a time and place . . ." I stopped speaking. His face was blank again, as if he had shut off.

I put the niggling thought behind me. We set off, and I enjoyed driving behind his BMW on the broad *Route Nationale Vingt*, enjoyed refreshing my memory with the various road signs for hotels and restaurants, and nearer Cahors the discreet one for the Chateau Mercuez. That was for a special dinner *à deux*, not a hurried lunch.

Cahors, when we drove in, was its usual self, busy, bustling, with that feel of the south in the air, a degree or so hotter than Meloir further north. In the Boulevard Gambetta the cafés were spilling over with people at pavement tables, but parking would have been hopeless there. Rick waved his hand to follow him, and we were lucky to find two places at the Allés Fenelon close to the Syndicat d'Initiative.

The restaurant he chose was in sight of the Pont Valentré. I was moved as always by its symmetrical beauty, its three towers and pointed arches, its battlemented stairs leading to the first storey of the towers. Ben's boyish voice came back to me from the past.

'*Have you heard of the pact the devil made with the master mason, Andy?*'

'*No. Go on. Frighten me.*'

'*The mason traded his soul for the prompt execution of his orders so that the bridge would be finished in time.*'

'*So the devil got the work done for the mason and collected his soul?*'

'*No, that was one wily mason. When he saw the bridge was nearing completion he gave the devil a sieve and asked him to fetch him some water. Get it?*'

'*So, ostensibly, the devil never did manage to finish the bridge for him?*'

'*Too right. But the devil got his revenge. See that stone up there? It has a little devil carved on it, trying to prise out the stone. That's to commemorate that the devil loosened it. But not to worry. It won't fall on our heads. Many years later, another clever mason came along and fixed it in permanently.*'

'*Ben, do you believe in the devil?*'

'*I believe in the powers of evil . . .*'

Remembering, a cold shiver passed through me in spite of the heat of the day. As Rick and I walked to the restaurant I had for the first time in my life, I think, a cognisance, as if a huge, evil bird had brushed me with its wings. The heat's addling my brain, I thought. The streets are busy with shoppers and people hurrying to lunch, Rick is striding along beside me, everything is normal and yet unreal, as if I was looking at a picture of normality. I was glad the restaurant was large and noisy. I should have found an intimate atmosphere embarrassing in my present state.

We were both quiet. I was still affected by the memory of that conversation with Ben, by the awareness of evil that it could still engender. I lifted the menu and held it out to Rick, tried to smile. "What will you have?"

He handed it back to me. "You choose."

We both agreed we weren't hungry, blamed it on the heat, and decided on a *cèpe* omelette and a glass of wine.

"That isn't going to break the bank," I said, making an effort to be light-hearted. He put his hand over mine, and when I looked at him, his face was sad. I felt a rush of sympathy towards him.

"You've changed, Miranda," he said. "You were the one bright light in my future, but it's gone."

"That's too melodramatic," I said. "Circumstances change, and it's a sad time for you. And we've both changed. I've been away for three years in London, different setting, different people. You've just gone through a particularly distressing bereavement. People don't just stay the same."

But you came to Meloir to be near him, I reminded myself.

"I'm the same." He shook his head. "I was hoping you would fill the gap left in my life, that perhaps—"

I interrupted him. "Don't. Rick," I said. "Give yourself time to get over your loss." He released my hand abruptly.

"You're putting me off."

I had got myself into such a mess that I decided to be frank. "This friend of mine who's coming to Meloir . . . I see quite a lot of him in London."

"I guessed as much." His voice was bitter. "Yours isn't really a mercy mission. It's an excuse for a holiday with this Chris."

"Oh, for God's sake, Rick." I was exasperated. "Don't make heavy weather of it. You'll find Chris most sympathetic. He has two weeks' holiday and he's visiting me. He's interested in speleology." He looked at me, his mouth working.

"When I think of those letters . . ."

"They were meant at the time. I was lonely. I had been so happy at Meloir with Ben, and you and Chloë."

"They were love letters."

"In reply to yours."

"Mine were genuine. Now I see you were just leading me on."

I gave up. Sighed. "I expected better than that from you."

"I could well say the same." We were like a couple of children now.

"Would you like some more coffee?"

71

"No, thank you." He got up from his chair and said, formally, "Thank you for the lunch. I'll have to go."

"Of course. Thank you for your company." There was no response to my smile. He turned on his heel and left.

I called for the waitress and paid for our meagre meal.

I enjoyed shopping in Cahors, renewing my acquaintance with the bakers, delicatessens and antique shops which I had patronised before. But afterwards, when I walked along the river bank with its pollarded trees, the unease I had felt at the sight of the Pont Valentré came back. Why was I allowing an old legend to upset me? Why should Ben's words come back to me? '*I believe in the powers of evil . . .*'

I felt guilty because Rick was sure I had let him down, but at the same time comfort at the thought that Chris was coming to Meloir. I told myself it was because I wanted to share my pleasure in this part of France with him, show him Cahors's hidden corners, its walks by the placid Lot.

I turned and looked back at the city, the roofs with their curved Roman tiles, the *pigeonniers* which are such a part of the architecture here, and wondered why this particular part of France had captured my imagination. I remembered reading that everyone had two countries in their heart, France and their own.

I walked back slowly to the old quarter of Les Badernes where I had parked the car while I shopped, and on an impulse decided to go into the cathedral. But first I had to refresh my memory by studying again St Etienne's wonderful north door. You never tire of art of this perfection, I thought, as I admired the symmetry of the two angels flanking the central figure of God, the cherubim flying down to meet Him, the delicate tracery of the carving.

Inside were the cupolas, admired and copied by St Sofia at Constantinople, the vast nave, the rose window, the paintings in the chapel, fifteenth century. I always say I am non-religious. Should I get even more pleasure out of this church if I were a believer?

But I was content with the feeling of calm which came over me, a non-thinking stillness of the heart. '*I believe in the powers of evil*', Ben had said. In this holy place it was easier to believe in evil being conquered by good.

With my mind now cleared of foreboding, I remembered reading that the Bishop of Cardaillac who had the cupolas built, had just returned from the Crusades with Bertrand, Count of Toulouse. It was pleasant to sit there and let my mind wander down the paths of history, to imagine the knights at prayer on their return from the Crusades, or being blessed before they set forth.

But the unease returned when I was driving back to Meloir. Adèle Bovier's description of Chloë's naked body with the missing piece of hair was there in my mind again. I decided I would stop at the Carvels' when I reached the village.

I had seen them only briefly at the funeral; also those friends of the Gillams, Guy and Lenore Machin, and the other couple, Yvette and Raymond Lavange – but not the American friend Chloë had spoken about, Ellen Lerner. It was strange she hadn't turned up. I regretted now that I hadn't fraternised more. I might have found out about her.

It was a good time to stop off at *Le Repos*, six o'clock, before the Carvels started to cook and serve, and I found them behind the bar, washing glasses. I sat down on a stool.

"*Bonjour*, Chantal, Alain. *Ça va bien?*"

"*Très bien, merci*," Chantal said, and Alain echoed her, adding, "*Un Ricard*, Miranda?" We were on first name terms at last.

"Thank you. I saw you at the funeral, but I didn't get round to speaking to you. I've come to apologise."

"*De rien*. We didn't spend much time there. I noticed the Machins and the Lavanges left early too. I think we all felt the same."

"Thérèse Knocke? Thanks, Alain." I accepted the Ricard.

"*Mon Dieu*," Chantal said. "That was embarrassing."

"Funerals are distressing occasions for everyone." I was being cautious, remembering how careful they are in French villages about what they say. "It surprises me, all the same, that no one noticed before Chloë's death how unhappy she was."

73

Alain shook his head. "Well, you know Chloë. She had great strength of character. She wasn't the type of woman to complain. And she was loyal. She never spoke ill about Rick when she was here, but we could see she was unhappy." He paused, lowered his lids. "The evidence was there."

"You mean she looked depressed?"

"More than that. Do you remember the first time we noticed, Chantal?"

"When was that?" Chantal was non-committal.

"A month or so ago. Rick burst in here, face dark, eyes blazing. Chloë was setting the tables and he strode over to her. 'So this is where you've been hiding?' he said. We could hear him quite plainly. She passed it off, perhaps for our benefit. 'You haven't looked hard enough,' she said. But she looked afraid."

Chantal had decided to remember. "And we have seen bruises . . ." She stopped. "Perhaps we should not mention such things, Alain?"

He shrugged. "Miranda is a friend." Chantal was saying no more on that subject. "She certainly was away a lot from home, frequent visits to Angers, but she told us her father was dying. He never recovered from his bankruptcy."

"I remember Chloë telling me about that," I said.

"Perhaps her visits to Angers were to escape from Rick." Alain examined a glass he was polishing. "But there you are, marriages go to the rocks sometimes."

"On the rocks," I smiled, "like a shipwreck."

"It is not uncommon." Chantal looked at her husband. "But we were rescued in time, *n'est ce pas, cherie*?"

"Where there is love one is always rescued," I said. I wondered if I should tell them what Madame Bovier had told me about Chloë's hair, but remembered my theory about French villages. Better not to spread gossip. They asked me to stay for dinner, but I refused. I wanted to be in my house alone and do some more reading about the Quercy knights. St Etienne at Cahors had fired my imagination. What about witchcraft? I thought, in the car again. Women were being burned alive at the time it was built because they possessed the evil eye – had made *fachilhas au mépris* with contempt of their soul. Fascinating, I thought, seeing the hooded figures of the Inquisition, the bearded white knights of the Templars . . . even Meloir looked like a medieval village.

I was brought back to the present when, driving past Madame Devreux's house, I saw Luc, her son, sitting on the wall. I drew up sharply, noticing how dejected he looked, his shoulders hunched, his feet scraping the ground.

"*Bonjour, Luc*," I said. "I'm glad I saw you." He didn't look glad to see me. He was pale, and he hung his head, mumbling. I could barely hear him.

"I knew you were in the village, madame, but it hasn't been possible to come and see you. I have not been well."

"Oh, I'm sorry," I said. "What is the matter?"

"It's Madame Gillam, you see." He wouldn't meet my eyes. "It has made me feel so sad. She was good to me. We talked together. She encouraged me to study . . ."

"Yes, we all miss her. Perhaps if you started to work again, Luc—"

He went on as if he hadn't heard me: "She thought if I went to Cahors and took a course, you know, I could set myself up in business around here. There are people who vacate their houses and go back to Toulouse or Paris, and . . ."

"It's a splendid idea," I said. "And I should be very glad if you would help me with my garden."

"But now she is gone." He raised his head and I saw his eyes were full of tears. Young men don't usually give up work when an employer dies. Or weep.

"I know how you're feeling, Luc," I said, "and you are quite right to talk about it. That's how grief goes. You remember when my husband was killed how sad I was, but people helped me, especially my mother and father. You met them."

"Yes. They were very kind to me. They asked me to make a wreath for Monsieur Stanstead, and they gave me far too many francs for it. I said, no, but they insisted."

"Well, there you are, you see. And you could do wedding bouquets as well. Build up the little business Madame Gillam talked to you about." He looked more interested. "And if I were you I should talk to your mother. She could help you."

"No, no!" He became agitated. "She does not like the soft son. She tells me to be a man."

"Well, come and talk to me. And I'd like your advice on my garden. Would you call round and see me?"

"I'll think about it." He was still pale, unhappy-looking. "It may take me a day or two to get myself ready so that I do not weep all the time, but I will come. Do not despair." His eyes were again tear-drenched.

If I'd been his mother I'd have given him a good hug, and tried to find out what it was that depressed him so much about Chloë's death. But perhaps she thought hugging was the wrong way to make him a man.

Ten

I was sitting happily in my *pigeonnier* study, the lamp on my desk shining over the dark garden, when I heard a knock at my door. My heart jumped. It was a quiet village. No one would call at this time of night (it was around half-past nine, I knew) unless there was something wrong. My mind flew to Chris, but I dismissed his arriving unheralded. He would telephone first. Chris was not the spontaneous type. All those thoughts went through my mind as I went slowly downstairs. I could have done with a knight or two, fully caparisoned, shielding me.

Because I had been immersed in my writing, I hadn't gone downstairs earlier to put on any lights. I did so now, also switching on from inside the light above the front door. I was contemplating shouting 'Who is there?' but not liking the idea – how many people are murdered because they are too shy or embarrassed to take this simple precaution? – when I heard Rick's voice. Immediate relief flooded through me, followed by apprehension. Had something happened?

"It's only me, Miranda," he was calling. "Rick."

"Oh!" I stammered, "It's you! Okay." I hurriedly undid the complicated bolt and chains which I'd had fixed.

His appearance reassured me. In the overhead light, as well as looking incredibly handsome, I saw his haunted air had gone, and even his dress was casual and reassuring, light shirt and trousers with a dark sweater knotted round his neck by the sleeves.

"Sorry, sorry!" I said. "I was dead to the world upstairs. Writing, you know how it is. Come in!" He stepped into the narrow hall. And, jokingly, I said, "Do you know the time?"

"Yes, I shan't stay long. I was restless, and thought of our meeting today. And our conversation. I wanted to set things right."

"Oh!" I said, leading the way to the sitting-room, and because I was puzzled, I started babbling nervously. "I was buried in the eleventh century. Raymond IV was just setting off on the First Crusade with an army of barons. I was working out their emblems. Cardaillac's was a silver lion . . . so as their vassals would recognise them . . . I didn't hear the car . . . the *pigeonnier* faces the garden . . . will you have a drink, or coffee?"

"A drink, please. It will save you fussing in the kitchen with a coffee pot, the way women do." He smiled at me. He had a disarming one-sided smile which lit up his dark eyes and caused a crease to appear at the side of his mouth. His whole demeanour was different, lighter than it had been at Cahors. He seemed . . . at peace with himself. Had I been the same when Ben died, swinging from one mood to another? It was difficult to know how one had presented to those around.

"Then, how about some vino? I only had some cheese and fruit for dinner, nothing to drink." For some reason I didn't mention my *Ricard* with the Carvels.

"Perfect. Let me pour it out for you." I waved at the table with bottles and glasses.

"Put your nose in that," he said, bringing me a glass of rouge. "I'd recognise it anywhere. "*Vin du pays*. You're wise to drink the local wine."

I sipped. "The essence of France," I said. 'The Carvels' *vin de la maison*. I bet it would be awful if you drank it anywhere else. Take Gaillac, for instance. You know, the flinty white wine? I raved about it when I drank it in Albi with Ben, and when we bought some in the local supermart in London I had to pour it down the sink."

"I call the Quercy wines the stay-at-home wines, except *Vin de Cahors*. That'll go anywhere, a truly classic wine, Roman."

We were so relaxed with this chit-chat that I stopped worrying about his sudden appearance. I well knew the restlessness which came with grief. "Did you have a good afternoon at your office?" I asked.

"Yes, and we're busy, thank God. Houses in this region are going like hot cakes, mostly to the English and the Dutch." He smiled and lifted his glass to me.

"Did Chloë like working there?" I didn't know why I had introduced her name into the conversation unless Carvel's rough potion had made me careless.

"Yes." He nodded slowly, consideringly. "She was very efficient. She tended to poke her nose into things which didn't concern her, but then women are like that, don't you think?" His smile had lost its charm. "Latterly, she lost interest, left me in the lurch often." He sighed. "But it's all behind me now and I must make a new life for myself." He sipped, twirled his glass, looked at me over it. He was making me nervous. What was coming?

"You'll stay on in Meloir, of course?"

"Yes. I don't like living on top of the office. And I'm fond of the house." He ran his finger round the rim of his glass. "I don't intend to let Chloë's ghost haunt it." His eyes were on me.

"Unless as a happy one? We had good times there, Rick, the four of us."

"Yes, we had good times there, Miranda." The smile, the pause.

I blurted out, or so it seemed: "I was sorry I didn't speak to your friends at Chloë's funeral, but you know how it is. You get stuck with someone."

"They left early. They came in one car and Guy wanted to get back to his office to sign letters. Raymond also. Le Credit Agricole, you know, my friend Raymond. Very astute."

"I hope he's taking care of my money." My joke fell flat. "I would be pleased if you would bring them here, Rick, say what day would suit."

"As a matter of fact they're both coming to me for lunch on Sunday. I could look in with them if you like."

"That would be fine. Will their wives be coming?"

"Not very likely. It's purely business."

"Unless they would like to come here with them and stay on with me for lunch?"

79

"Well, that's very kind." He gave me his charming smile.

"Not at all. I'd enjoy it. Shall I leave it to you to arrange? By the way, I remember Chloë had an American friend, Ellen Lerner. I never met her, strangely enough. Was she at the funeral?"

"No." He looked round the room. "Pleasant, the way you've done this. French Provincial? It has your quality, Miranda."

"What quality is that?"

"A capacity for getting things right. *Savoir faire.* 'Laid back'. Isn't that what they say nowadays?"

"Sometimes. Well, thanks for the compliment."

He looked at me. His glass was empty, but I ignored that. He said slowly, "You've changed, you know. Even your living alone is different. You aren't afraid?"

"Afraid? No, why should I be?

"Alone here, outside the village. If you screamed your head off no one would hear you."

I laughed, convincingly, I hoped. "I don't let my imagination run riot. I've a sanguine temperament, I've been told."

"That's good." He twirled his empty glass rather ostentatiously, but again I ignored it.

"Is it, good?" I said. He nodded, lips pursed and nodded again, as if he were thinking.

"You see," he was holding me with his eyes, "I haven't told you why I came here. Actually *I* have a vivid imagination, and I don't have a sanguine temperament, at least not all the time – like now."

"Do tell," I said, and for some stupid reason asked, "Would you like another drink?" What I meant was that *I* should have liked one.

"No, thank you."

"So?"

"It's about those letters, Miranda."

Oh, God, those letters . . . my heart gave two significant thuds, like the preamble on a tom-tom drum. "Yes," I said. I met his eyes. "What about them?"

"I was thinking over what you said, that you had written them under peculiar conditions. Well," his eyes were still on me, "I've begun to think it was the same with me." What's he playing at? I thought. "You were recovering from Ben's death; I was using my letters as an antidote to Chloë. I was worried about her behaviour, and thinking that we might break up, and if that happened perhaps you could take her place . . ." He gave a small laugh. "I see it all now."

"What do you see?" I was calm, wondering when the crunch would come, trying to be ready for it. Was he going to say that this feeling for me couldn't be controlled, and now that Chloë was gone there were no restrictions? His words came back to me, 'living outside the village . . . No one could hear if you screamed your head off . . .'

"It's as if I had suddenly come to my senses. Chloë has gone, but I have no intention of making any demands on you. That's over and done with. I hope we'll remain good friends – special friends because we helped each other at a crucial time." He smiled. "So, there it is. *Mea culpa.* I'm looking forward to meeting your new friend – Chris, isn't it? – when he comes."

I rushed into relieved speech. "Of course, of course! Chris would love it too. I've told him about you. I value your friendship, Rick, believe me. We're linked in a way by Ben and Chloë. I'm so happy that we know where we stand."

"That's why I felt I had to come. Let's try and bury the past. It's early days for me yet, and I'll need friends." He got up. "Now I'll have to go. It's been a busy day, but I like being a working man again, taking up the reins. My mind is calm. I shall always miss Chloë, of course, but I'll take you as an example of how to behave when one's partner dies."

"I'm glad for you, Rick," I said as we went into the hall. "And remember, make that arrangement with your friends. I'm looking forward to it. I shall expect you all at twelve."

"I'll see to it." We kissed sedately, and I walked with him to his car. The French air was soft on my face. I took a deep breath of relief. "Shall you go back to your desk?" he said as he got in and wound down the window. 'Mmh. Beautiful night."

"Yes, lovely. No, I've had enough for tonight."

81

His smile was white in the darkness. "Do we ever get enough?" he said, as he turned the ignition, let in the clutch. He waved as he drove off.

Had I imagined that last remark? Cryptic, but then it had been a peculiar call. But welcome all the same. I stood watching the car disappear round a bend in the road. It was open, and the back seat was empty. Leo had stopped coming with him. Was he still lying at the side of the pool, head in his paws?

I went slowly into the house.

Eleven

I had two telephone calls the following morning, one from René Bonnard, and one from Adéle Bovier. René was first. "I take my *congé* tomorrow afternoon. I wondered if you would like me to drive you to Les Eyzies, and possibly have a look at Font de Gaume. You said you were interested in *grottes*."

"Yes, I am." I talk too much at times. I didn't really want to go; that is, I wanted to go but not so quickly, and preferably with Chris. I was getting really embroiled with my research now, and I am like a terrier down a rabbit hole when I get started. There were all kinds of delicious side issues, such as how the persecution of the Jews really started with the Crusades, and whether the power of evil might have been the driving force of the Crusaders. Which was the stronger, the power of evil or the power of good?

The only one who really understoods this obsession with an idea was Chris. Once, we had discussed the book by Yukio Mishima about the Zen acolyte who, being ugly, couldn't bear the beauty of the Golden Pavilion and had set fire to it. I said that I thought the real obsession belonged to the author who had committed hara-kiri.

Back to René. I said I would love to go to Les Eyzies with him.

Adèle's call was also an invitation. I thought the sparkle had gone out of her voice. "I have to go into hospital in Paris next week."

"Oh, I'm sorry," I said, "I do hope it's nothing serious."

"No, just an investigation. My doctor in Cahors has fixed it up."

"I hope it's an unnecessary journey. Can I do anything to help?"

"Yes, you can come for dinner this evening, if you're free."
Something about her bleak, almost brusque tone disturbed me.

"No," I said, "I wouldn't dream of coming again. Let me give
you dinner."

"Some other time. I want to show you the library and then if
I'm away for any length of time, you'll know your way about.
Jean and Marie will always give you access."

"But won't you be back after Paris?"

"No, I'll go straight to Antibes. I have promised my English
friend." She never said his name.

"In that case, thank you. I'll see you this evening."

"Seven o'clock?"

"*Parfait.*" My social life in this remote part of south-western
France was fuller than in Bloomsbury, I thought. I felt sorry
about Adèle's news. But I still had a good day's work ahead of
me. Every writer or researcher knows how one longs to have an
uninterrupted run, and as I went upstairs to my *pigeonnier*,
(feeling like Daudet in his old mill near Arles), my thoughts
went to Rick. Why had he bothered to call so late at night simply
to tell me that I needn't worry about his intentions. Had that
become an obsession too?

Of course I understood how in our correspondence our feelings for each other had developed. Wasn't that why I was here?
But why the urgent need to tell me that I needn't worry, that he
was now able to draw a line under that episode?

Draw a line. That was it, of course. I had found out at first
hand that grief makes one erratic in one's behaviour, in one's
thinking – unsure of one's judgement, like a straw in the wind, as
if one is in the epicentre of a storm which grief is, a storm of
feeling. He had come out of it. He was back to himself. He had
wanted to tell me.

But could a line really be drawn? There was that disturbing
fact about Chloë's missing hair. I had heard of someone tearing
out their hair in anguish. Was that what had been decided at the
post-mortem when they gave the verdict of suicide?

My mind was going round in circles as I got my books out and
sat down at my desk, but the beautiful landscape seen through

the window calmed me. It rolled beyond my semi-wild garden, with that stone shape of the *gariotte* at the foot, to the faraway Pyrenees. Was it my house which obsessed Rick? The thought sprang out from nowhere.

There were plenty of houses in south-west France to equal mine in age and character. Quercy was only being discovered. The Dordogne had monopolised the attention of the English so far, so much so that they were making a little England out of it and spoiling its charm.

Give it up, Andy, I told myself, and get on with your work. Writing a book is like ploughing a field. Your mind gets disturbed, it turns up all kinds of peculiar thoughts. Life's interesting. You're making a go of it without Ben, and you have Chris coming soon, probably next week. He can be a sounding-board for all those random doubts you're having, he can set your mind at rest. And then I remembered Leo and I was away again. 'He is my constant passenger,' Rick had said when we had driven across the valley for dinner. But he hadn't been in the car last night. 'I can't go anywhere without him,' Rick had said.

Had he forbidden the dog to come because he had disobeyed him by rushing round the back of the house? But I hadn't minded and it wasn't a great sin his making a beeline for the *gariotte*. There was nothing to spoil there. Was it that Leo had refused to come and was he still lying at the pool, his head between his paws? Too many suppositions. I went back to the eleventh century. The Crusades were less disturbing.

Or were they? That setting off on the first Crusade with Raymond of Toulouse at their head. The barons proudly emblazoned, with their vassals around them. Off to the Holy City, blessed by the Popes – a long-lasting religious stag night, Chris had once said. There I was, ploughing again, turning up stones, starting off hares. I called my thoughts to order and started writing.

I thought what a pretty village Meloir was as I drove through it later on my way to have dinner with Adèle Bovier. That was what struck me when Ben and I had first seen it, *un si joli village*.

You dipped into *la place* from the high road, a large expanse of baked earth with a huge sycamore roughly in the centre and surrounded by old Querçyois houses of golden stone with Roman tiled roofs. In between the houses was the *épicier* – Madame there called it a *supermarché* because she had invested in some wire baskets – and Monsieur Fecamp, the *boulanger*, and on the corner was the café for the young – the Carvels didn't encourage them because they didn't eat. The school had a prominent place in the middle of the square.

Behind the sycamore, the rest of the square except for the space for *les boules* was taken up by the huge Norman church with its arched door and the rose window above, the whole edifice far too large for the few women who turned up regularly. On the road to Lafont there was a small *tabac* and a *quincaillerie* usually surrounded by a few trucks and gossiping farmers.

My house was on the other side of the village, what we called the Cahors side, and beyond it there were only fields and a small château, a dilapidated place which came alive every August when the Parisian family who owned it came for their holidays. But the gates were beautiful, fanciful wrought-iron with a heraldic crest of a strange animal surrounded by lilies – a salamander, I thought.

I passed Luc Devreux's house but there was no sign of him, and a little further on Colette Jourdan's, the young woman who had looked after my house when I was in England. She was now helping Rick. I had paid her through the Credit Agricole, but so far I hadn't seen her, although she must have heard I was back. I remembered the lovely zinnias she had put in a vase for me. As I drove through the valley which dipped between Meloir and Le Petit Ouisselac, it occurred to me once again that my life in Bloomsbury was quiet in comparison with my social whirl here.

I knew the way now, take the turning at Les Trois Lapins – I still hadn't figured that one out – and along the quiet road leading to the hamlet, with the occasional farmhouse nestling in a fold. I met a *troupeau* tinkling along, followed by a young lad who had probably sat out most of the day to guard them. "*Bonsoir,*" he said cheerfully to me. Where in England would you get a boy of sixteen to sit in solitude looking after sheep without even a radio? I hoped he was looking forward to an evening spent in the village café with his friends.

Adèle Bovier met me wearing a long dress of white splashed with large black flowers, her hair drawn smoothly back from a white face with coral lips. She reminded me of the picture on an old record sleeve I had of Maria Callas, the shape of the face perhaps, the large accented dark eyes. I remembered reading that the prima donna had had a struggle with her weight. The resemblance stopped there. Adèle Bovier was painfully thin. Her wrists and ankles looked as if they could have been snapped like twigs.

Her welcome was sincere. "You are a kind girl to take pity on me," she said, leading me to the terrace which ran outside the *salon.* "The thought of driving anywhere was too much for me, on top of the amount of packing I've had to do, first for Paris and now Antibes . . . do sit down." And waving her hand towards the wrought-iron table, "You see we are having champagne tonight. And here is Jean to open the bottle." He had followed us in.

"*Bonsoir, madame,*" he said. "*Je suis heureux de vous retrouver.*"

"Now, now, Jean," Adèle waved a finger at him, "No making of the sheep's eyes at madame here."

His laugh was at least sheepish. "*Je vous demande pardon, madame.*" He opened the bottle expertly and poured each of us a glass.

When he had left the room she said: "You see I don't stand on ceremony with Jean and Marie. They have seen me through bad times and good. Sometimes Jean tries to deputise for my Yves."

"You are lucky to have them." I sipped the champagne appreciatively.

I'm no judge of champagne, I don't drink it often enough, but this seemed to be excellent. After a few sips I became light-hearted and I noticed Adèle's eyes also had brightened.

"*C'est une tonique sans reproche,*" she said, holding up her glass to me. "How are you getting on at Meloir?"

"Very well. Life is amazingly busy. I've been to Cahors with

Rick Gillam." I didn't mention last night. "I've seen the Carvels, Luc Devreux and Dr Bonnard. He's invited me to go to Les Eyzies with him tomorrow."

"He's a palaeontologist, of course. Everyone must have their passion. That is his. As far as I know, women don't come into his scheme of things, but I'm not a close friend of his."

"I thought he was your doctor?"

"No, too provincial. I prefer to go to Cahors." I wondered if there was a little reserve in her manner.

"I'm sorry you have to go to Paris. Are you worried?"

"I don't allow myself to be worried. I remember my dear Yves and how he bore his illness so uncomplainingly. It is necessary to emulate him. I am returning to Antibes because the weather is gentler there now that we approach autumn." She smiled. "And there is my English friend. He will come to my apartment each day as his is adjoining, and sit with me and make me laugh – so necessary, don't you think? And in the evening he will drive me somewhere smart to dine which will raise the spirits. How is your lover?" she said, hardly drawing breath.

I laughed. "I telephoned him after I saw you. You must have made me envious of yours." I noticed that she showed not even the slightest flicker of embarrassment.

"Will he come to see you?"

"Yes, sometime next week. It will probably shock Meloir."

"I should not worry. Besides, things go on in Meloir and here which are far more shocking, I can tell you that. One looks at the tranquil countryside and thinks all is peace, but do not believe it. It is like turning a stone. Marie has told me some tales which make my hair stand up, but I think: yes, Marie, you don't say a word about yourself, ah, no!" What can she mean, I wondered, preferring not to let my mind roam too far.

Jean came in and announced the meal. "A light *repas* as you ordered, Madame," he said.

"*Bon.* I hope Marie has followed my request and not made her famous *pissaladière* as well."

He laughed appreciatively. "Who am I to say, madame?" He bowed and went out, still chuckling.

The meal was light, various pâtés and salads, cheese and a delicious ice pudding. I noticed again Adèle merely picked at her food, all the time encouraging me to pay no attention to her. Marie's ice pudding, she told me, was famed throughout the region.

When we were having coffee in the dining-room – I was glad as I could continue to admire the vaulted ceiling – I told her about my call at the Carvels': "They told me of an incident with Chloë and Rick. He followed her to their place once and accused her of hiding from him." I looked at her. "But it's three years since I saw them together. Marriages can deteriorate in that time."

"There is no doubt there was trouble. Madame Devreux confides in Marie, who confides in me." She gave me a rueful smile. "How we gossip in the country! Luc's an observant boy, but he refuses to talk to her about Chloë's death. It's obviously had a great effect on him."

"Perhaps I'll get him to talk when he comes to work for me – if he does." I stirred my coffee. "I wonder why Rick's behaviour changed towards Chloë. Do you think he had a long-standing grudge against her?" Here I go, I thought, gossiping too. "He told me once in a letter that when they were both at university she tricked him into marrying her because she said she was pregnant."

"And she wasn't?"

"No."

"It doesn't sound like Chloë." She was resting her chin on her hand. She looked tired, but her eyes were interested. "Did *she* ever tell you that?"

"No, she was always circumspect, always loyal." A thought occurred to me. "Is Rick rich, do you know?"

"Now he is. His business does well, but I believe it was an aunt who paid his fees at Toulouse. I've never heard him mentioning his parents."

"Perhaps he thought Chloë was rich?"

"If so, he would have been disappointed quite soon. Her father became bankrupt."

"Yes, I remember." Could Rick have advised him wrongly, or even borrowed from him? This is your friend, Rick, you're thinking about, I reminded myself, charming, well liked. You've caught some of the Meloir disease – speculation, gossip.

"He's charming, Rick," Adèle said, "well liked by most people. Small villages . . ." she was echoing my thoughts. She waved her cigarette in its ebony holder at me. "This is the great evil, the cause of my trouble. And yet I cannot give it up." I smiled in sympathy: it had taken me a year.

"I'm sure your visit to Paris is wise." And because I had grown to like her very much I said, "You and I were lucky. We both had happy marriages."

"Yes, lucky. I have a sadness for Chloë. There was a poignancy . . ."

"I feel the same about her. She wraps herself round your heart." I had a vivid memory of her as I spoke, when I had imagined her coming towards me in the station yard, arms outstretched, beseeching . . ."

"Shall we go next door and see the library?" Adèle got up abruptly and I followed her. I had noticed she staggered.

"Are you sure?" I said. "I don't think you look at all well."

"I am really sure." She smiled, and her smile dazzled me with a rich enveloping kind of beauty. That was how she had been when her Yves had been alive. I liked her very much at that moment, and felt an unaccountable sadness.

The library was barrel-vaulted also, and she told me there was a further one where her stock of wines was kept. "It was the oldest part of the house, probably as old as some of the knights you are studying." She sat in a chair while I went from row to row exclaiming in amazement at the abundance of books.

"But this is a wonderful collection. I feel very privileged to be allowed to look at it."

"You must do more than look at it. You must come here whenever you like and work. I cannot allow the books to leave the library. Yves had strict rules there. His father had been a professor at the Sorbonne, and books were his life, especially this collection."

"I'm humbled. You're sure you don't mind me coming occasionally?"

"I'm sure and Yves is sure. I have asked him and he agrees."
She cast her eyes upward. "Now, this evening, I am sorry we
cannot wait to see Monsieur Reynard for I must get to bed and
rest for my journey tomorrow."

"Of course." I saw the dark rings under her eyes. "Oh, I do
hope I haven't over-tired you."

"You have stimulated me. I have been worried about Chloë. It
was fortunate you came into my life. Now I give my worries to
you, but I ask you to keep in touch with me by letter or telephone
and tell me anything you find out. Will you do that for me?"

"Of course."

"Enjoy your visit with René Bonnard to Les Eyzies – I wonder
what is the interest he shares with Monsieur Rick? I'm sure it's
not palaeontology. And perhaps Luc Devreux will come to work
in your garden." She smiled at me. "You are much more
compatissante than his mother."

We walked slowly to the hall and at the foot of the stairs she
put her hands on my shoulders and kissed me on either cheek. "I
have grown fond of you, Miranda. I hope we will meet again."

"I'm sure we shall."

"I am glad you are so sure. I'll ring for Jean."

"No, please. I can let myself out."

"Very well. He helps Marie in the kitchen. It is still not time for
him to take his place in the hall. *Au revoir.*" And, mischievously,
as she turned to go upstairs: "Have a good time with your
'lovaire'."

My eyes were wet as I started the car. The sadness was deeper
than conscious thought.

Twelve

T he telephone was ringing as I opened the door, and I went quickly to it. I heard Chris's reassuring voice. "I was on the point of hanging up. Where have you been gallivanting to?"

"Since when have I been accountable to you?" I laughed, with relief. Why did words like 'reassuring' and 'comforting' always spring to mind in connection with Chris, and was that a bad thing?

"Black mark. I'll rephrase it. I was worried when there was no reply. I'm ringing from Chichester, but I hope to be back in London tomorrow. I'm missing you, Miranda, badly. This place makes it worse. It's so prosperous, everybody looks well fed, and the shops have such quality goods in them, nothing shoddy nor shabby like some parts of London. Too well bred for me."

"Poor Chichester. I've hardly had time to miss you. Village life is absorbing. Have you fixed your date for coming here?"

"I'm hoping for the middle of next week but I'll ring you again."

"You're not thinking of surprising me, are you?"

"Would you like that?" Did *he* wonder if he was too reassuring, too comforting?

"I'm getting enough of that here."

"In what way?"

"Before I came, Rick had told me – in his letters, of course – that Chloë had changed towards him. Now to my surprise the Carvels tell me he made a scene in their hotel when Chloë was helping them there. Barged in. Shouted at her. It's not like Rick."

"Do you believe them?"

"I've only their word for it, of course, but there would be no point in their making it up, would there?"

"That's the trouble with small villages. Make a drama about anything. Give me London every time." Is he right, I wondered, or is there something peculiar about Meloir? *The power of evil* . . . Ben's words came into my mind. "Married couples squabble, Miranda," Chris was saying.

"It's par for the course."

"That's true." Still, there were all those confidences in Rick's letters, from the marriage onwards. I decided to keep quiet.

"Did Chloë ever confide in you?"

"No. And she never wrote." It was a second or two before Chris replied.

"How do *you* find him?"

"Charming. Everyone seems to like him. He's coming to terms with Chloë's death, he's gone back to work. He's built up a good business in Cahors. He's industrious."

"Maybe he's turning towards you?"

"No. I admit he confided in me – and I in him, but we were both . . . vulnerable at the time. That's over now. He's told me so."

"Wiped the slate clean?"

"Yes. His business is important to him. He'd even like to buy back my house."

"Really?" Chris always said less than what was going on in his head. I changed the subject.

"I've been to Adèle Bovier's again. She's given me the free run of her library, and I think you could come along too. I mentioned that you would be here."

"That's good. You're seeing rather a lot of her, aren't you?"

"This was to tell me that she's going to Paris for a medical check-up and would be away for a time. She looks far from well. I've grown fond of her."

"Oh, I'm sorry. Worry about my health is something I've never known. I used to have kittens if Sophie or Jon were ill. Anne was much more stoical than me." I rarely thought of Chris's former wife although I had met his children. I suddenly saw him as an anxious parent. Supposing he and I, eventually, had children? Who would be the anxious one then?

"Has the local doctor sent her?"

"No, she prefers to go to Cahors."

"Well, people have preferences for doctors. It's a personal thing."

"I suppose so. We talked about Chloë a lot. She was fond of her too. You know, Chloë, in spite of being quiet, had a very definite personality. Pervading . . . We can't understand her suicide."

"Well, the poor girl's dead and buried. If there had been any doubts—"

"No, there couldn't have been." Only mysteries, I thought. "Remember I told you about the missing hair? I keep wondering if she had pulled it out in some kind of anguish, and then I think, not Chloë. She was too . . . self-contained."

"You're friendly with your local doctor there, aren't you?"

"Yes, I am. René Bonnard. He's taking me to Les Eyzies tomorrow. Why?"

"You *are* having a busy time. Ask him if he ever thought Chloë was depressed?"

"I have. He says he knew she was unhappy, but not depressed."

"Was he her doctor?"

"I don't think so. Rick would tell him. They're friends."

"I'm beginning to get the picture – everyone knowing everyone else's affairs. Have you managed to see any of Gillam's friends yet?"

"Only briefly at the funeral, but I've invited the wives for lunch on Sunday. Their husbands are Rick's solicitor and banker. They're going to him."

"Did Chloë leave any money?"

"No, I shouldn't think so. I think they were rich once, but her father lost it all." Should I tell Chris that I had wondered if Rick was implicated in that? "There are so many angles, Chris. You're right about small villages. I'd really like you to be here so that we could talk."

95

"Is that the only reason?"

"No."

"When you dashed off to France I was jealous of that Gillam." He sounded boyishly unlike himself.

"How nice, but I told you: he's no longer interested in me, except as a friend. But it's the . . . mysteries. You know, 'underneath the smiling face of Meloir' kind of thing."

"You need the other kind of thing. What mysteries?"

"Well, it's back to Chloë. Why did she never write? Was she perhaps unhappy because she wanted a child, and what was it that changed the marriage, and what happened to her hair . . . ?"

"Don't let yourself become too involved. As far as I'm concerned, it's music to my ears to know that Rick only wants you as a friend. Help him in any way you can and get on with your book. Have you lost interest in writing?"

"Oh, goodness, no. I can become completely absorbed in it. But even in that there's a link with Meloir. It's a medieval thing."

"Naturally. It's a medieval part of the country."

Actually it was a primeval thing. Evil.

I wanted to say to Chris that I needed him, couldn't say it because I didn't know quite why. "Come soon," I said instead.

"I will, my darling. Sleep well."

That touched me, left a pleasant warmth. But it was Chloë whom I thought of before I went to sleep, or maybe afterwards. Again I saw myself in that railway yard with those overhead lamps casting strange elongated shadows, saw her coming towards me . . . a pervading presence. There was an ache in my heart when I woke next morning.

It was a golden peach of a day, with that fecundity which late August brings, a feeling that nature has given her all, has reached the peak of the symphony, and now there would be the long coda of winter before the rippling sounds of spring began. Beethoven, here I come.

I went out the back door to drink in my view across the fields, and on an impulse bent down and patted the grass, short, springy, like fur. Mine, I thought, my land.

The sun slanted on the stones of the *gariotte* and I went to the shed and got a rake. I went close to the opening and, crouching down, pushed it in as far as it would go, twisting it as I did so. It became entangled in the brambles, and I turned and twisted in the hope of dislodging at least some of them. Brambles have roots which go down to Hades. When I looked in I didn't see that I had made much difference.

I kept peering, and saw I had been wrong. There was one place which seemed bare, for I could see a small gap in the mass of shoots, but whether I had done it with my rake, or Leo had made the hole when he was foraging, I couldn't say. What did I expect to find in any case? A seat for some old shepherd sheltering from the elements? I gave it up and went in for breakfast. I was sitting at the table munching some of yesterday's baguette – a heinous sin in France where yesterday's bread is chucked out in appalling quantities – when there was a knock at the door. When I opened it Luc stood there, looking sullen rather than willing.

"Well, Luc," I said, "how nice to see you! Have you come to work?"

"I shouldn't have been here at all but my mother pushed me out this morning. '*Paresseux!*' she shouts at me until I'm sick of it."

"I've been thinking, Luc," I said – I had decided on diplomacy, "I ought to pay you more if you come back." He didn't look gratified, only more miserable, if possible.

"*Pas d'importe*," he said, "I've plenty of money. I work for Monsieur Gillam, you know. He pays me very well, you have no idea." He stuck out his chest with a pitiful bravado. "As a matter of fact, I'm only doing you a favour because your parents were kind to me. So gentle. I have not known parents like that." He looked wistful.

"Well, at least you'd be doing the garden a favour. It's becoming neglected, brambles everywhere. Have you seen them on the wall at the bottom? And this morning I tried to pull them out of the *gariotte*. They spread, you know." His head shot up.

"No, no!" Alarm was in his face. "Monsieur Gillam says it is not allowed to clear *gariottes* of brambles. Anywhere! They should be left as nature intended."

"But it is *my gariotte!*" I was astounded at his reaction.

"*Gariottes* have not to be touched! Monsieur Gillam knows best. He has been here with the doctor and they warned me. I have to tell you, madame," his voice was trembling, "it is impossible for me to work here if you ask me to clear yours out!" He looked so distressed that I pretended to give in.

"Very well, Luc. But please remember it is my *gariotte* not Monsieur Gillam's. However, we'll leave it for the time being. There's plenty for you to do besides that. I should start on the grass, but first of all you will have to clean and oil the mower. That should keep you busy all morning. Will you start now?"

"I begin." He kept all the tools in the shed in apple-pie order.

I retired to the house to think over his outburst. Was Rick activated by some civic duty or was there something else? I had never known that he took any interest in the fabric of the countryside. He was essentially a commuter type who liked the activity of a town but enjoyed retreating to his house in the country in the evening. He was a charming host, liked to entertain. I thought of the many parties we'd been invited to, and how Ben and I had enjoyed those evenings and Sunday afternoons round the swimming pool.

'Monsieur Gillam has been here with the doctor,' Luc had said. And no doubt Leo. Did my *gariotte* increase the value of my house, and was it René Bonnard who was interested in buying it? And since Rick was a good businessman was he interested in selling it to him . . . if he could persuade me to sell?

But, I remembered, he had made no point about its importance when he had sold the house to me and Ben.

I was now very glad I had an appointment with René tomorrow. Perhaps I could bring the conversation round to my *gariotte*, see how he reacted. Chris was right. Small villages and intrigues. In spite of myself I was being drawn into it.

Thirteen

I was ready for René Bonnard. He called around midday, and we set off. He was pleasant, with that certain quality to be found in some French professionals, an extra formality. Although he was on *congé*, he was dressed formally in a suit of French cut, the wide shoulders, the jacket shorter than the English style, polished black shoes. With his neat goatee beard, sharp bird's eyes, he looked every inch a doctor.

"I thought we would stop off at Sarlat for lunch," he said, "since it's on our way. Sarlat is reassuring, and I always like to see how Etienne is getting on."

"Etienne?" I said with raised eyebrows.

"La Boétie. Montaigne's little friend. *Charmante!*" I remembered the statue in the square.

Sarlat is a completely satisfying small town, overrun by tourists but a model of how the English imagine French towns to look. It's the epitome of why the English like the Dordogne. The old quarter, the Renaissance buildings, the shops full of curios and the numerous art shops inducing you to buy replicas of the Renaissance buildings. It can't be faulted.

We had lunch near La Boétie's house, and then had a brief look at the cathedral. "One never visits Sarlat without a brief look at the old episcopal seat of the Archbishop Cambrai," René said. "The Salignac Fenelon family, you know. The Salignacs came from a village near Meloir. It has a fourteenth-century belfry, flat-fronted. You should have a look." Not my period, I thought of saying. The French are proud of their history and never tire of displaying their knowledge. How many people in England live in a historic town but know little about it?

Even London. I don't know the history of Bloomsbury, except for the tiresome Bloomsbury Set. Typically I'm too busy with my research in far-off Aquitaine. It is a fact that it is sometimes easier to write about places when one is distanced from them.

We had a pleasant run along by the Dordogne to Les Eyzies, with René expounding on the various châteaux we passed. I learned more about the Venus of Laussel which was found in the château of that name than I did of him. I was beginning to tire of his pedantic manner, and in a pause changed the subject.

"I had Luc Devreux working in the garden when you came, thank goodness. It's badly overgrown."

"Ah, yes," he said, "a quiet lad. Ruled by his mother, of course. His sisters married and left Meloir, probably to get away from her sharp tongue."

"He says Rick Gillam has told him not to touch the *gariotte*. I expect you've seen it . . . round the back."

"I believe so." He wasn't giving anything away.

"It must be of interest to you with your knowledge of local history," I persisted. "How old do you think it is?"

"Not very old. Certainly much more recent than the Magdalenian age." He laughed. "Long after Cro-Magnon Man." He polished his little joke.

"Was it a shepherd's hut?"

"Yes, that's all. To shelter from the weather. Your property is really part of the Causse fenced off."

"Why do you think Rick would tell him not to go near it?"

"Oh, I imagine out of respect for your property while you were away. That's all, I should think." He put on a puzzled face.

"But even Leo, his dog, went rushing behind the house and into it. Could there be anything buried there, do you think?"

"*Pas du tout.* He accompanies Rick everywhere, and possibly when he was keeping an eye on things for you. Wolfhounds are intensely curious. The *gariotte* would intrigue him."

I pursed my lips, looked, I hope, as if I was considering this. "I suppose so. Luc tells me you've been with Rick when he was 'keeping an eye on things' for me." I emphasised this slightly.

"Yes, I suppose I did. Perhaps I'm intrigued too with 'my knowledge of history'." We were fencing. "It's rare, you know, very rare to have it on one's property. Quite a selling point . . . *Mon Dieu!*" he peered close to the windscreen. "That was an oriole! On a main road! Can you believe it?" I am used to side-tracking. Research is full of it.

"Poor Leo was very sad the day of the funeral. Do you remember how he lay at the pool with his head in his paws?"

"Ah, yes, a sad day for all of us. And dogs are faithful animals, you know."

I nodded. "How do you think Rick is coping?"

"By working. He's back at his office, you may know. It's his life. He's worked hard to build up the business, and he won't want it to slip back if he isn't at the helm."

"I can understand that. I'm researching in our area about the barons of Quercy. It's been my solace too. I started it when we were first here, but since I came back I find I'm being steadily side-tracked . . . by puzzling incidents." I kept my eyes on him.

His blandness seemed genuine. "Perhaps the sad death of Chloë? And there is the beauty of the countryside as well. I, too, would like to write a book on speleology, my passion, but, alas, I'm a village doctor, always at the beck and call. That is why I am so grateful that you agreed to accompany me today on this expedition." I gave up.

"What marvels do you intend to show me at Les Eyzies?" I smiled round at him.

"I'm sure you've seen the paintings before, or reproductions. My destination is the museum. I should be delighted if you would come too, but if that is too dull for you, I could drop you at the entrance of the Font de Gaume. One can never see enough of it."

"It takes rather a long time, René, and it's such a glorious day to be swallowed in the bowels of the earth. Ben and I used to save our visits there for rainy days."

"If you wish, then, I could leave you at the Grand Roc for half an hour. Do stalactites appeal to you?"

"Yes, I'm a child at heart, really. It's like fairyland."

"*Bon.* We'll go our separate ways for about an hour and then you and I will have the English tea at the hotel by the river. Would that suit?"

"Yes, thank you," I said. "I would like the English tea." And their pâtisseries. They are streets ahead of ours.

There's nothing more pleasant than sitting outside a riverside hotel and having 'the English tea'. Delicate Limoges china – what else in a four-star hotel? – *les tranches de citron*, and those scrumptious pâtisseries. Scrumptious is the only word for them.

I made a small pig of myself, and when I said this to René he looked alarmed and then laughed uproariously, his small eyes twinkling. "Then we must have dinner sometime at *Le Repos* and perhaps then I shall see you make a large pig of yourself."

Jumping straight in I said, "I've been having dinner at Madame Bovier's once or twice. She has a wonderful cook."

"Ah, yes, Marie. And there is her twin, Jean. Inseparable."

"Madame Bovier's appetite is very poor. She picks at her food like a bird."

"You have the peculiar metaphors in England," his eyes were still twinkling, "for food. Pigs and now birds."

"Very descriptive, though, you must admit."

"Did you enjoy your visit to the Grand Roc?" He didn't want to talk about her.

"Yes, I did. It was good of you to let me have your car. There's a wonderful view of the Vézère from the stairs leading up to it. And I'd forgotten how striking those coral formations are. I was quite right. It is just like fairyland. It took me back to my childhood. Was your visit to the museum profitable?"

"Very."

"Tell me, René," I was making conversation now, "which came first, *Homo sapiens*, or *Homo erectus*?"

"Ah, my dear madame, I confine myself to research for my own little book. I understand *Homo sapiens* is the generic term for man as a thinking creature. As for *Homo erectus*, you must have recourse to a library. As far as I'm concerned I've had a most pleasurable outing with you and I must thank you sincerely." I could see his Aunt Leonie at his elbow.

"It's been a lovely outing for me too."

In fact my visit to the Grand Roc had made me sad because the last time I had been there was with Ben. I remembered he had put his arm round me and said, 'Magical, isn't it?' I had heard again his young, hushed voice.

'Were there many people there?'

"Quite a lot." Go on, Andy, I told myself, say it. "A man I spoke to beside me was telling me about Lascaux. He was greatly intrigued by how it was discovered. I knew, of course, but I had never known the local name of the hole which the boy's dog went down – an *aven*."

"An *aven*," René repeated politely. I was looking at him, and I noticed that the sparkle went out of his eyes. "Yes, I have heard it. *Garçon?*" He hailed a passing waiter, "*S'il vous plaît.*" They engaged in conversation for a second and when he turned to me the twinkle was back in his eyes. "I have been enjoying your company so much that I have forgotten the *clients* come to my house at 6.30 p.m. My housekeeper will have the chairs arranged. Do you mind if we go?"

"Not at all," I said, rising. "I have telephone calls to make. I must get back too."

We chatted on all kinds of subjects on the way back, two civilised people used to avoiding awkward pauses. But the tension was there. We had reached that flat period when the pleasure had gone. Even the comical sight of a field packed with waddling geese failed to make him smile, although I was amused how they pushed and shoved each other like women in a queue.

The heat was still in the air as he drove into Meloir. The old stone houses seemed to exude it. The village was like a cat lying in the sun, seemingly peaceful, and yet in its very stillness I thought there was a menace. I thanked him for the delightful lunch and the even more delightful tea, and we shook hands amicably in front of the house. I went straight to the telephone hoping against hope Chris would be back in London. I got him, luckily, at his flat.

"Chris," I said, "I know why there's such an interest in the *gariotte* in my garden."

"What's a *gariotte*?"

"Remember, I told you. A stone shelter for a shepherd."

"A dead shepherd?" he suggested helpfully.

"No. I think there may be a hole in it, which may go into a tunnel which may lead to a cave which may be an undiscovered one." There was a pause at the other end.

"You," he said slowly, at last, "may be sitting on a gold mine."

"Something like that. The hole is called an *aven*."

"Whatever." He wasn't wasting any time on its nomenclature. "And, presumably, you are not the only one who thinks so – your friend, Rick, and the doctor perhaps?"

Neither of us spoke for a second or two.

"Something like Lascaux, for instance," I said.

"I'm sure I can get to you by the middle of next week". I heard the receiver clicking at his end as if he were on his way already.

Fourteen

On Sunday morning I was up early and drove to Lafont to buy some food for my lunch party. I had been so busy that I hadn't been much in the kitchen, and it was too late to plan a menu. Besides, I liked Lafont, I liked the Sunday bustle, the shops all being open until midday, and as I manoeuvred through the parked cars in the busy main street I saw it hadn't changed.

There was the usual buzz at *Maison de la Presse*. I remembered how Ben and I used to like to go there and browse through the books and magazines and buy the Sunday papers – the local ones because the English papers didn't arrive until the following day – look at the postcards, laugh at the earthy humour of some of them – a row of peasant women in a field, skirts up, bottoms up – have a chat with Monsieur Maurois, the proprietor, in the flowered waistcoat and bow tie, smiling, bowing, king of his small territory.

The windows of the shops were brimming over with Sunday fare, and women were going in and out with laden baskets to the *boulangerie* and the *pâtisserie* for bread and those huge tarts which were a special feature of many Sunday lunches.

It was to Madame Lacouche I went first, she of the bouffant hair-style and exotic earrings, there to buy a selection of her mousses, pâtés, individual quiches, her pickles, sauces, canapés – all the ingredients for a cold *repas*, or even a hot one, judging by the golden corn-fed chickens glistening on the rotating spit. Afterwards I made my way to *Le Self* to stock up on the staples, the wine and soft drinks. I had a loaded boot when I started on my way back to Meloir.

But I am a Speedy Gonzalez in the kitchen, and by midday I was seated in the garden having a glass of wine to bolster my confidence to meet the ladies, Madame Machin, the solicitor's wife, and Madame Lavange, the banker's – Lenore and Yvette respectively. Fortified, I rose when I heard their car drawing up at the front of the house and went to greet them.

A smartly *coiffured* and fashionably dressed young woman was driving, and she got out to greet me, smiling. "Are we too early?" She held out a beringed hand. "I'm Yvette Lavange, and here is my friend, Lenore Machin." The other woman had come round the car as she was speaking.

We shook hands.

"I'm so glad you were able to come," I said. "It will give your husbands a chance to talk on their own with Rick. Business is boring, don't you think?" Social small talk, I thought, as I said it. I liked talking business. Since Ben had died I had looked after my affairs, and it had been a salutary lesson.

"*Ennuyeux!*" agreed Madame Lavange, laughing. She had a pert face with the pointed chin and prominent teeth which often go with that type. Her hair was lint white cut short, her earrings were jade green to match her short-skirted suit. She was attractive, outgoing. She would talk enough for two, I thought.

"Shall we have an aperitif in the garden?" I said, leading them round the back of the house. "By the way, my name's Miranda. Could you bear to call me that instead of Madame Stanstead?"

"*Pourquoi pas, eh, Lenore?* All girls together?" She looked as if she were accepting a dare.

"*Très à la mode?*" Lenore Machin smiled. She was less outgoing than her friend, also smart, dark-haired. Middle-class women in France are invariably well turned-out, with an attention to detail, and don't mind spending money on perfume. Theirs was rivalling my flowers. They exclaimed at the size of the garden and the view. They were tired looking at 'that old Lot', especially now they had a steamboat chugging up and down it. 'Can you imagine?'

The *gariotte* intrigued them. Lenore thought it was 'bizarre', but when I told her Dr Bonnard had said that the garden was actually a piece of fenced-off Causse, she nodded. "Ah, well, we all know René. He is an authority on everything, don't you think?" I thought it was a tongue-in-cheek remark. I didn't mention my *aven* theory. That I was only sharing with Chris. We sat down and I poured them some Monbazillac and passed the regulation boudoirs. "René Bonnard took me to Les Eyzies yesterday," I told them. "We stopped off at a restaurant near La Boétie's tower for lunch, then we went on to Les Eyzies where he went to the museum and I had another look at the Grand Roc."

"*Vous avez de la chance,*" Yvette said. "*That* restaurant! *Très chic. Je l'adore!*"

"Didn't he bore you talking about speleology all the time?" Lenore Machin asked. She was a bit sharp, I thought. If I wanted to find out anything, she would be the one.

I smiled diplomatically. "I'm always willing to learn."

"You must feel sad to be back without your husband," Yvette Lavange said. "I remember meeting him at Rick and Chloë's. Charming. Very handsome."

"Yes, he was," I nodded, "and yes, I do feel sad, often." I met Lenore's eyes which were sympathetic. "But I'm very busy in London. I work in the British Museum. This is going to be my second home, I hope. I don't want to give it up."

"You are very courageous," Yvette said. "I can scarcely go anywhere without my Raymond."

"Oh, nonsense, Yvette!" Lenore smiled at her. "You drive all over the place without him."

"Yes, because I know he is there when I return, but for Madame Stanstead. . .*je m'excuse!*" she put a hand with painted fingernails up to a mouth which matched their fuschia colour, ". . . but for poor Miranda, in a foreign country, this is quite different."

"Chloë was like you, Miranda," Lenore looked at me, "composed, you know, able to direct her own affairs. There is an English expression for that?"

"I admired Chloë very much. An English phrase?" I racked my brains, "perhaps, 'very much her own person'. That might do."

"*Un style particulier? Bon.* You speak French very well."

"Thank you. Perhaps it's because I feel at home here," I said. By the immediate warmth in her eyes I saw I had said the right thing. "I was very fond of Chloë. It was because of that I came to see if there was anything I could do to help Rick. How do you think he'll get on with living in their house alone?"

"He'll be all right. He's self-sufficient. And engrossed in his business. Isn't he, Yvette?"

"Yes, I know that from Raymond. It's going from strength to strength. I mustn't say another word. 'Be discreet,' Raymond says. As if I'd ever be anything else!" She burst into a peal of laughter, accepting a canapé from the plate I was holding. "Mmmh! *Délicieux!* I always think people who have not known a happy childhood have more ambition."

"Yes, he's told me a little about that," I said.

"Well, of course, he always put you on a pedestal. Didn't he Lenore?" she appealed to her friend.

"Yes, he talked a lot about you." Lenore's eyes were amused as she looked at me. "I wonder Chloë didn't become jealous. Of course, Rick's always been popular with the ladies. But then again, Chloë wasn't the jealous type. She had a kind of. . . inner dignity."

"That's very true," I felt uncomfortable remembering those letters now so much regretted. "It describes Chloë. I'm so sad she's gone . . ." The three of us looked at each other. I felt near to tears. "Well," I said, getting up, "shall we go in for something to eat? It's in the kitchen. The dining-room is so formal for three women on their own, don't you think?"

"*Bonne idée!*" Yvette said, looking surprised. "Perhaps you'll start a new fashion in Meloir."

"*Le dernier cri,*" Lenore said. They followed me inside.

By the time they'd had another glass of wine and helped themselves from the various platters I had laid out, we seemed to be the best of friends. Grown-up women together always seem to feel slightly naughty when there are no men there. We still haven't shaken off their presence. We are inclined to tell silly jokes and laugh at them too much, to become a little confidential. Before long the talk turned back to Chloë without any prompting from me.

"You and Chloë were very close, weren't you?" Lenore said when we were drinking coffee, again in the garden. It was too good a day to be indoors for long.

108

"Yes, I think we understood each other," I replied. And because I too had been drinking and was enjoying their company, I said: "A strange thing . . . when I got off the train this time when I arrived I thought for a moment I saw her. Rick was meeting me . . ."

There was a pause. Lenore spoke first. "Perhaps that means she is not at peace."

"She couldn't be at peace if she drowned in their pool." Yvette looked at both of us, her mouth hanging slightly open. "You can imagine how Rick felt when his gardener told him that he had found her . . ."

"Yes." I met Lenore's eyes. They were on me, questioning, they seemed to be asking. 'Do you know more about this?' Or was I imagining it? "Did you both know her well? I asked, looking from one to the other.

Yvette spoke slowly. "I can't say we knew her well, apart from socially. She was a very private person, wasn't she, Lenore?"

She nodded. "She worked in Rick's office, and we both work part-time. I'm in the hospital at Cahors. Yvette teaches. There wasn't much opportunity during the day." I had to change my opinion of them as social butterflies.

"What do you teach, Yvette?" I asked.

"Gymnastics. I was a champion at one time. You wouldn't think so now, would you?" She laughed.

"Why not? I think you have a lovely figure." She had the taut, slightly muscular frame of someone who kept themselves trim by sport.

"And when Chloë stopped working for Rick," Lenore said, "she seemed to withdraw into herself. She took no part in village life, apart from helping the hotel here. Madame Carvel said she was glad to get away from Rick and the house. I do not know why she said this. It was not to me. I always thought they were a happily married couple. Didn't you find them so, Miranda?"

"Certainly when I lived here. Do you know anyone she might have confided in?" I waited.

Lenore appealed to Yvette. "Do you remember that American girl who came one evening when we were there? But she wasn't at the funeral."

109

"I remember. Ellen Lerner she was called. But I don't know where she lives."

"Cahors," Lenore said. "I remember she said she lived in Cahors. She teaches, but not at your school, Yvette. At the *lycée* . . . if she's still there."

Yvette shook her head doubtfully. "I've no idea. Chloë certainly looked sad at times. I hope she did confide in someone. Rick never said anything, although sometimes I felt their relationship had changed. But he was a good host, always welcoming. People liked to go to their house."

"Do you think she was depressed?" I asked.

"Oh, I should say so. Wouldn't you, Lenore?" She looked at her friend. "But then she was worried about her father. His bankruptcy had made him ill. She spent a lot of time in Angers and I don't suppose Rick liked that. Oh, and did you see her sister at the funeral? Something was upsetting her. What a commotion! It must have been terrible for Rick." She looked at her watch. "*Mon Dieu*! Do you see the time! We have strict instructions to be at Rick's by three. It's ten past already."

"So it is!" I got up. "I mustn't keep you. I've enjoyed you being here. You must come again."

"But you have to come back to Rick's with us! He said to insist."

"Do you think I should?"

"Of course. Let us help you to wash up and then we shall go together."

It was useless to resist. With a fair amount of girlish giggling, mostly on the part of Yvette, they helped me in the kitchen, then each went to the bathroom to '*faire la toilette*'. We eventually left in two cars (I took my own so that I could leave when I liked). It had been fun, but I knew I would appreciate being alone when I got back to think things over.

I hadn't found out much. There was no explanation, as far as I had learned, as to why Chloë had committed suicide, unless she had been clinically depressed. But at least I knew Ellen Lerner taught at the *lycée*. I thought I might try to track her down, at the same time wondering why I should want to. Was it the Meloir atmosphere?

Fifteen

I was surprised to see Rick and the two husbands sitting round the pool. And Leo, I noticed, was still there. He flicked his tail but didn't rise when we joined the men.

"Well, here come the ladies," Rick said. I thought he was surprisingly cheerful for a newly bereaved husband. "Let me introduce you, Miranda. Monsieur Lavange and Monsieur Machin." We shook hands.

Monsieur Machin was taller than the usual Frenchman, stout and cheerful; Monsieur Lavange was quieter-looking than his wife, and had a slightly worried expression, almost a guilty one. Did he feel like me, I wondered, that it was in rather bad taste to be sitting round the pool where Rick's wife had so recently drowned? It was difficult to shake off an embarrassed feeling as I sat down with the rest of the party.

"It was so hot indoors," Monsieur Lavange said, "and the chairs were here." His brows were knitted.

"Did you ladies enjoy yourselves together?" Monsieur Machin asked. He struck me as the kind of man who enjoyed female company, perhaps because his wife was not demonstrative.

"Oh, yes, Guy," Yvette sparkled. "We had a lovely time talking about you." He laughed with her.

"I hope you heard nothing but good, Madame Stanstead?" He beamed on me.

"Actually," I said, "we were wondering how Rick was coping on his own, and if there was anything we could do to help?" I still felt uncomfortable. "It's a big house to run." I had to avert my eyes from the pool, the curse of a vivid imagination. The image of Chloë floating there, hair outspread, was strong. Did any of the others feel it, I wondered. I was sure Raymond Lavange did. He was very quiet.

"That was sweet of you," Rick said. He was almost debonair. "I hope I'm not depriving you of your intended good works, but Colette Jourdan comes daily and tidies up for me and leaves an evening meal ready if I'm going to be in. I often dine out in the evening in Cahors. People are very kind."

Lenore, who hadn't spoken so far, said suddenly, echoing my thoughts, "I can't help thinking of Chloë when we're sitting here. And Leo . . ." she pointed. We all turned and looked at the dog who was the picture of utter dejection. He raised his head, but let it fall again. "Oh," she said, looking around, "I'm sorry. I'm being tactless."

"Very tactless, *chérie*," her husband said. "We are all making an effort . . ."

"No, I'm glad you spoke." Rick's handsome face had become suddenly sad. "I feel strange too, Lenore. It took a real effort of will to come and sit here. I couldn't have done it without my dear friends." He looked around us.

"You must admit, Lenore," this was Raymond Lavange, "that it takes a great effort on Rick's part, but life goes on. We all admire him for it."

"And to be practical," Yvette chimed in. "This is the best place in the garden for chairs. The lawn is rather steep. Chloë loved this patio with the umbrellas and chairs and tables. And she did those tubs herself." We all dutifully admired the tubs with their trailing pelargoniums, lobelias and felicias like stars against the brilliant blues and pinks.

Nevertheless, the talk became desultory, as if by saying what we thought, we still had to get used to the actuality, and after Rick's bright welcome he hardly spoke. The traitorous words occurred to me: perhaps he feels he got his act wrong. I felt ashamed.

"Did you get all your business affairs sorted out, Rick?" I asked him. "I remember how difficult it was when Ben died." He brightened immediately.

"Oh, yes. Thanks to my good friends here."

"And thanks to Madame Stanstead also," Guy Machin said.

"It would have been dull for our wives. Besides, Yvette wouldn't have kept quiet." He smiled at her.

"*Tu est très méchant, Guy!*" She pouted at him.

"It was a pleasure for us to be entertained by Miranda," Lenore said, smiling at me. "See, we are on first name terms already, *comme les Anglais.* She must visit us soon."

"And us also," Yvette said. And to the men: "She may be in Meloir part of the time. We'll make her very welcome."

"Thank you," I smiled around.

The conversation limped along. There was no doubt that none of us was at ease; even Guy Machin's light remarks from time to time seemed to fall on stony ground. I saw him look at his watch, start theatrically.

"*Mon Dieu!* Four o'clock already! We really must be on our way. The children . . ."

"Yes, we must," Lenore said.

Raymond Lavange was on his feet, as if he had been given a release.

"*Chérie*, are you ready? We came in one car, remember?"

I got up too. "I really only came to say hello to Rick. And to see if I could help with clearing up. But now that I know Colette is here—" I paused because at that moment I saw her walking towards us, a short sturdy figure, her dark luxuriant hair piled on top of her head. I remembered that she'd had a faint moustache. "She must have heard me mentioning her." I smiled towards her.

"*Bonjour, tout le monde!*" Colette said as she stopped beside us. "I came to see if you would like drinks, or the tea. As you asked me to do, Monsieur Gillam, at four o'clock."

"No, thank you, Colette," Monsieur Machin said quickly, "We are just going."

Colette spoke to me, "How nice it is to see you again, Madame Stanstead. The tea for you?"

"No, thanks." I got up to shake hands with her. "I'm just going too. It's nice to see you, Colette."

"What's the rush?" Rick said. "Stay and talk."

I suddenly felt I couldn't stay at the pool for another minute. "I really must go, Rick." And to Colette: "Monsieur Gillam tells

113

me you're helping him out. It's good to hear." I was aware of Rick's eyes on me.

"I can also come to you, if you like, Madame Stanstead."

"Thank you, but you're busy enough . . ."

"Have her by all means," Rick said. "Don't mind me." When I looked at him he was sullen. Was he angry at Colette? I was embarrassed, unsure how to act. I turned to Colette.

"I tell you what, look in and see me. I'm really grateful to you for looking after my house."

"Tomorrow?" she said, "if that's convenient?"

"Fine." I looked at the two couples. "Sorry about this, but Colette was very good . . ."

"Well, if you're all deserting me," Rick said. I almost changed my mind but I met Lenore's eyes. Her face was expressionless but there was something in them which I couldn't fathom.

"I'll give you a ring very soon," I said to Rick. "Remember I'm at your beck and call whenever you need me."

"I shan't forget that." He gave me his charming smile.

I said goodbye to the Machins and Lavanges at the front of the house where we had parked our cars. We all seemed awkward, unable to talk naturally to each other. The women repeated their invitations to me, and I was polite and said I would love to visit them. I noticed Monsieur Lavange seemed subdued but that Monsieur Machin, perhaps impervious to atmosphere, was now chatting gaily.

"We needn't have left so early," I heard Yvette say to her husband as they got into their car. I waved as I drove off in mine, glad of the prospect of going upstairs to my *pigeonnier*, but still worried. Had I annoyed Rick by not staying on? He might be afraid of solitude. And should I have turned down Colette's offer?

It's doubly difficult, I reminded myself, for a man left alone. Today would be his first attempt at entertaining on his own, and that could be fraught. Chloë had been quietly efficient. Rick had always been the front man. Everything had always run on oiled wheels behind the scenes.

If he was annoyed, I thought, put it down to the vulnerability of the psyche in bereavement – it was a phrase I had read somewhere. It's like groping in the dark, as you well know.

I telephoned Chris later, hoping he would be back at the flat, but there was no reply. I left a message on his answering machine, and had a late supper which I didn't enjoy, eating leftovers. The visit to Rick had left me unsettled in some way. Had it been because of sitting round the pool? But it was a brave effort on Rick's part, I reminded myself. You should respect that, give up worrying and get on with your work.

The following morning when I was engrossed in studying Eleanor of Aquitaine – now there was a woman who knew her own mind – I heard someone knocking at the door. Was it Rick, I wondered, and if it were, I would apologise for not staying on yesterday. The bright morning had dispelled any doubts of his behaviour, or indeed the wisdom or otherwise of us sitting round the pool. As Yvette had said, it was the best place to sit; it wasn't bizarre, merely practical.

But it was Colette, I found, when I opened the door, standing there in her navy-blue pin-spotted cotton, the kind of dress housewives bought at the Lafont market on Thursdays. "*Bonjour*, Colette," I said, "Come in." I led her into the kitchen. "Sit down and we'll have a cup of coffee. It was good of you to call."

"I'm on my way home from Monsieur Gillam's residence. I do not have to return until five o'clock when I prepare a meal. He'll be at home this evening. It is a nice little job for me."

"Of course." I had the kettle boiling and, sacrilege in France, was making instant coffee. "Excuse this," I said, holding up the jar.

"I prefer the instant," she said.

"Me too, except in the evening when I like the real thing. I call this 'lazy coffee'."

"Monsieur Gillam won't drink it. Everything must be just so."

"He is a perfectionist. Here you are." I put down a mug and a tin of biscuits. "Have one." I was trying by my chatter to put her at ease. For some reason she appeared nervous.

115

"Do you mind if I ask you something, Madame Stanstead?" she said.

"Not at all. Fire away."

"I wanted to ask you, do not you think it strange to sit at the pool where Madame Gillam drowned?"

"To be honest," I said, "at first I thought that. But then I realised it was brave of Monsieur Gillam, and since the chairs and table are situated there—"

"But they are not," she said.

"But Madame Lavange said it was their usual place."

"It used to be, but when Madame Gillam . . . died, they were carried to a shed because people came to examine the pool. Monsieur Gillam asked me to put them back again yesterday morning and serve lunch there. He helped me."

"I see." I looked at her worried expression. "It was rather brave of him, don't you think? You know what they say, 'Life must go on'." She didn't look convinced. "Do you like working for Monsieur Gillam?" I asked her.

"Well, it is a question of money, Madame Stanstead. My husband had an accident and broke his ankle. He drives a van for Madame Lacouche in Lafont, and she doesn't give him his full pay, you know, now that he has been off for over two weeks. It is a bad fracture. The money I earn is useful. But I don't think I will continue when Didier goes back to work."

"Why is that?"

"I feel . . . *mal à l'aise*. There is an atmosphere. Sometimes Monsieur is pleasant, and other times he is impatient and angry. I know he has lost his wife, but I do not like when he is this way and that way."

"He is bereaved, Colette. It affects people different ways. No one could have lived with me when my husband died."

"You had your parents."

"Parents are different."

"Perhaps. Didier says not to stand for it, that we can manage."

"Well, of course it's your decision, but if I were you I should be patient," and to change the subject, I said, "By the way, I must pay you for any extra work you did for me." Perhaps that was why she had come.

"No." She waved her hand. "That was taken care of by Madame Gillam. She said you had arranged it with the bank."

"Yes, I had, but I wondered if it was enough . . . those lovely flowers, and fresh linen. Would you be able to help me occasionally while I'm here?"

"Yes, as I said to you, when I'm not at the home of Monsieur Gillam."

"Once a week would be fine. At any time to suit you." I remembered what I wanted to ask her. "By the way, Colette, do you ever recall meeting a friend of Madame Gillam's when you were working for her – a Madame Lerner?" I had noticed her face change while I was speaking.

"It's Mademoiselle Lerner." She was definitely taken aback. "Yes, I do. She was a friend of Madame Gillam's, yes . . . I should say a very good friend. Well, I must be going . . ."

"Why was she a *very good* friend, Colette?" I was deliberately nonchalant.

"I shouldn't have said that as if there was something . . ." She put down her cup, looking troubled.

"I hope I haven't upset you, Colette?"

"No, no. You were a good friend of Madame Gillam's. She spoke of you to me. 'I miss her, Colette,' she said to me once."

Why hadn't she replied to my letter?

"I was very fond of Madame Gillam. But if I have upset you in any way, please say."

"No. You haven't upset me. I've not told anyone . . ." she hesitated. "It was something that happened when I was working for Madame Gillam . . ."

I encouraged her. "She always spoke highly of you, Colette."

"I did my best. She needed me when she was working in their office in Cahors. That is where Mademoiselle Lerner lives. I never spoke of the matter to anyone, I do assure you." She looked so distressed that I decided not to press her.

"If it worries you, please don't tell me anything. So," I smiled at her, "you'll come once a week to help me, morning or afternoon, whichever you prefer." I watched her face, the doubt, then the decision. She spoke as if following her own train of thought.

"But I have been disappointed in how Monsieur Gillam treats me. After all, I am doing him a favour as well. But I should not have been surprised, you know; there were disagreements, quarrels which I overheard. Madame Gillam sometimes asked me to help with guests in the evening. I never actually saw anything happening . . ." she had lowered her voice on the word, "but sometimes Madame looked very pale, and once I saw bruises . . ."

I remembered how the Carvels had told me the same thing, and I felt a twist in my heart, a sick little lurch. Was it from Colette their story had come? Small villages – Meloir, a smiling village on the surface . . . And bruises . . . where? I didn't want to believe this.

"I don't know if you should tell me any more . . ." but Colette hadn't heard me.

"Well, one day I went to work there, when Madame was alive, of course. She had told me she would be at the office, and I began with the sweeping downstairs. The machine was going when I heard above its noise a voice upstairs, and I went to the door and listened. I was fearful, alarmed. I had thought the house was empty. I thought I was being called, but it wasn't my name, it was someone moaning, like this –" She made an eerie long-drawn out sound. "It was someone in pain. I thought, it must be Madame, and I went running upstairs, thinking she must be ill and had been unable to go to the office."

"And it was?"

"Yes, I met her staggering out of the bathroom, and her night-dress was . . . you know . . . stained with . . ."

"Blood?"

"Yes, Madame. I said, 'Oh, dear, Madame, whatever is wrong?' She was as white as a ghost and staggering, and I went towards her. 'Let me help you to your room,' I said. 'There is no need.' She waved me away. 'I want you to telephone my friend . . .' she was panting '. . . Ellen Lerner. She lives in Cahors.' 'The number, Madame?' I said. She whispered, 'My address book . . .

bedroom,' but she was now in so much pain that she allowed me to help her back there and get some towels which I spread on her bed. She crawled in, moaning, groaning . . . it was pitiful."

"Didn't you ask if you would call Dr Bonnard first?" I was trying to appear calm.

"No, she had a Cahors doctor. I suggested calling Dr Bonnard, but she said I was to ring Mademoiselle Lerner and say to bring the doctor with her. Perhaps it was her husband?"

"I wouldn't know. You rang this Ellen Lerner?"

"Yes, I did, as soon as I had looked up the number."

"Can you remember it?" I didn't for a second think she could.

"I can because it was an easy onè. Twelve twelve, fourteen fourteen. My memory is excellent. Didier always says so. Especially for numbers."

"That's good. Did you get Mademoiselle Lerner when you phoned?"

"Yes, I did, and she said she would come right away with the doctor. I sat with Madame, holding her hand . . . well, it was evident what it was." She looked at me.

"A miscarriage?"

"Yes, I have had two. We keep hoping." At least your Didier is alive, I thought. "She began to feel a little better. I fetched her some tea, and she talked to me – she had a sense of humour, that one. 'Please Colette,' she said, 'don't go round Meloir like a town crier telling everyone this has happened.' I said I wouldn't, and I haven't. But you are different. You do not belong to Meloir, and I know you and Madame Gillam were good friends. I will not say any more about what I saw when I laid the towels under her, or what my opinion is. On that my lips are sealed." She leant back in her chair.

I decided not to voice my opinion either. "Did Mademoiselle Lerner take a long time to come?"

"The best part of an hour. She arrived with this doctor, a youngish man, dark-haired, who went running upstairs and bent over Madame and said, 'What's been happening now, Chloë?' I heard that as I followed him."

"Did you stay on in the house?"

119

"No, Mademoiselle Lerner thanked me and said she would look after her, and I was glad to go as it happened because Didier gets impatient if his lunch is late. When I next went back Madame Gillam seemed all right, but pale, which was not unusual. She gave me some extra money and said it was for my kindness in helping her, and reminded me not to talk about what had happened. 'What we women have to put up with,' she said, and I told her about my two miscarriages. We had a nice little talk."

"Did she ever mention it again?"

"No, never again. The matter was closed. It was not long after that she lost her life in the pool. I grieved, you know, Madame Stanstead. There was something sad about her. She should have been happy. You will keep quiet about what I have told you?" She looked anxious. "To anyone?" I reassured her. Chris wasn't 'anyone' I thought. For the first time I longed to see him, to tell him about the deep-seated ache I had felt when I was listening to Colette, how I too felt Chloë's sadness. I should have tried harder to get in touch with her when I was in London.

Sixteen

I telephoned Ellen Lerner at lunchtime but there was no reply to the number Colette had given me. Perhaps she had got it wrong. I checked it in the *annuaire* and certainly there was an E. Lerner under that number. There are some days which seem purposeful from the time you rise until you go to bed, an endless procession of tasks to be accomplished, interests to be pursued. This was not one of these.

It wasn't helped by the weather, a grey day with a hint of autumn chill in the air. Mist hung over the Pyrenees, and I had the impression of being enclosed in my own little world, a foreign world, I thought. For the first time I missed my work in London, the urban bustle, and there was an undercurrent of anxiety about Chris. Why hadn't he telephoned me? Could he still be in Chichester? Could it be that he was unable to come to France this week after all?

I thought I might call in at the Carvels', and again that I might telephone Rick, but I did none of these things. I had been disturbed by what Colette Jourdan had told me. Why had Chloë not asked her to ring Rick? It would have been the natural thing to do, and had Colette's seeming dislike of him stemmed from that incident – '*I will not say any more about what I saw when I laid the towels under her*'. Bruises? I felt like an alien, as if I was being drawn into something which didn't concern me, even the view from the window which normally I liked so much seemed strange, unfamiliar, foreign. And my usual writing seemed impossible today. I felt English in a foreign country.

I tried my other solace. I went into the kitchen, donned a checked apron and made a batch of Banbury biscuits, resolutely

121

English, then when they were ready and I'd had a cup of tea with two of them – I hadn't lost my cunning, I noticed, enjoying their rich crumbliness – I changed to walking shoes and set off. Surely the French countryside was bound to work its usual charm.

It really was a very pretty village, I thought, walking through it, the houses attractively grouped round the too-grand church, and set in a hollow with those winding lanes leading off the *place*. Ben and I had obtained an old ordinance map of the district, and had tried to discover the original village roads, cart-tracks – the skeleton of the land.

The area had always fascinated us, the idea that there were two worlds: this snug one through which I was now walking with its tangled hedges, no longer rich with eglantine and honeysuckle (though the purple berries were beginning to appear); and the limestone world higher up, the mysterious limestone Causse, the turf of which when walked upon released the pungent smell of thyme. And underneath, a third world of underground rivers and caves where our ancestors had lived in firelit darkness.

The gateway to that world was by *avens* discovered by speleologists, or by a curious dog. Had René and Rick discovered one concealed by my *gariotte?* Or, rather, had Leo? You can walk up an idea as I had often done with writing, develop it, like winding up a ball of wool. Could it be that they had formed some kind of partnership which would involve persuading me to sell? Chris had said when I told him of my belief in the *aven* that I would be sitting on a gold mine. But there was French law, different from ours. If the *aven* existed, would it become the property of the State?

I stopped on the path which I had taken out of Meloir and turned in the direction of Lafont. I was on what I took to be the highest point, beside a deserted barn, and looked over the quiet fields and woods with the occasional farmhouse towards the market town with its church on the hill, its Norman tower clearly visible. Utter tranquillity, I thought, hardly a sound but the distant bleating of a sheep on a far-off hillside.

And yet the deserted barn demonstrated another side of this region I loved – its inhabitants, their earthy hardness, their acquisitiveness. When we had been looking for a house here we had offered the farmer who owned it a reasonable sum, thinking it could be converted, but he had refused. The English were moving into the area. He wasn't quite ready to sell; if he waited he might do better. He had the patience of the seasons, a hard practicality which Rick might have acquired in the course of running his business.

I started walking again, my mind playing around Rick. Chloë had worked in his office. She would have had access to the files, have overheard telephone conversations, perhaps read letters lying about. Had she found out that René and Rick were planning to get me out so that they could cash in on my *aven*?

I had now convinced myself that it existed. I didn't have the necessary tools for excavation, nor the strength to clear away the accumulation of tangled shrubs which would conceal it – if it were there. And Luc had refused. I needed Chris to help me.

I started downhill again, my footsteps quickening. I had to telephone Chris at his flat again, and if there was no reply, ring the British Museum. In the evening I would again ring Ellen Lerner's number, and sometime soon I must try to get in touch with Adèle Bovier to find out how she was. Then there was Rick. My original reason for coming to Meloir had been to support him, but now that Colette had told me that he had asked her to put the chairs back round the pool, had even helped her . . . did he *need* my support? Didn't that mean he had come to terms with Chloë's death? Then there was Chloë's miscarriage. Was Colette unduly prejudiced against Rick and was it she who was spreading the story about bruises. I had heard only her side, I reminded myself. Chris, I thought, I could do with you here.

I rang him immediately I got in but there was no reply. I began to be seriously worried, and looking at my watch I saw it was five o'clock. Perhaps I would still find someone in the BM who would know his whereabouts. Luckily, Fiona, a sensible Scottish girl in the office, answered when I rang. She had the national trait of intense interest in what went on around her, and she was immediately able, and willing, to relieve my anxiety.

"Oh, is it Miranda Stanstead? I know they've been trying to

get you for ages! Three days in fact. Mr Balfour wasn't able to give them your address."

"Not able?" I was alarmed. "Why not?"

"Ach, well, you won't know. You see he's in the U.C.H." My heart jumped.

"What on earth's he doing in hospital?"

"He was mugged." No leading up to it. Dramatic effect. "Aye, mugged. As far as I know he was on his way home, now, let me see, which night was it, Thursday, or, no—" I interrupted her.

"Never mind, Fiona. I'll ring right away. I can't understand why they couldn't contact me."

"I don't know the ins and outs. I think it was the French telephones. The system's different . . . or maybe he couldn't remember. When you've been mugged—" I interrupted her again.

"Could you give me the number of U.C.H.?"

"Just a mo. I've got it here . . . no, it's on the board. Here it is . . ."

I rang straight away and to my surprise they asked me if I would like to speak to Chris. In a few seconds I heard his voice. I imagined it sounded shaky, perhaps an echo of how I felt. "What on earth have you been doing to yourself?" I asked.

"Minding my own business. I gave them your telephone number but they said they couldn't reach you. Am I glad to hear from you!"

"They wouldn't know the code. Tell me what happened?"

I must have sounded shaky because he said, "For heaven's sake don't panic. I'm being discharged tomorrow."

"They said at the BM you had been mugged. Is it true?"

"Yes, worse luck. The street was quiet. I had stayed late at the BM and the next thing I knew was my head striking the pavement with a resounding whack. Do you know those cartoons with heavy black zigzags and 'Ouches!' and stars? Like that. I didn't even see my mugger. He took my wallet when I was down and out for the count and buggered off."

I laughed with relief. "It could have been worse. I'll come back right away. You need someone to take care of you."

"What is this nonsense? I'm okay. Apparently I have a cast-iron skull. Tell me about you. Have you found out any more about your *aven?*"

"No, nothing further . . ." I didn't want to go into details about Colette.

I could hear him thinking. Chris was acute. "Okay," he said, "not to worry. I'll be with you within a week. I've to take it easy for a day or two then I can jump over the moon for all they care. This is Monday. I'll be with you definitely on Saturday."

Because I was glad I said, "No, I wouldn't hear of it."

"Why wouldn't you hear of it?"

"Because you've been mugged. And I . . . care about you."

"Are you serious?" He sounded pleased.

"Deadly. I'd love you to come, but see how you feel."

"I know how I feel. A permanent need, a hole in my life when I'm not with you." I felt foolishly happy. He went on, "I've been giving what you've told me a lot of thought while I was lying in my bed of pain. I get a kind of aura coming from the direction of Meloir, a something-nasty-in-the-woodshed kind of feeling, bad vibes . . ."

"Like the powers of evil." They were Ben's words, coming out of my mouth.

"Why did you say that?"

"I don't know." I gave my head a quick shake. "Okay, Saturday, but remember, if you have a relapse or anything . . ."

"Nothing's going to keep me away."

I hung up, well pleased; no, more than that, very happy. Ben, my dearly beloved young husband had died cruelly and precipitately. I was lucky to be given a second chance. It was odd, I thought, that I had been willing to sleep with Chris without committing myself, and yet not until I was here in France where my memories of Ben were so strong was I able to come to terms with having lost him, and think of filling his place.

I heard the loud rat-tat of the knocker and instantly knew who it was. My car was parked at the front of the house. I had to go to the door.

It was Rick, of course, looking extravagantly handsome. It is difficult for anyone as handsome as Rick not to look too good-looking. Everything about him was impossible to fault, lustrous dark eyes, strongly marked eyebrows, chin ever so slightly squared. It could have been called a male model handsomeness except for something strange in his expression, and an uncertainty in his smile.

"Hello, Miranda." He stood. The smile was even wistful.

"How lucky to have caught me!" I said. "I was just going to the Carvels' for a bite."

I was still wearing my suede jacket and scarf. I remembered an old precept of my mother's, rather, a con trick, that if you're uncertain about answering the door, you should wear some outdoor garments, then you had two options. If it happened to be someone you were pleased to see, you could say, 'How lucky! I've just come in', or if the opposite applied, 'What a pity! I was just going out'.

"I was hoping you would take pity on me," he said, "and let me take you for dinner."

"That would be nice." I smiled, thinking how difficult it was at this moment to believe what Colette had told me, or for that matter, Luc.

"Great!" He waved a bottle. "How about an aperitif? I've brought my own." His manner still seemed uncertain, and slightly shy.

"Oh, there was no need, but thanks. Come in! Do you mind if we sit in the kitchen?" I led the way. Kitchens were less seductive than sitting-rooms with their cushioned furniture, I thought, and then felt mean, thinking that.

"This is by way of being a pact," he said, sitting down on a stool and placing the bottle on the counter while I rummaged in cupboards for glasses and titbits.

"A pact?" I handed him a corkscrew. "Do you mind?"

"I felt I had been a bit touchy about Colette yesterday." He was expertly opening the bottle. "Of course I'm glad she wants to work for you."

"I didn't give it a moment's thought." I noticed it was a Cahors wine he had brought, a heady wine which went with

126

cushioned sofas rather than a kitchen stool. "How are things with you now, Rick?"

"You mean am I coming to terms with Chloë's death?"

"Yes."

"Materially, fine, but you have to make an effort. Colette looks after the house, then people are very kind. I dine out quite a lot. But, you'll know, it's the loneliness which gets you. I couldn't stand it this evening. I had to get out. Here, try that." He handed me a glass of the wine, dark, like blood.

I sipped. "Lovely. I understand that. Still, you're lucky having friends in Cahors, and the village. René Bonnard?"

"Yes, but he's difficult to get hold of unless it's his *jour de congé*."

I wanted to say, 'But you do share an interest in my *gariotte*', or even, 'Why did you tell Luc not go near it?' but couldn't. I changed tack: "I'm worried about my friend, Chris Balfour, who was coming here. He's been mugged in London."

"My God!" He was genuinely shocked. "Is he all right?"

"Yes, fortunately. He's getting out of hospital tomorrow and hopes to be here before long."

"He would be unwise to make such a long journey before he's quite fit."

"I told him that, but I doubt if he'll listen to me. Men always think they know best." I smiled.

"But we do most of the time." There was no humour in his voice, no answering smile. "You're like Chloë. She never acknowledged that I knew best. Life would have been much easier if she had." His eyes were flat.

"We're entitled to our own opinion." I steered the conversation away. "How are those charming friends of yours I met last Sunday?"

"The Lavanges and the Machins? Did you notice how mismatched they are? Guy Machin is outgoing, Lenore . . . well she can be a bit of a bitch; then Yvette is full of fun compared with her solemn partner." He laughed, "They should wife-swap."

"How do you know they're not happy as they are? Opposites attract, you know." I was at it again, being provocative. Had it been the same with he and Chloë? "*She never acknowledged that I knew best*" I didn't remember Rick being so opinionated three years ago, but then people grow into themselves. That had been another saying of my mother's.

"You need another drink, sweetie." He had sensed my annoyance.

"No, no." I shook my head vigorously. "I love Cahors wine but unfortunately it doesn't love me. Makes me heady. We should be lying on couches like Romans when we're drinking it."

"Well, what are we waiting for?" He laughed. That was the old Rick.

"We're just friends now, remember?" I looked at my watch. "I think we ought to be going. Chantal expects me around this time. She gets shirty if she's kept waiting. Once, she phoned me . . ." That was embroidery. I stood up, lifting the two empty glasses and putting them at the side of the sink.

"Ah, well, party's over." He was amiable again. "Well, you're the boss."

I laughed. "Am I bossy? Sorry. But since Ben died I expect I've changed. We all have to grow up. A salutary experience. It's different for a man, of course."

"Yes, we're used to being in charge." He was bland.

"I'm sure you are, but remember, if there's anything I can do for you while I'm here, please tell me. I know the sadness, at times, the agony."

He became serious. "Agony is the word. Night after night . . ."

"It'll pass. I'll never forget the happy times the four of us had. But we were young. It wouldn't have lasted. We have to come to terms with what happens to us as we pass through this vale of tears . . ." I became deliberately mawkish through a kind of embarrassment. "Well, come along. We'll reminiscence in *Le Repos*. I'm starving. I haven't eaten all day."

He got up and followed me into the hall. I chattered like a mad thing on our way to the hotel to cover this odd sense of embarrassment. What was wrong with me? Of course we had both changed. The charming young man I had known then now seemed much more complex. But then, wasn't that what was called growing up? Perhaps I had been too immature myself to recognise that aspect of his character.

I thought Chantal and Alain were rather reserved when they greeted us, and Rick seemed to feel it. "This was Madame Stanstead's choice," he said. "I hope you don't mind me coming along?"

Alain Carvel had more *savoir faire* than his wife. "We're always glad to see you, Rick," he said. "Anything we can do."

Chantal took her cue from her husband. "Are you managing on your own?" she asked. Alain had brought aperitifs to our table which we hadn't asked for, two *Ricards*.

"Life goes on but thank you. Everyone has been very kind." Neither of the Carvels had sat down, which they sometimes did with old customers.

"Well, of course, you're well known and respected," Chantal said. "Now, if you'll excuse me I'll go and attend to the meal. A simple roast chicken, Miranda? I haven't been to Lafont today to shop."

"Your simple roast chicken is far from that. I can smell it already. Can't you, Rick? That and a piece of *cabecou* and I'll be in heaven. Do you still get it from Monsieur Vivier?"

"Yes, old Vivier. He has the art. Crusty outside, melting and rich inside. *J'y vais.*"

Rick was telling me something about old Vivier, the farmer, and I watched him as I listened, sipping my *Ricard*, comparing him with the young man I'd known. I was puzzled. Very handsome still, but different – a detachment, as if he inhabited a world of his own. But the world I'd known three years ago had contained Ben, that laughing, loving young husband; this one contained Chloë, floating lifeless in the pool with that damaged fan of hair outspread. We were both different.

"How is Leo?" I said. "He used to go everywhere with you in the car – so you told me."

"That dog!" He was suddenly angry. "He's no use to me now, disobedient, won't eat. I'm thinking of sending him to the vet to be put down."

"But he's a beautiful dog! You can't end his life like that."

"I've no use for dogs who don't fulfil my expectations. Or people."

"That's hard, Rick." I refused to take his remark seriously. "You must be constantly disappointed."

He shrugged. "Not at all. There are other things in my life. Interests . . ."

"Like René Bonnard with his speleology?"

"Yes," he smiled, nodding. "René is full of ideas on that. An enthusiast. I must admit he comes up with one or two good ones."

Chantal brought the carved chicken on a huge platter surrounded by string beans and small potatoes. Alain followed with a bottle of house wine which he opened and wished us a swift *"Bon appetit"* before going away. I looked round the sparse room, a few locals, a few visitors. They couldn't claim to be busy.

We finished with Monsieur Vivier's *cabecou*, two pots of crème caramel and black coffee. The rough wine, not so heavy as the Cahors, had loosened my tongue, and I managed to feel comfortable as we chatted and ate.

"Have you heard from Ellen Lerner recently?" I asked, with my capacity for saying what came into my head at the moment. "Chloë's friend," I added.

"No," he said, draining his coffee cup, "nor do I want to." He was abrupt. "How did you know about her?"

"From Chloë, of course. I never met her."

"If I never met her again that would be too soon. She was the cause of most of the trouble." He looked around and raised his finger to Alain for the bill.

He brought it in a few minutes on a plate which he placed before Rick. The two men scarcely exchanged a word as Rick examined the bill and laid down the money. I had intended to offer to share, but decided to stay out of it. I had caught Alain's glance as Rick's head was bent, a lowering of his eyelids, a sideways glance.

As Rick and I roared through the village in his open car I wondered if I should ask him in. He was lonely, in the early stages of bereavement, and yet . . . While I was still pondering he had drawn up in front of my house, turned off the engine and turned to me. "If you don't mind, Miranda, I'll get off," he said. "I've a lot of things to attend to."

"Are you sure? A last drink?"

"No, thanks. You're sweet, but . . ."

"Some other time, then." I quickly got out of the car before he changed his mind. "I must admit I'm rather tired. Thank you for my dinner."

"Thank you for giving me your company. I do appreciate it." He turned on the ignition, gave me a brief wave and roared off.

There was nothing wrong with that, I told myself as I walked up the path towards the house.

Seventeen

I telephoned Ellen Lerner at eight-thirty next morning and an unmistakably American voice answered. "Ellen Lerner?" "I'm Miranda Stanstead," I told her, "I was a friend of Chloë Gillam's—" She interrupted me.

"Yes, I remember. She spoke about you often. Where are you calling from?"

"I'm in Meloir. We have a house here. I'm on my own. My husband died three years ago." I could never bring myself to say the more brutal, 'he was killed in an accident'.

"That was tough. Yes, I remember. And now Chloë . . ."

"Yes. That's why I'm ringing you. I came here to see if I could help Rick in any way. I was devastated when I heard the news . . ."

"He's all right." She was dismissive.

"I wondered if I could meet you in Cahors for lunch. I'd like to have a talk with you . . . about things."

"Me too, but can't be done at lunch, I'm sorry. I teach, and lunchtime I'm on duty. But if you like to make it later I could see you around three-thirty?" We fixed our rendezvous at a café bar in the Boulevard Leon Gambetta near the *lycée* where she taught, and then she hung up with a swift, "Be seeing you." I got the impression of a long-limbed, squeaky clean, blond-haired super-efficient American expatriate; a prototype, I know, but one I was familiar with.

But I felt relieved. This was the link I needed, someone who had been a friend only of Chloë's, and who would give me her opinion about Rick. And according to Colette it was she whom Chloë had wished her to call when she had the miscarriage.

133

I went upstairs to my *pigeonnier* in good spirits and buried myself in my work, becoming part of that turbulent medieval world which had always fascinated me. I had decided that Raymond, Duke of Toulouse would be the principal character, but as I riffled through reference books I found I was being sidetracked, just as I had been in Meloir ever since I had arrived. I had come out of sympathy for Rick, and yet there were incidents which disturbed me, strange undercurrents, a darkness under Meloir's smiling face.

Witchcraft? I had come across as I turned pages the strange tale of Guillemette, the young girl who had been burned as a witch near the church with the Norman tower in Lafont. '*Fachillera*,' they had taunted her as she was bound to a stake, 'ape of God.'

She lived alone at sixteen in a clearing in the woods, having been cast out by her mother, and on the Fête of Fools, during Lent, the young men of the village, disguised as satyrs, had raped her, one by one. A gang bang, medieval style.

She had earlier been seduced by a knight wandering in the woods who had promised her a hare in payment, but had failed to keep his promise. When he got home, three live toads jumped out of his hunting bag. Guillemette had asked for the aid of the Devil.

Then strange things began to happen. A monsieur from a nearby village was found near one of the narrow *portes* leading up the hill to the church, and the dagger planted in his heart was found to belong to the knight who had seduced Guillemette.

The knight returned to Guillemette, received a magic potion from her, was cleared of the crime and stayed three weeks in the forest with his saviour 'in sweet payment'.

But fame and suspicion grew in the minds of the villagers, not least in that of her doughty knight who betrayed her in the end. Her last conscious sight was of her lover turning his head away as she burned to death.

The stuff of legends, knights, hares, magic toads and all, but in medieval times they believed in the Devil, and their burning of a young girl was done in the hope of conquering that Devil. Was there something of this fear still lingering in the old stone of Quercy villages, in the one where Ben and I had bought our house? Ben had believed in the powers of evil. Did I?

I was a modern young woman, widowed, but happily in love again with Chris. My attachment to Rick which had brought me here was temporary – a wish to confide in someone who had known my husband, who could share memories with me; and sympathy towards someone in a similar situation.

I felt confident, mistress of my own fate, as I sat back and gazed over the fields with the far-off line of trees where the sheep sheltered from the heat of the sun. It was a Book of Hours scene. I had been in its thrall ever since I had seen those illustrations of gothic castles, the ladies whose tall pointed headgear echoed the towers of their castles, the caparisoned horses ridden by doughty knights, a land of Cockayne. Poor Guillemette, I thought.

My mood was so serene that I crossed to the iron cot which Ben had installed there for an extra guest. He had meant to replace it sometime with a more luxurious divan. 'Don't change it,' I had said, 'an iron cot is right for me when I'm thinking great thoughts. A divan is too erotic.'

I stretched out on my back so that I could still see the great arc of sky over the grape-coloured mountains, and felt the soft air on my face from the wide-open window. I thought I heard the tinkle of sheep bells, certainly incessant noise. Nowhere are insects busier than in France, that evocative susurration.

I thought of Ben with a soft, melancholy sadness. What plans we had made. Children enjoying this house as they grew up, bringing their school friends on holidays, their parents sitting outside in the cool of the evening. Before the children were born just Ben and myself, relishing being together, being happy, being in love.

It was too self-indulgent. Ben was gone – I didn't know where except that he was dead. "Dead." I repeated the word. It had been a mistake coming here, although well intentioned. My relationship with Rick had changed, or had it been necessary to come here to change it?

My future lay with Chris, the man who had said only yesterday

135

that he loved me, and there was no reason to believe that it was a lesser love than Ben's. As he had said, he was not the type for a fly-by-night relationship, and although I had gone to bed with him for our mutual pleasure I had realised only yesterday that I cared for him, loved him. He could be a continuation of Ben, what Ben might have been. I had given my love to Ben. I had enough surely to continue to give it to Chris.

When he came to Meloir this time I would be honest. Caring was a middle-aged thing, all right in its place. I would be honest with myself and start afresh, think of Chris within his own parameters, a talented young-middle-aged man, divorced with two children whom I already liked very much. 'I love you,' I would say to him, make a commitment.

I got to my feet, feeling purposeful. I would drive to Cahors now and have lunch on my own there. I would wander round Les Badernes and look again at the thirteenth-century houses, peer into shops like caverns. The time would soon go until I had to meet Ellen Lerner. I was looking forward to that.

Ellen Lerner, I felt, was the key. I got myself spruced up in a short skirt and linen military top with epaulettes which I liked – women always dress to please women, who are far more critical than men – and got into my car. I loved the road to Cahors, driving along that spur with the land falling to either side of me, that vast French land which always made England seem too neat and tidy in comparison, a tight little island.

Contrary to my stereotypic imaginings, Ellen Lerner was small with mouse-coloured hair, large grey intelligent eyes and a determined chin. In spite of her smallness she had an intrepid air; I could well imagine her leaving her native soil and being able to settle in south-west France – or anywhere – if there was a reason. Perhaps I would find what that reason was.

"Hi, there!" she said coming forward to where I was sitting at a corner table. "You must be Miranda."

"How did you know?" We shook hands. "Have a seat."

"You can spot the English a mile away. I daresay you can spot Americans?"

"Yes, there's a certain something. And you all have lovely

teeth." She had the *de rigueur* dazzling white smile, even more striking in her small brown face.

"It's all a question of finding the right dentist. I can give you the address of one in Cahors . . . not that you look as if you need it. Unless you intend to stay. What are you drinking?"

"A *Ricard*. It lasts the longest. I get a flagon of water with it." I indicated the one at my elbow. She beckoned the waiter.

"Hi, Paul! *Un Ricard, s'il vous plaît.*"

"*Comme d'habitude*, Mademoiselle Lerner?" He grinned at her.

"Don't give my secret away!"

"I expect you need it after teaching?" I said.

"It's not bad. Fortunately I like children. So far it's other people's."

"I should think you'd have a lot of French boyfriends here . . . not that it follows!" We both laughed.

"None that I like. *Merci*, Paul." Her *Ricard* had arrived. "Terrible about Chloë, wasn't it? You would feel it especially badly."

"Yes, the four of us were good friends. It seems like another world. I felt I had to come. Chloë was the sort of person who got under your skin."

"Yes, great strength of character. That's why it doesn't fit. And I get really angry when I hear Rick painting her quite differently."

"You don't like him?"

"Do you?" Her wide grey eyes were fixed on me, probing into me.

"Yes . . . to be honest with you, after Ben's death we started a correspondence which developed into a kind of . . . paper love affair. Ridiculous, but I now see what it was, something to do with a link with the past. I had falsified my memory of him, either that or he had changed since I last saw him. He's . . . different."

"Memory can play tricks. He's still very handsome, of course. Most women think so, which pleases him." I thought she was a bit tart.

"I have a feeling you have a reason for not liking him." I looked at her over my glass.

"Has Colette Jourdan been speaking to you?"

I nodded. "She told me of Chloë's miscarriage, and of telephoning you."

"You and I have to stop pussyfooting. Yes, when she called me I came as soon as I could with Matthieu – he's her doctor and police pathologist here. Not in Lafont, though."

"Is the Matthieu you mention Dr Pinard by any chance?"

"Yes, it is. Why?"

"A friend I've made in Meloir, Adèle Bovier, had a doctor in Cahors, and I'm pretty sure that's the name she mentioned." I wondered if that explained her confidences about Chloë. She and this Dr Pinard could have been friends.

"Chloë didn't start to see Matthieu at my instigation. It may have been your friend who recommended him. I gather she didn't want René Bonnard because he was a friend of Rick's. Matthieu was convinced Rick was ill-treating her. He challenged her about it several times, but she never admitted it. She was a bit of an oddball, Chloë. She thought it was too shameful to talk about marital relations, or that if she did that no one would believe she wasn't a willing party." The grey eyes were fixed on me. "Do you get the scenario?"

"Yes, and I don't like it." I was finding what she was inferring hard to believe.

"I advised her often to clear out but she wouldn't. Then the pregnancy. I wouldn't be surprised if that was rape." I stared at her, but her eyes, meeting mine, were unfaltering. "She tried to get rid of it because she didn't want his child."

I found what she was saying incredible. Why were women so loyal? Why, if what Ellen Lerner was saying was true, didn't Chloë leave Rick? I would have done. But how can you put yourself in anyone's place? How could you know that you wouldn't feel so tainted that you would want to stay put and hide the whole thing?

"If you couldn't get her to do something about it," I said, "I don't suppose it would have been possible for me. How long has it been going on for? You'd have thought I should have noticed something."

"Don't beat yourself about the head," Ellen Lerner said. "No one could get her to come clean, not even Matthieu with his professional clout. She was stubborn as all hell."

"She fought her own battles." I felt suddenly near to tears thinking of Chloë and what she had suffered.

"I think she fought until she was found dead in the pool. That she died fighting." That's a bit strong, I thought, but before I could comment she went on: "Look, I'll have to have a sandwich. I didn't have time for lunch. I'll have a coffee with it. Would you like to join me in one or the other or both? Or another *Ricard?*"

"No, thanks. I'm driving. I'll join you in a black coffee. It helps me to think."

Ellen's sandwich came, the usual baguette split lengthways with a slab of ham between it. She tackled it vigorously.

"To see you get round that," I said, "reminds me of an anaconda tackling something twice its size." She laughed at me, showing those marvellous teeth.

"What a fabulous analogy. That's exactly how I felt." She put it down, wiped her mouth with a tissue. "French sandwiches are not for the dainty eaters. Matthieu and I have been giving Chloë's death a lot of thought," she said, practically in the same breath. I nodded.

"In view of what you've told me about Rick, I'm doing the same right now."

"The bastard," she said slowly, "the mean cruel bastard." She looked at me. "I can see you aren't quite convinced. Oh, yes, he's charming, but I have to relieve my feelings of downright venom from time to time. That lovely girl. Matthieu and I felt powerless . . ." Obviously there was more than a professional understanding between her and this Matthieu, I thought. Was he the reason why she was not interested in boyfriends? "If I were you I might clear out back to London," she said. "Where do you work?"

"The British Museum. I can't go back meantime even if I wanted to. I have a friend coming to stay on Saturday. He works there too."

"Well, that's all right. The British Museum?" Her eyes lit up. "That's fascinating. What do you do there?"

"Research."

"Is that why you don't want to go home?" Her smile came and went like a lighthouse beam.

"Yes, I'm curious by nature. And pig-headed – like Chloë. Chris, my friend, will stay for about a week then we'll travel back together."

"That's nice. Well, as long as he's big and strong and forbidding that's all right."

"He's just been mugged."

"No! Well, that's London for you."

I felt protective of London. "It's not so bad."

"No? To tell you the truth, I always feel much more vulnerable there than in New York. It's a matter of atmosphere. Dickens has a lot to answer for, those dark alleys and Fagan."

We had both finished, and I had the feeling I should be setting off back to Meloir. I wanted to be home before dark. For a moment I thought of asking Ellen if she would like to have dinner with me, and then I'd stay in Cahors for the night, but that was too feeble. Like Chloë, I had my pride.

I suddenly wished I had Adèle Bovier to visit or to speak to, a woman friend, a mature woman friend. Ellen had the positivity of youth. I thought she would be in her middle twenties at the most.

"I'm afraid I have to go, Miranda," she said. "I'm meeting Matthieu. His wife has dinner with her old school friends to-night."

"Oh," I said, "well, that's okay. I have to go too. It's a bit of a drive back. It's been good to speak to you. We must meet again."

"We shall. Call me if there's anything worrying you. And as soon as your friend arrives, I should fill him in, you know, about Rick."

"I already have."

I got up and we shook hands again. "Aren't we French?" she said. "Next time it will be air-kissing. I'll call you later."

"Oh, for goodness sake, don't worry about me!" I shrugged.

"It's a busy road, that. And if you ever want me to drive over to Meloir I'm free most evenings this week. I know your house. Don't hesitate."

"Thanks." We smiled at each other. My smile wasn't as dazzling as hers.

I walked along the Boulevard towards the car park. It was strange how such a small slight young woman could be so positive, could inspire such confidence in me. I would take her advice and be wary. It was only when I was nearly home that I remembered I hadn't told her anything about the *aven*. Maybe I would next time.

Eighteen

I had one or two halcyon days after my meeting with Ellen Lerner. They had that rare quality which I had felt that evening on Adèle's terrace, an extra something which would linger. Was it something to do with the essence of France, so difficult to find in England nowadays, less civilised – an un-hurried feeling of everything falling into its proscribed pattern and taking its time about it. No rush.

The first day began, like the others, with the birds calling. In France they seem lazier than in England, none of that frenetic song which can waken you with its enthusiasm, and which you can surprise at intervals during the day, with an added last rallentando before night comes. In France they seem to sleep the afternoons away.

Then there was my morning visit to Monsieur Lacolm, he of the floury complexion and taciturn greeting, for my baguettes and croissants, and to exchange the time of day with the villagers before I walked back past the school. Inside, I could hear the children singing lustily and Madame Rossignol's disappointingly strident voice, '*Doucement, mes enfants!*' Further on I met a *troupeau* being herded down the road by Madame Henriot complete with knitting bag to take up her seat on a convenient tree stump in the pasture behind my house.

When I got back I drank some coffee and ate my baguette spread with golden butter – very non-French – did some neces-sary chores then went upstairs to my *pigeonnier* where I worked diligently – no, that's the wrong word – with enthusiasm. I was researching Richard the Lion-Heart's unsuccessful attempt to take Lapopie, the fortress in St Cirque Lapopie. I remembered spending an afternoon there with Chloë, and how we had climbed the path to see the view from the cliff where the ruins of the fortress still stood, the village with its church nestling at the foot, the river winding its way towards the Causse de Gramat.

I worked in the garden after my lunch, thinking of Ellen Lerner and Adèle, which made me think of Rick, but somehow in the gentle sunlight he had lost his importance for me. My books beckoned, and I climbed the stairs once more. Before starting I sat at my *pigeonnier* window looking towards the Pyrenees covered today with a pearly mist. The view was my elixir.

I bent my head again, but after an hour's work I made a decision. I hadn't enough information. I would drive over to Le Petit Ouisselac and ask Jean and Marie's permission to use Adèle's library. She was much in my mind, and perhaps they could give me some information about her.

The village was having its afternoon sleep. A few old men were dozing on benches round the *place*, waiting for the younger men, no doubt, to get back from the fields to liven them up with a game of boules. The children walked sedately through, led by Mademoiselle, en route for a nature walk. "*Bonjour, Mademoiselle,*" they chorused to her prompting as they passed, followed by a burst of giggling, subdued by her "*Mes enfants! Soyez sage!*" Some were carrying butterfly nets. I hadn't seen so many of the tiny Causse Bleus this year, and wondered if they would be luckier.

I crossed the Route Nationale, stopping for *l'essence* at the hotel garage, then dipped down into the valley and sailed up the other side, turning left when I came to Les Trois Lapins. A farmer was cutting his tobacco plants in a field beside the road, and I remembered they had three harvests every year. My neighbouring farmer had told me he was giving up their cultivation as there wasn't the same demand nowadays. Perhaps he was intending to turn that deserted barn on the high road into a holiday home for letting.

Ahead of me I could see Adèle's house, set in its *boiserie* of trees. How sad that she would not see it as often as before, if ever. An apartment in Antibes could not have the same attraction. But she had her English friend there, and friends were more important than houses. I drew up outside, having gone slowly to avoid Jean who was raking the gravel in front.

"*Bonjour, Jean,*" I said. "I have come to use Madame's library, if I may."

"*Bon!*" he said, resting on his rake. "Madame has told us to expect you. Please go in. You will find Marie in the kitchen."

"Thank you." What would happen to them eventually? I wondered, as I knocked then entered the stone-flagged hall.

Marie came to greet me, wiping her floury hands on her apron. "*Bonjour*, Madame Stanstead. I thought it was you. Madame has told us to expect you."

"It is not inconvenient, Marie? If not, I should like to use the library."

"*Pas du tout.* Any time, Madame said. And I have to offer you refreshment. The English tea, perhaps? I have the Earl Grey. If you care to follow me to the *salon*?" Her rosy face was bursting with excitement. I was a welcome break in her routine, obviously, and Jean's also, because he was standing at the door nodding and smiling.

"Marie will look after you," he said, taking a delighted part in the exchange.

"I'm sure she will." I began to feel I had done them a favour by coming.

"Get on with the drive, Jean," Marie said. "You have the pool to clear after that. There are the leaves. Madame does not like the leaves." She turned to me. "The tea, Madame Stanstead? English afternoon?"

"Yes, please, but only if you give it to me in your kitchen. I know you're busy."

"This is the baking day, certainly, and there is a *tarte des pommes* and a casserole in the oven. Each day has its own task." Regardless of whether Adèle was there or not, evidently.

"Good. I'll follow you, Marie." I was aware that Jean melted away behind me. Had she the natural superiority of age, two minutes older perhaps, or was it simply a female ascendancy? In any case, her word seemed to be law.

145

There was a glorious smell of baking apples in the large kitchen, and Marie sat me at the scrubbed wooden table while she made tea. "Have you spoken to Madame Bovier recently?" I asked her.

"Yes, last night. She now goes to Antibes. Perhaps that is best. It is where Monsieur Bovier passed on."

"She'll be back in the spring, probably, if not before." Marie shook her head as she filled the teapot at the stove, a sorrowful shake.

"She does not expect to be back here at all, Madame Stanstead. She said her goodbyes to her favourite places – the *salon*, the library, the bedroom which she shared with Monsieur Bovier for so long, the garden and the pool, especially the pool. They made it together. Such excitement. They were like children when the water was filled in. She clapped her hands and they embraced. So touching, like lovers. Jean and I watched from this window.

Jean said, "There is no need to cry, silly one." But it was *très emouvant*.

"Had you known she was ill for some time?" She placed a tray in front of me with a cup and saucer and some tiny sponge cakes on a doilied plate. "Oh, thanks. You have gone to too much trouble."

"It is as she wished. Help yourself to sugar and lemon. Is the tea to your liking?"

I sipped. "*Parfait*."

"Did I know she was ill? Well, of course. When she sent back my dishes from the table untouched, I knew. Her appetite before that was good. 'I eat like a peasant,' she would say. She liked my soups, particularly the sorrel made with cream and eggs. But when she stopped eating I knew something was eating her. Then she told me. Jean sat by my bedside all that night while I wept and wept. I had to get it all out before morning. 'No tears, Marie,' she had said, and her word was law in this establishment, I can tell you. Ah," she lifted her head and sniffed, "The *tarte* smells just right. *Excusez-moi*." She removed an enormous apple tart from the oven and placed it at the other end of the table. I wondered how on earth she and Jean would get through it.

"That looks lovely," I said, "and I know you have something else in there. I caught a whiff of it." A rich succulent odour had flooded into the kitchen when Marie opened the oven door and peered inside.

"That will take some time longer. It is a lamb casserole." I thought that if it were as big as the apple tart it would last them a week, unless they had gargantuan appetites. Perhaps it was Marie's way of overcoming her grief, by pretending nothing had changed.

"If it's convenient I'll go to the library now," I said, and rose.

"*Certainement*. Please follow me." As we passed a window in the hall we could see Jean raking the pool. He looked up and saw us, then bent to his task. "He's intensely curious," Marie said. "You have to watch him." I smiled behind her back.

It was a delight to be in the barrel-vaulted library again, such a beautiful room with its walls of books, its library ladders on runners, its pale oak furniture and floor. The chairs were upholstered in red velvet and studded with brass nails, and several comfortable armchairs were placed in alcoves with lamps covered in old linen placed strategically above them.

I spent half an hour assembling the books which appealed to me, and another hour reading about the knights of Quercy, Lapopie, Gourdon, Cardaillac and the Hebrard of Saint Sulpice. Still that feud today between religions – I thought of Ireland.

I filled out what I already knew about that peripatetic king, Richard Coeur de Lion, who without the aid of telephones or web sites contrived to be in so many places where there was trouble. I learned how he had been given a hard time at St Cirq, and an even harder at Chalus, where D'Ademar, Vicomte of Limoges and owner of the château at Chalus, refused to give up part of the booty to his overlord.

This was a challenge which Richard could not ignore, but, unfortunately, one of D'Ademar's arrows from a new type of crossbow found Richard sheltering some distance away. Three days later gangrene had set in. '*L'enflure gagne le coeur, c'est la fin . . .'* Sad words. He was forty-two when he died, the first victim of a new 'secret weapon'.

I sat taking notes until my eyes and wrist tired, then straightened my back and got up. I carefully replaced the books, enjoying climbing the ladders which gave me a closer look at the wonderful ceiling. I had been at peace in that lofty room. I am a student by nature. Nothing gives me more pleasure than being with books, the feel of them, the riffling of pages, even the ache at the back of my neck is pleasurable. Some of the older books here had calf-covers and the musty, bookish smell was better to me than the finest perfume.

I went into the stone-flagged hall. I heard the murmur of voices in the kitchen as I walked towards it. I tapped at the door, and there was the sound of a chair being pushed back over the stone floor. Jean appeared in the doorway, chewing vigorously. He gulped and bowed, his hand over his mouth.

"I have finished, thank you, Jean," I said. Marie joined him.

"Everything was to your satisfaction, Madame Stanstead?" she asked.

"Yes, perfect, thank you. It's a wonderful library. I'm so grateful to Madame Bovier and to you two for helping me."

"She will be pleased you came." She looked at her twin sorrowfully. "Alas, no more reading lessons this winter, Jean."

"Those evenings with the firelight flickering on the pages . . ." He sighed.

She sighed also, wiped her eyes, then straightened her shoulders. "May I offer you some further refreshment, Madame Stanstead?" The picture of a well-trained servant, a tribute to her beloved mistress, I thought. "A glass of wine? Madame would wish it. Such a fine cellar, eh, Jean?"

"Assuredly." He looked at me, "There is a Chablis beyond compare?"

"No, thank you." I felt I had caused enough disturbance. "I must get home before it is dark, but if I may, I'll return."

"We are at your service." He bowed. "Permit me to show you to your car."

I shook hands with both of them, and realised immediately that I had stepped out of my role. They both looked nonplussed, then recovered quickly and smiled. Their smiles were identical, wide, ingenuous, even childlike.

Jean preceded me, opened the door of the car, shut it behind me and waved me off with dignified aplomb. In fact they both waved, for Marie was now at his side. Tweedledum and Tweedledee, I thought, waving back.

I wasn't long in when the telephone rang. To my surprise and pleasure it was Adèle Bovier.

"*Ici Adèle*. Miranda?" Her remembered throaty voice sounded bright.

"Yes. What a lovely surprise!"

"Here I am in Paris. I have permission to go to Antibes tomorrow to recuperate."

"How good of you to let me know. You sound cheerful. Is everything all right?"

Her voice changed. "No. The cancer progresses."

"I'm so sorry." I was devastated.

"Thank you. I knew, of course, but now I am *à l'aise*. Can you understand that?"

"I think so. But there are cures now . . ."

"Not in my case. It is too far gone in the lungs. Well, of course, it is the punishment for smoking. An addiction I could not cure – nor, since my dear Yves left me, did I want to." There was no reply to that.

"You prefer to go to Antibes?"

"Yes, I have my English friend there who depends on me and I on him, and there is the climate. It is agreeable. You haven't seen Meloir much in winter. Don't believe it when they say the sun always shines in France! It can be cold, and rainy, and that lowers the spirits. In my dear Yves' case, when he became ill we bought our apartment in Antibes because he said that if he died it might as well be where it was warm." She laughed, a chuckling, smoker's laugh.

"Perhaps I can come and see you?"

"Perhaps. In any case we must keep in touch with one another.

When I think of dying, I think only of leaving my dear friends. You and I had an immediate rapport. Sisters beneath the skin."

"I felt that too. Adèle, I had some things to tell you, but I . . ."

"If it is about Chloë, please do tell me."

"You're sure? All right. I met Ellen Lerner and she says the Cahors doctor—"

"Matthieu Pinard. Mine also. I have known him for a long time. He has tried so hard to persuade me to give up smoking."

"I thought he must be your doctor. He was Chloë's also, and it appears Rick was ill-treating her. I find it hard to believe. Dr Pinard knows the Lafont pathologist, the one concerned with Chloë's death."

"He is also a pathologist, Matthieu."

"Perhaps the Lafont one has consulted him . . . would you think?"

"It would be very likely. Matthieu works closely with the police. He is highly respected. Such a pity his wife won't give him a divorce. There is no love left in that marriage."

"Are he and Ellen . . . ?"

"*Naturellement.* Why else did she stay on in Cahors? She came on an exchange post and met him. There is true love between them. Let us hope he is not too full of rectitude." I was learning quite a lot.

"She didn't look unhappy. Full of spirits. You know, Adèle, what with this and that, I'm beginning to doubt what Rick told me in a letter a long time ago . . . that Chloë had tricked him into marriage by saying she was pregnant."

"That is not Chloë. Definitely not."

"Another thing: Colette Jourdan called to see me, and she says when she was working at the Gillam's Chloë had a miscarriage. She asked her to get Ellen Lerner who would bring Dr Pinard with her. It seems strange that she didn't ask Colette to telephone Rick?"

"Nothing surprises me. Whatever was the initial reason for that marriage it wasn't a happy one later. That at least I gathered from Matthieu. I have known him since he was a boy. Sometimes he calls me 'Aunt' as a joke, you know."

"Does he? I mustn't keep you talking, Adèle. It will tire you. It was good of you to telephone me."

"Good for myself also. Have you used my library yet?"

"Yes, I've been today. I saw Marie and Jean and they were most hospitable. And your house looks wonderful. Thank you so much for giving me permission to go."

"How I wish . . ." her voice was choked ". . . well, I'm glad you've been."

"Will you let me have your address in Antibes when you get settled? Only if it's not too much trouble." There was no reply, but I was sure she was there. "Adèle," I said, "please hang up. I'll get your address from Marie. We'll keep in touch. I'll think of you. . ."

I could hear her smothered coughing. I listened for a time, then slowly hung up the receiver. I was deeply affected by her call. It took first place in my mind as I went upstairs and prepared for bed. How unfair life seemed. She wasn't an old woman. My mind went back to the evening when we had been sitting on the terrace and the fox appeared beside the pool, one of those scenes which stay in the memory, truly magical. I knew it would often come back to me when I thought of her.

I saw the scene clearly, the dark background of the cypresses partially obscuring the moon which slipped in and out, as no doubt the fox did to sit motionless by the gleaming water. I felt again the warm companionship which had existed between us, which sometimes takes years to grow with other people, if at all.

I was aware of my own mortality as I undressed, realising the futility of most worries which in the end seemed trivial. Ben, at least, hadn't had to face death daily, like Adèle. I was still shaken by the thought of her illness. Better, when one's future was unknown, to extract the essence of living from each day.

I was in the mood for asking myself questions. What was important in my life, really important? My work? To live life to its fullest extent? To realise and appreciate the importance of one's parents, and friends? Perhaps it was no denigration to Chris to place him in that category. Friendship in the end, that rare union of minds, that caring, could be more important than love.

Nineteen

L uc Devreux turned up unexpectedly the following morning. I had given him up and was tackling the garden myself. I was shocked at his appearance. He was pale and drawn, and as if aware of this, he seemed to have adopted a jaunty, cocky air, quite foreign to his usual demeanour. "Just thought I'd come along and give you a tidy-up," he said, hands in pockets. "You'll be leaving soon."

"As a matter of fact I am," I said, "next week. Well, if you feel like it, you can join me."

"I don't need you to help," he said, still with his off-hand air.

"But I feel like being in the open air." I looked around. "I'll miss this place."

His lip curled. "Not me. The whole of Meloir can go to the Devil for all I care. I've had it up to here." He left me abruptly and went to the tool shed, returning wheeling the barrow. He bent slowly and began to pick up the weeds I had dug out. He was the perfect picture of a reluctant gardener.

"You pull out those petunias," I said, pointing, "they've had their day." We worked together for about ten minutes without speaking.

"What prompted you to come today, Luc?" I said, straightening up.

"*Que voulez-vous*? My mother. Who else? She gets mad when I stay in bed in the mornings."

"I don't blame her. A young lad like you should be full of energy. And your mother works, doesn't she?"

"Yes, she goes to one or two of the big houses, scrubbing.

That's what she is, a scrubber." He laughed at his joke. He said, "*Une putain*", thinking I wouldn't understand.

"What time do you generally get up?" I asked, ignoring this.

"When she drags me out of bed. Thing was, she came back from scrubbing out Madame Ferrier at *dejeuner* when I was still there. She flew into a rage."

"You can see her point."

"Can you?" He glared. "Can you see her point in taking a stick to me, eh?"

"Well, no. That's different." I looked at him again. The jaunty air had gone, his lower lip was quivering. He shovelled up some dead plants, put them in the barrow and trundled them across the grass to the bottom of the garden. He came back, head bent, and took up a spade. I thought I might be better to keep off the subject of his mother.

We worked away without much talk for an hour or so, but at eleven o'clock I called a halt. "I think we both deserve a break, don't you?"

"Not for me," he said. "I've changed my mind after all. I can't stay long. I've better things to do, and as I told you before, I don't need the money."

I wanted to say, 'Go to hell, then', but I felt sorry for him.

"Suit yourself," I said. "I have some pâtisseries in the kitchen. Japonais. I thought I might have one with my coffee. Would you like to change your mind?" He shrugged, didn't reply. I left him.

When I was halfway through with my coffee, he knocked and walked in.

"I've got to go now," he said. The peculiar tone in his voice made me look up at him.

"Sit down first." I pointed to a chair, but instead he began to walk about the kitchen, head lowered. I saw he was in a state of some agitation. "Luc," I repeated, "sit down, please. You're making me nervous." The face he lifted to me was agonised, tears running down it. "What's wrong?" I asked.

"I told you, didn't I?" he shouted. "How would *you* like anybody to take a stick to you and beat you like a dog?" I wondered if he were exaggerating. "I wouldn't like it at all, but your mother was upset. Did she hurt you much? Tell the truth."

"Luckily she didn't." His mouth turned down like a recalcitrant child. "She was waving it about a lot all the same. She could have hurt me, broken my arms, for instance. I had them up in front of my face to protect it."

"Poor thing. But put yourself in her place. She lost her temper because she came back after working hard herself and found you in bed."

He looked at me, then turned away as if I were talking nonsense. It dawned on me that the hurt he claimed his mother had inflicted on him wasn't the real cause of his present state. There was something preying on his mind, something which terrified him to think about.

I got up and poured out some coffee, put a plate with the succulent pâtisseries in their paper cups on the table. "Come on," I said, "sit down and have a rest." I took a bottle of aspirin from a nearby shelf and put two on his plate. "You've worked yourself into a state, Luc. Have those. They're good for calming the nerves. Wash them down with your coffee and then have a Japonais. They're delicious."

He sat down, slumped down, rather, stared at the plate for a second or two, then took the pills in his hand and swallowed them, followed by a drink of coffee. He sunk his teeth into one of the cakes, looked at it approvingly, then ate the whole thing in about two bites.

"Good, isn't it?" I said. I felt I was talking to an infant.

"*Pas mal.*"

"When you've finished we'll go into the garden again. Fresh air and exercise is better for you than lying in bed brooding, isn't it?" I went on, "Lying in bed worrying, regretting that—"

"Yes!" he shouted, interrupting me, "That's what I do. You're right!"

"Have another Japonais," I said, "they're as light as a feather. Madame Lacouche is an expert at making them. A young man like you could easily put two under your belt."

He took another one, bit into it and said conversationally,

"The Lacouches had a boy the same age as me, Pierre. They lived in Meloir. He died of polio. Then his father and mother split up."

"I didn't know." I remembered Madame Lacouche's frivolous appearance, the bouffant hair style. Was it a desperate kind of courage on her part?

"He played the guitar, Pierre. He wanted to start a group. His mother used to sing along with it when she'd had a skinful. It was fun to visit them . . ." At the thought of Pierre and his parents his mood had become brighter.

He joined me in the garden until lunchtime, when we lunched off some more of Madame Lacouche's offerings, sausage rolls and hare pâté. I gave him a glass of red wine.

"I'm glad you turned up, Luc," I said. "I didn't want to go away without seeing you. Now we're going to leave a tidy garden. While I'm away, if you want to come occasionally I'd be happy to pay you for that. That is," I added, "if Monsieur Gillam can spare you."

There was no reply. When I looked at him I saw the trembling was back. He pushed back his chair and rushed out of the kitchen. When I followed him he was standing beside the *gariotte*, his head against it.

"Luc," I went up to him, "I'm so sorry I've disturbed or upset you. Please turn round." He did, slowly, drawing a dirty hand down his face, causing black smudges from his tears to streak his cheeks. He was a pathetic figure. I took a risk.

"You could tidy up the *gariotte*, if you wish. I've tried, but it's . . ."

"No no no!" he shouted through his sobbing. "I told you before I have to keep away from it. It's his orders!"

"Why should Monsieur Gillam give you orders for *my* garden?" I tried a bit of shouting myself. His face was working. The tears were still streaming down his face.

"He's my employer, that's why! He pays me handsomely – that is his word, handsomely – not only for gardening!" I went cold as I watched him waving his fist at me. *Not only for gardening.* "But that's a secret!"

I heard my voice, cool, no trace of the alarm I'd felt a second ago. "He pays you to keep your mouth shut, is that it? You know something he wants you to keep quiet about?" My subconscious was still putting words into my mouth, "It's to do with the swimming pool, isn't it? Madame Gillam? He's only frightening you, Luc . . ." I stopped because the tears were there again, coursing down his cheeks. I felt ashamed of myself.

He flung himself away from me, seized a spade and began digging furiously in the bed beside the *gariotte*, and I hadn't the heart to tell him that he was digging up the bulbs I had just planted. It was nothing compared with the hornet's nest I had just stirred up.

"You saw something," I said, "and Monsieur Gillam is paying you to keep quiet, but let me tell you, the police are looking into this . . ."

"You mean about the time?" His eyes were starting out of his head.

"Yes, about the time." My mind was working at a furious rate. "You weren't supposed to be there . . ." I was using words, sentences, which I hoped would fit.

"It was because I couldn't sleep." The words came like a sluice-gate being opened. "I was in bed that night and I remembered I had left the greenhouse window open where his special vines were. I thought if they got spoiled he'd kill me . . ."

"So you got up?" I had to keep him talking.

"It wasn't really so late, only ten o'clock, so I got out my bicycle and was at the Gillam place in no time. There was a moon behind the trees. They were waving about in the wind. The village was deserted but it looked pretty with the church. It reminded me of Christmas. A cat ran across my wheels. Nearly killed the brute . . ." He laughed, a boyish laugh.

"Poor cat . . ."

"I pushed my bicycle up the drive so as not to make a noise, but before I reached the greenhouse I heard voices coming from the pool. I peered through the trees shading it – Madame Gillam loved those trees but he always wanted to cut them down – I saw them in the pool . . ."

"Who?"

"Monsieur and Madame. At first I thought it was a lover's thing – they were naked – I saw her . . ." he darted a look at my breasts ". . . his arms were round her, but her cries weren't those of pleasure." He smiled slyly. "I've seen lovers, you know. Pierre and I used to spy on the couples down by the river . . . but never mind. Her cries were different, not groans, but high-pitched screaming, and yet smothered, then spluttering, then long, drawn out . . . made your blood run cold. Then there was a scuffling amongst the trees which frightened me – I know now it was only a bird, or a rabbit – and I grabbed my bicycle and went quickly to the greenhouse. I shut the windows and raced down the drive."

"You didn't stop and look at the pool again?"

"Not likely. I was shitting myself with fright. I just wanted to get home quickly. Next morning the police were there. Madame had drowned and I was questioned."

"Did you tell them what you had seen?"

"Catch me! Benoit, the butcher, had warned me that if he caught me snooping by the river again, he would report me to the police, not to mention flaying me alive with one of his big knives. And Monsieur Gillam always said he would do the same, only he would take a gun to anyone snooping around his property. No, you have to watch your step with the police! In any event Monsieur Gillam would have docked my wages if he'd known the greenhouse windows had been left open . . . Oh, yes, you have to have your wits about you as far as the police are concerned!" He stuck his chin in the air.

"So you didn't tell the police anything?"

"No, not me. Besides, when I got home that night I thought maybe I had imagined the whole thing. I told Monsieur Gillam in the morning all the same, in case he had seen me passing the pool. But I said to him not to worry, I wouldn't say anything. He was very nice. Gave me a hundred francs and said to keep my mouth shut because it would only get me into trouble with the police who were hot on snoopers. 'One day you'll know all about sex games,' he said, when I kind of . . . hinted that I thought that was what they'd been up to . . ." Luc guffawed. Poor, silly boy, I thought.

"I don't know how you convinced the police, all the same," I said.

"I'm not simple, you know. Monsieur Gillam told me what to say, that I had finished work at four o'clock the day before, and it was seven o'clock the following morning when I went to clean the pool that I had found Madame Gillam. He said that was best, then I couldn't be accused of snooping . . ."

"So you told them that?"

"Yes, as cool as cucumber. It was true, too, except I kept mum about having seen them in the pool at ten o'clock the previous night. I think I gave a good account of myself." His chin was raised. There were no tears now. I remembered Chloë talking to me about him – 'He's a bit odd, poor soul. Lacks something. Maybe love. But he's a good gardener, he has an affinity with the earth, with plants . . .' – "Monsieur Gillam has been very generous to me," Luc was saying, "I wouldn't say a word against him . . . but that doesn't help . . ." The tears were back again, his face was shapeless with tears. I gave him some tissues.

"Wipe your face, Luc." He did, sniffing as he wiped.

"*C'est ça.* Maybe I should have told them everything . . ." he shrugged. "But I described how that morning I'd run into the house and brought Monsieur Gillam and how upset he was when he saw his wife. I cried watching him crying . . ." He snorted, wiped again. It was Rick who had reduced him to this, I thought, frightening the life out of him, telling him to withhold information.

I put my arm round the boy's shoulders. "Come into the house with me," I said, "you've done enough for today."

I seated him in the kitchen, made some tea and gave him a cup with plenty of sugar in it. When he seemed calmer I sat opposite him at the table. "Do you remember," I said, "seeing a friend of Madame Gillam's at any time? Mademoiselle Lerner. She's American."

He blew a breath which was half a sigh. "Yes, I remember her. Colette Jourdan told me her name. She gave the two ladies tea in the garden when I was working there."

"Good. Well, listen, Luc. She lives in Cahors, and she has a friend, a doctor, who would give you something to make you sleep at night. You're wearing yourself out worrying, and there's no need for it."

"Would he ask me any questions?"

"Nothing that you didn't want to tell him. You're letting yourself get into a nervous state through worry. He would give you some advice."

"I wouldn't want to see anyone who would question me about that night then tell the police that I'd been there and what I'd seen . . ." I could see he was becoming agitated again.

"He's a doctor, Luc," I said. "He would only be concerned about your welfare. Now, suppose you go into the cloakroom and have a wash and I'll ring to see if we can make an appointment." He didn't move. I was pushing him too much. "I would drive you to Cahors. It would be a little jaunt for you. He might even fix you up with a gardening job there. You'd be better away from Meloir."

He raised his head. "That's what I need. To get away from this place. Away from Maman. I'm driving myself crazy about that night." I felt miserable that I was manipulating him. I should insist on his going to the police.

"Well, go and tidy yourself up and then I'll take you home."

He got up and shambled out of the kitchen, shoulders hunched. His whole appearance made me feel more miserable than ever.

By great good luck I was put through to Ellen Lerner just as she was on the point of leaving the *lycée*. I quickly told her about Luc. "He says he saw Rick and Chloë in the pool the night before she was found dead. They were either struggling or having a spot of sexual capers."

"Hey! Wait a minute! What did *he* think?"

"She was groaning, and screaming . . ." The enormity of what I was saying struck me.

"This Luc should go right to the police! Can't you insist, drive him there?"

"He's scared stiff. Rick has told him some cock-and-bull story about the penalties of snooping. The poor soul believes them."

"If they were just having fun and games in the pool why should Rick want to keep it quiet? Has that occurred to you?"

"Yes, it has. It was ten o'clock when Luc says he saw them. So the police will presumably know from the autopsy how long she had been dead in the water. He's such an unreliable lad, Luc . . . schizoid. On the other hand, why should he make up anything like that. He's scared out of his mind . . ."

"Are you beginning to change your opinion about Monsieur Gillam?"

"I don't know. Everything's circumstantial. And this lad's close to being deranged."

"He ought to go to the police."

"Ellen," I spoke softly and hurriedly. "Luc's in the house now. I was wondering if I could drive him to Cahors tonight and if you could persuade Doctor Pinard to speak to him. I've said to Luc he might be able to find him a job in Cahors. He wants to get away from his mother . . . she's unsympathetic, to say the least."

"Say, that's not a bad idea. Matthieu will jump at the chance to talk with this guy, decide if he's on the ball or not. Could you meet us with him around seven-thirty at the Café Bergère, the smaller one across from the station? His surgery finishes around seven."

"Great. I've tried to talk him into it already." I turned. Luc was at the door, his face shining. The wash must have had a good effect. He looked more hopeful, and with his diffident, gawkish air, about ten years of age. I put my hand over the receiver. "I've fixed it up for Cahors, Luc. Okay?" He nodded dubiously. "Okay, Ellen," I said, taking my hand off, "we'll be there. I'll hang up now. I'm very grateful."

I drove Luc home. He talked quite animatedly, as if a load had been taken off his mind, and I was relieved, although I thought he was still in an agitated state. He kept fidgeting, his hands went to his face, his hair, he moved his shoulders. "Once you're feeling well, Luc," I said, "everything will seem different. This doctor is well known for sorting out people's problems, especially young people. It's better to see him than Dr Bonnard who might tell Monsieur Gillam. They are friends."

161

"*C'est ça*," he agreed. "I think they do business together. I'd rather steer clear of him."

We had reached his house. "Tell your mother I'm taking you to Cahors for an outing," I said, "because I'm pleased with your work."

"It's more than she ever was." I saw his mouth was trembling as he banged the car door.

"I'll call for you at six o'clock," I said as he stood uncertainly beside the open window of the car. "Now, don't worry. You'll probably find your mother's in a good mood now. On you go." He nodded. I sat and watched him shambling into the house, shoulders hunched. His mother was certainly going the wrong way about inspiring confidence in him.

When I got back I sat down to think things over. Ellen would tell Doctor Pinard about Luc's confession and I was pretty sure he would get on to the police. Or was I? Might he not wait to judge whether Luc was telling the truth or not? And what did I think now about Rick? He was showing all the usual signs of bereavement. Wouldn't he look guilty if he had *drowned* Chloe? My mind found it impossible to accept. Not Rick, that charming man who had been one of a happy foursome a few years ago. Don't let emotion cloud your thinking, I told myself. At least take the idea on board, entertain it. Nothing is impossible, and how well do you really know him? There has been a gap of three years.

I wished I could ring Chris, but he would be on his way by this time. Adèle Bovier was a person to confide in and perhaps give me advice, and on an impulse I rang the number of her apartment in Antibes. There was no reply. I hoped it wasn't a bad omen, and on second thoughts I doubted if I should have confided in her in any case. She had enough on her plate.

I was restless. I wished I had never left London, at least for the reason I had; I wished I had waited until Chris and I could have come here together. I should go upstairs and do some work, but there was only an hour before I was due to collect Luc. To-morrow I would go again to Adèle's library, and perhaps also get news of her from Jean and Marie. The day after that Chris would be here. I was conscious of a great sense of relief.

It was strange, I thought, that I had spent the best part of a month in Meloir embroiled in Chloë's death when my original intention had been to comfort Rick. But there had been advantages. I had done some work on my book, and being in Meloir had taken me back to my life here with Ben, the happy life of two people deeply in love. I had returned with an idea, nebulous, certainly, that Rick might take his place. But just as I now knew that was impossible, I knew also that living in Meloir in the future was impossible. There was an atmosphere here which troubled me despite its beauty.

Those times spent with Rick and Chloë I now realised were far from what they had seemed at the time. I had been so absorbed in my own happiness that I hadn't looked under the surface of theirs. Even then Chloë must have been far from happy. Now my only image of her was her floating dead in the pool. My heart lurched, sickeningly. Don't think of it, I told myself. Chris will be here in two days' time. All will be well.

I went upstairs to get ready to collect Luc. What a relief it would be to pass my worries over to this competent friend of Ellen's, Matthieu Pinard, and let him deal with them. I would much rather concentrate on the Knights of Quercy.

When I knocked at the cottage door it was Madame Devreux who answered.

"*Bonjour, Madame*," I said. "Is Luc ready?"

"*Bonjour, Madame*." Her face had an uncertain look of recognition. "Ready for what?"

"Didn't he tell you? I'm Madame Stanstead, remember? He works in my garden and I had promised him a little treat. I'm going to Cahors and I said I would take him with me."

"I know nothing about little treats." She was taciturn. "He wasn't here when I got home. Nothing unusual in that. I expect he's gone round to that café again to meet his *copains* . . . if he has any left."

I ignored this. "Perhaps he misunderstood and he thought I was going to pick him up at the café. I'll go there at once."

"Well, *bonne chance*, Madame." She nodded tersely and shut the door.

He wasn't at the café when I went. I hesitated. Should I alarm his mother? But she might expect me to let her know. I drove back, but when I told her that I hadn't found him she didn't seem unduly disturbed. "That is the kind of boy he is," she said. "You see what I have to put up with?"

I said goodbye to her, and drove alone to Cahors. It seemed the best and only thing to do.

Twenty

E llen was sitting in the café when I arrived. I'd had trouble with the traffic in the Boulevard Leon Gambetta. French people going home after a day's work are a very determined lot, and I had been obliged to crawl along at five miles per hour.

I thought how pretty her mouse-brown hair looked in its shining bob, much more original than bleached blond, and the smile which she turned on me was dazzling. No wonder Dr Pinard was smitten. I had long ago given up blanket opinions about women's affairs with married men. Each one was different.

She was having a *Ricard* and I joined her. It was a typical railway 'caff', many of the men still in uniform or blue work-clothes. I could see it would not be a preferred habitat for Cahors's uppercrust.

"You've certainly found out a lot since I last saw you," she said. "Matthieu was surprised too when I told him on the telephone. He'll be along later."

"It was good of you both to meet me at such short notice. Unfortunately Luc Devreux wasn't at home when I called for him. He hadn't said anything to his mother."

"That's worrying."

"Yes, it's just another thing. I'm like a Causse Bleu flitting from fact to fact and unable to tie it all up."

"For instance?" Her hair swung forward as she bent to lift her glass, swung back again to let her eyes rest on me.

"I was thinking about Chloë's sister on the way here. It's as if she's dropped out of the picture."

"She's not a matey character, but I know the police interviewed her when Chloë was found. I don't think she has anything

165

to contribute other than her deep-rooted dislike of her brother-in-law."

"Yes, that's true, and it may have been only her own opinion. French people tend to put up a front about their marriages."

"It was certainly Chloë's way. She was stoical."

I nodded in agreement. "Then there was Leo, the dog. Chantal Carvel told me Rick was having it put down. I haven't been to his house recently so I can't vouch for that."

"I have a theory. You know a piece of Chloë's hair was missing?"

"Yes, Adèle Bovier told me."

"It's true. The police verified it at the post-mortem."

"So, what's your theory?" I took a sip of my *Ricard* to hide an involuntary shiver.

"That Leo got hold of her hair to try and pull her out of the water. He had to let go but there would be some of it still in his mouth. If the police decide to search Rick's house because they're suspicious, they'll look everywhere . . . even in the dog's kennel."

The image of Chloë's body floating in the pool was back again. I took another sip of my *Ricard.* "That would be why Leo wouldn't leave the pool and it would get on Rick's nerves?" I looked at Ellen, trying to be matter-of-fact. "And so he might remove the source of his irritation. Or maybe the poor dog died of a broken heart. It can happen, you know. There was a dog in Edinburgh, Scotland, who lay on the grave of his master day after day, and died."

"Yes, it's possible . . . Hi!" Ellen's voice was suddenly animated as she looked up. "Here he is!" A stocky, youngish man had come into the café, looked around, saw us and came quickly over to our table.

"I'm sorry I'm late. *Je vous demande pardon.*" Their eyes were locked for a second, and then she was saying, "This is Miranda Stanstead, Matthieu."

"*Enchanté.*" He bowed. "The Private Eye?" he said, his eyes dancing.

"Sit down," Ellen said. "You won't embarrass Miranda. She's cool."

"Thanks!" I laughed, looking at him. He had a sallow complexion, a large nose, teeth as brilliantly white as Ellen's (that Cahors dentist again), and brown eyes as large and intelligent as her grey ones.

"Would you rather I spoke English, Madame?" he said. His speech was rapid.

"Spare the poor girl that!"

I envied that smile, and the look in their eyes. Chris, you're needed here . . .

Dr Pinard answered his own question. "Perhaps Ellen is right. But then we aren't all teachers in a *lycée, n'est-ce-pas?*" He turned to the waiter at his side. "*Café crème,*" he said, turned back again. "This Luc Devreux you've been telling Ellen about, your gardener, I gather he saw Chloë and Rick Gillam in a, let us say, compromising situation in the water the night before the morning she was found? There is this fashion to make love in the water, but we don't think it was that, do we? And this Luc didn't tell the police when he was questioned? Why was that?" He was firing questions.

"He says Rick told him to keep quiet because they would accuse him of snooping. And I don't think Luc's conscience is quite clear there. Young boys . . ."

"*C'est ça.* This information is very useful. I've already passed it on to the police."

"Can Rick be charged?" Ellen asked.

"On the evidence of this boy? It will place him under suspicion certainly. By the way," he turned to me, "I thought you were bringing him this evening, Madame Stanstead?"

"So did I. When I called at his house for him as arranged, he wasn't there."

"*Quel dommage.* Ellen tells me you found him nervous?"

"Yes, agitated, weeping. I told him you would be able to give him something to calm his nerves. I hope I find he's at home when I get back to Meloir."

"If not, the police will set a search in motion. This is serious."

"I can't quite believe what's happening," I said. "One thing after the other. I never saw Rick in this light at all. When I first knew him all I saw was a charming young man in love with his wife."

"Monsieur Gillam has a reputation for charm, even in Cahors. He is well thought of. But we have to face the fact that his wife has drowned in their pool under what now proves to be mysterious circumstances, if we are to believe your gardener." He shrugged, and smiled engagingly. "I'm hungry. I haven't eaten all day. Will you join us in a snack here, Madame Stanstead? It is rather, how do you say . . . ?"

"Basic," Ellen offered.

"*Merci.*" he shot her a glance which was certainly loving. "But I haven't time to take you ladies elsewhere." Their glances were locked again and I thought they would prefer me to refuse.

"No, thank you," I said. "I ought to get back to Meloir and see if Luc has come home. And I'm expecting a telephone call from a friend who is on his way to see me." I introduced Chris for my own *amour propre.* "Also I might get a call from Adèle Bovier. I believe you know her, Dr Pinard?"

"Ah, yes, Aunt Adèle. I adore her. Such good fun always, but now, alas . . . I wish you had known her husband, Yves. What a charming couple. He also died of cancer."

"That's sad. Have you heard how she is?"

"She has had to be admitted to the hospital in Antibes. She was brave to travel there but she wanted to be beside her lover, someone from your own country, I believe."

"They make good lovers?" Ellen grinned at me.

"Not as good as French ones, I'm told." I might as well live up to my reputation for being cool.

"That goes without saying." Their eyes met again, and this time two hands lying on the table. Which one would inch forward first, I wondered, but I wasn't waiting to see.

"I am so sorry you will not join us," Dr Pinard said as I got up. He seemed genuine. "You have been very helpful. As for the boy, Luc, if you find out he is not back home would you be good enough to let the police know?" He produced a card. "That is the number. They won't want another death on their hands."

I put the card in my pocket. "I'll do that. By the way, there's a doctor in the village whom you may know. Perhaps Luc has gone to him?"

"That's possible. He's a friend of Monsieur Gillam's. Do you know why?"

"You tell me."

I thought his glance might be admiring. "My theory is they're interested in your house because there might be an *aven* concealed in the *gariotte*. The idea came to Dr Bonnard first, and he shared it with Monsieur Gillam as he is a house agent. Be ready for developments."

"I expect rumours get around. Meloir is like most villages, I imagine, a hotbed of rumour." I laughed. It sounded uncertain in my ears. "I thought at one time I was fond of Rick. Now I'm beginning to . . . doubt him." I really wanted to say, 'be afraid of him!'

"And so you should. When does your friend arrive?"

"The day after tomorrow."

"Until then be very careful. Be sure to lock your door at night."

"I always do."

"Would you like me to come back with you, Miranda?" Ellen said. She looked sincere. Her hand was no longer on the table.

"That is a good idea." Dr Pinard nodded at her. And to me, "Why don't you accept?"

"No, thank you." I smiled. "I'm not easily alarmed."

"I still think you should let me come," Ellen said.

"There's really no need. If I'm at all apprehensive later I'll sleep at the Carvels'. That's the hotel in the village."

They seemed reassured, and I said goodbye, my brave front making me feel brave, and cool. Ellen kissed me on either cheek this time, and Dr Pinard shook hands formally. I thought they made a likable couple, but then I hadn't met his wife.

I sang on the way home, and drove to Luc's house before I went to my own. His mother said he wasn't back yet, but that she wasn't worried. 'He sits in the café until it closes. Who would have a son?' Nevertheless, when I got back to my house I immediately rang the number Dr Pinard had given me and

169

reported that Luc was still not at home. A grave voice assured me that they would take the matter in hand. Over to you, I thought.

I decided to indulge myself. I went into the kitchen, got the ingredients together and started to make myself a meal. I could have gone to the Carvels', but I was hoping Chris would telephone and I didn't want to miss him.

If anyone asked me, I should have to say that the kitchen is my favourite room. Even in my Bloomsbury flat I had spent some time on it – white walls, old cupboards I had painted, plenty of bright ware and bottles, and most important of all, a large table. I have to have a large table so that there is room for someone to sit and chat to me when I'm cooking, if they drop in. A country kitchen, even in Bloomsbury, with the proverbial string of onions and dried flowers hanging from the ceiling.

I had in my fridge a good slice of Prosciutto which would do for my first course, garnished with gherkins and a pat of butter; then a salmon trout which I had bought from the old man who had a fish farm tucked in a village on the way to the Causse. It wasn't exactly a wild salmon trout, but a good-sized stream runs into his lake, so it could lay claims to being at least half wild. Fennel. *Cabecou*. Melon. Gaillac. The telephone rang. It was Chris.

"I'm on my way," he said. "Crossed the Channel this evening and I'm bedding down south of Rouen. I've made good progress."

"You have." His voice made me feel good. "You'll be here easily by Saturday."

"Earlier, if you like."

"No, you must take things slowly after concussion."

"Okay. What did you do today?"

"Well, it's becoming fraught here." I was sorry I had said that, but went on since I had started. "Luc, the gardener, confessed to me that he'd seen Rick and Chloë in the pool at ten o'clock the night before her body was discovered."

"Both of them?"

"Yes. He said they seemed to be . . . playing around. She was making . . . odd noises." There was a pause at the other end.

"Chris?" I said.

"I'm thinking. Chloë's death, asphyxiation presumably, could be either of two causes – suicide, or . . . have you passed this information to the police?"

"Dr Pinard has. I saw him this evening with Ellen. They have a thing going. He's a pathologist. I was taking Luc to see Dr Pinard, as a matter of fact, but when I called for him he wasn't in his house."

"Scarpered? That's serious."

"I looked in again when I got back tonight but he still wasn't there. I phoned the police. Dr Pinard had told me to do this."

"And what did they say?"

"That they would take the matter in hand . . ." my voice cracked. "I'm bloody well fed up with all this!" I was suddenly angry. "It's ruined Meloir for me completely. It's as if there was a jinx on it, or me, some kind of undercurrent . . . evil. I'm terribly sorry about Chloë's death as you know – but I just want to be back in London. The British Museum would seem like heaven." I didn't mention the *aven*. I would keep that until he arrived.

"Where is Gillam in all this?" Chris sounded as angry as I felt.

"I don't know. Ellen thinks they'll take out a warrant to search his house. There's the business of Leo as well. If only dogs could talk! Remember I told you about part of Chloë's hair missing? It's out of my hands, Chris, the whole thing, thank goodness." I pulled myself together. "I'm not at all worried. Dr Pinard's very much on the ball. Look, I've got a nice meal ready for myself, and I'll have that, and some wine with it and go off to bed."

"Wish I were going with you."

"Me too," I said, sounding girlish, I knew. "Have you missed me?"

"Like hell. Life is no good without you, my love. Flat as a pancake."

"That's good. See you soon." I was surprised how tremulous I felt speaking to him.

When I looked out of the window as I was going upstairs I saw the silhouette of a uniformed man sitting in a car across the lane. I knew instantly it was a guard the police had laid on for me, probably at Dr Pinard's instigation. He didn't have to go to that length, I thought, but I felt reassured.

After I'd had my bath I looked again, this time out of my bedroom window. The car was still there. How did they avoid going to sleep? With the thought I yawned. It had been a busy day. I must have dropped off immediately, and when I wakened in the morning and looked out, the policeman was standing at the door of the car looking over at my house. I waved and he saluted, then got in and drove off. Very satisfactory. I took off my hat to Matthieu Pinard.

Twenty-One

T he next morning was pale gold, opalescent as befits late autumn. I looked across the fields from my *pigeonnier* where I had gone early. It is situated at the back of the house and looks away from the garden and the back door. The incomparable view had a poignancy, a feeling which often inflicts me in France. I have tried to understand what it is, an ancient, atavistic feeling which may have something to do with this ancient part which I know best.

I thought of Jacques Coeur, that entrepreneur who helped Charles VII with his finances, and how from his house in Bourges he sent out pigeons from his loft all over the world. His trading brought the rich damasks and silks from the Middle and Far East which so delighted the Court at that time. No modern-day financier could surpass him in his daring. Above his door, seen to this day, are the words, 'To the Valiant Heart, nothing is impossible'.

I thought of the words this morning, but all I was sending from my *pigeonnier* was loving thoughts to Chris on his journey through the heartland of France in order to keep me company. I knew that journey so well, stopping at little hotels each night (never brash glitzy ones), always later that one had intended. The open road is a magnet. Either one deviates to a hamlet with an enticing name, or one is seduced by the golden cornfields – never the Brasso-brightness of rape, bad cess to them – to keep on driving. Just another mile, one says, in a happy high-road blur, only to find that the little hotel planned for one's stop has a sign up: '*Complet*'.

Pas de problème. Around the corner is another one with a

flower-filled terrace where we are welcomed, taken up a dark, creaky, wooden staircase to a dimity-decorated bedroom and told that we may dine outside on the flower-filled terrace at our convenience if we do not mind the traffic. Mind? Whoever hasn't known the delight of watching the life of a small town pass before one's very eyes as one tucks into a *quennelle de saumon* hasn't lived.

I planned my day. I would do some essential shopping in Lafont, go to the Carvels' for lunch and to tell them I would soon be leaving, then spend the afternoon at Adèle's house. Before that I would have to make out a list of all the information I had to look up there in preparation for my work when I got back to London.

I couldn't telephone Ellen as she would be at the *lycée*, nor even Dr Pinard to thank him for arranging my guard as he would be busy in his surgery. Or perhaps with the police. I hoped the information I had given him about Luc had been a help to them, although the tragedy of Chloë had never been my business, only my concern.

When I got into the car I decided to drive to Luc's house to see if he were back. His mother came to the door almost immediately when I knocked.

"*Bonjour*, Madame Devreux," I said, "Did Luc return?" I knew by her face he hadn't, and my heart sank even before she answered.

"No, he hasn't, Madame." Her voice rose in exasperation. "Why would he do this to me? The police called this morning to inquire about him. I suggested he might be working at Monsieur Gillam's house – although goodness knows why he wouldn't come home first – but the policeman said there was no one there."

"No one?" I echoed, my heartbeats quickening.

"No one answered the door. That was all he said. 'That doesn't find my son for me,' I said, and he assured me everything would be done and drove away, just like that!"

"I'm sure he'll turn up." And now Rick. Presumably they had also checked at his office. The sense of exasperation dulled my fear for a moment. Really, it was too bad . . .

174

"You know what young boys are like," I said. "Maybe he slept with a friend last night. Have you anyone who would come in to be with you, Madame Devreux?"

"Why should I need that?" She bridled. "I have to work. We have to eat, after all, and there is no point in sitting here worrying. That's all that boy has caused me, worry. Just like his father. Went off and left me. It must be in the blood."

There was nothing more I could do or say. I left wishing her Luc's speedy return. My good wishes were cut short when she shut the door in my face.

I tried to banish the niggling unease I felt as I drove to Lafont, shopped, and then drove back to the Carvels'. It looked as if Luc had gone to Rick's house, perhaps broken down and confessed to having told me about the night he had seen Rick and Chloë in the pool together. It wouldn't have been difficult to get it out of the boy. But where were they now? Were they hiding somewhere, or . . . Do not get yourself further embroiled, I cautioned myself. Leave it to the police. But how did one quieten a fearful heart? I remembered Jacques Coeur's motto, but it didn't fit. There was nothing for it but to go on with my day's programme.

The Carvels were both behind the bar when I parked and went in. "Just a sandwich, Chantal," I said after greeting them, and to Alain, "*Un bière, s'il vous plaît.* Will you both join me?" Alain accepted.

"Sorry," Chantal said, "I have lunch to see to in case anyone comes in." She disappeared into the kitchen.

"She's still talking about leaving here and getting a place in Cahors." Alain opened two beers. "On and on." He pushed a brimming glass towards me. Was Chantal another person who felt uneasy in Meloir because of recent happenings, I wondered, but then remembered Dr Bonnard had told me of her son who had died. That could explain it. "And now we hear both Luc Devreux, that lad who does gardening, and Rick Gillam can't be found. The police looked in here for a *vin rouge*."

I shook my head in pretended disbelief. "News travels fast in Meloir," I said. "I'm not sorry to be going back to London soon."

175

"It's strange, though, don't you think?" He wanted to go on about it, "Two of them missing, I mean . . ." He looked at me and I shrugged, as if dismissing it. He changed tack. "Well, if you ever think of selling your house I'm sure René Bonnard would jump at the chance to buy it."

"So I understand. My friend is coming tomorrow from London, and we'll talk it over together."

"A good friend?" He gave me a masculine look.

"The best." I was cryptic.

Chantal came back from the kitchen with my sandwich. I always ate top and bottom separately as I hadn't Ellen's expertise. She watched me critically as she spoke. "Madame Devreux is in the kitchen and she's telling me about Luc having gone missing. And now Rick Gillam too."

"Maybe he's taken Luc for a jaunt?" I said. I wondered if Madame Devreux had implicated me.

"Of course, Luc has gone off before. She's pretty heavy handed with him." Her eyes saddened. "I've told her. Children need love."

"Perhaps Rick was more sympathetic with him."

"Perhaps. Rick Gillam used to look in here, as you know, but not lately." She leaned her elbows on the counter. "There's something strange about him now, ever since Chloë's death. Not ordinary grief. People are talking. And now if he's gone off somewhere . . . with Luc . . ."

"People are always talking," I said. "Especially in villages like this." Perhaps the anonymity of a city was the better bet for me in future . . . and then I thought of the view from my window this morning and the deep delight it had given me. "My friend, Chris Balfour, from London, is coming here tomorrow," I said, just to say his name.

Afterwards I drove up and down the valley towards Le Petit Ousselac in a resigned state of mind. Chris and I would talk it all out, everything that worried me, I would tell him about the possibility of the *aven* and he would advise me what to do about that. I was surprised at my melting heart when I thought of him, unlike my former attitude of refusing to be melted. It must be love, I thought, with what I hoped was a wry smile, not a smirk.

Jean and Marie welcomed me with their usual beaming smiles, but they faded when I enquired about Adèle.

"We feel very sad," Marie said, "that our dear Madame Adèle is in hospital in Antibes. She ought to have been in the one in Lafont where we could have visited her each day with little bakings to tempt her appetite. She loved my bakings, didn't she, Jean?"

"Very much, dear sister, as I do." She gave him a girlish smile which excluded me.

I spent about two hours in the library, and in spite of my worries about Luc and Rick I became completely engaged. The calm atmosphere under that vaulted roof brought a nun's calm to my soul. I blinked in the sunlight flooding the hall when I emerged – or should I say, surfaced – and made my way to the kitchen. Marie was there. Jean, she said, was in the garden.

"You must have the four o'clock," she said, putting her fat bottom in the air as she bent down to take from the oven a tray of golden cakes. I watched her prise them neatly from their tray, cut each one in half, spread strawberry jam on the bottom and split the top half in two which she inserted upright on top with a blob of cream to anchor them. "*Voilà!*" she said.

"Angels' wings!" I smiled at her. "I'm glad I was here at the right moment."

Over tea she talked about Adèle, the tears standing in her eyes. "I must not grieve. Jean and I will remember her always with gratitude. We were born to her *bonne*, you know, who was without husband – he had left the district for Marseilles – and she gave us a home here along with our mother, with the approval of Monsieur Yves, naturally. Such a lovely young couple, so much in love. Alas, they had no family. Our mother became the cook, and the three of us were given a cottage in the village. From an early age we were trained to help in this house after school, and when our mother died I took her place, a girl of eighteen. Jean became the gardener. We were never very good at lessons, but we had good hands, I for the kitchen, Jean for the garden. 'Everyone has a talent,' Monsieur Yves said to us. 'Adèle and I will help you to realise yours.' Of course, they travelled a lot, and so it was not too important at the beginning to be skilled. When my first soufflé collapsed on the dining-room table they laughed and clapped. Can you imagine the goodness?"

"I can. You were fortunate."

"Fortunate and so happy. 'Happiness is more important than skill,' Monsieur Yves said when I cried at the collapse of my soufflé. 'You must laugh with us, Marie.' He was a *philosophe*, you understand. And when he died that cruel death, we did our best for her. We have had a lovely life, don't you think?"

"The best of lives."

When I said goodbye to them I asked permission to sit on the terrace for a few moments. The pool was serene, shaded by the tall spruces, but so beautiful. I closed my eyes and thought of the young couple sitting here long ago and watching for the fox to slip in and out in the moonlight.

Twenty-Two

I was restless when I got back home, walking aimlessly about the house, uneasy for no reason, for several reasons. At six o'clock I saw that the policeman had taken up his position across the road, and, feeling happier, I went upstairs to my *pigeonnier* to collate the notes I had taken at Adèle's library.

There is a pattern scored in my brain, or, rather, a pathway. Perhaps psychiatrists have a word for it, but when I sit at my desk my worries switch off. The opening of a book, the taking up of a pen, is like a signal. It calms me. I am in my own world, one of medieval figures and scenes, the twentieth century fades away. I know serenity.

But not tonight. I was worried, miserable, lonely. And apprehensive. Rick had disappeared, so had Luc. Were they together? Had Rick decided that Luc was too dangerous to be going about, possibly telling the police what he had seen that night – he and Chloë together in the pool, her cries. But it might have been sex games . . . something was niggling at the back of my mind, something I had read in Rick's letters . . .

One of Ben's earliest gifts to me was a green Morocco writing case. I had found it useful when I was travelling. I never went without it. I got up and pulled my suitcase from under the iron cot where I had stowed it away. The bed in the room where I slept was modern, deep, no room underneath. I found the writing case, unzipped it, looked briefly at the snapshot of Ben I had slipped into the celluloid pocket – that smile, that ingenuous, lovely face – and I rummaged through the larger pocket where I kept old letters, praying . . . Yes! Here were some of Rick's. Keep calm. I took the case over to my desk, spread out the letters, read here and there, muttering, 'No, not there', 'Did I believe all that about Chloë? I must have been mad', despairing, no, the letter I was thinking of wasn't here . . . and then my heart raced, and almost stopped. This was it!

' "You monopolise the pool every morning," she said. "This is *my* time." I resented her attitude, her cutting me out of her life. It was a sultry evening. Tomorrow, Saturday, I made up my mind, tomorrow I'll go in when she's there . . . after all it's my pool . . . give her the fright of her life . . .' I looked at the date of the letter. Friday, 9th September 1994. Luc had seen them on the following evening, the tenth, Saturday – as Rick had said – in the pool, both naked, around ten o'clock, when he came back to shut the greenhouse window. And it had been Luc again who found Chloë dead in the pool on Sunday morning.

When had Rick phoned me? I have good recall, better if I shut my eyes. What was my *aidé-mémoire*? Carol, of course (Miss Dior in a mini-skirt), therefore a working day. 'You do look poorly, Miranda', and my poor quip, hiding my trembling because of the news I had just been given by Rick: 'Who wouldn't on a Monday morning?' *Monday*. Rick, now I remembered, had said on the telephone that day, 'Yesterday morning at seven,' in reply to my inquiry about when Chloë's body had been found. It fitted.

I had my working diary here on the desk, a big, one-page-a-day affair, and I flicked the pages over quickly.

'Monday, 12th. Morning. Dictated notes from American files. Trembling badly because of terrible news.'

I made myself work after a while to take my mind off the damning fact that I had written evidence that Rick had been seen in the pool with Chloë the night before she was discovered officially, again by Luc. Another part of my brain wondered whether I should let the police know or wait until Chris arrived tomorrow, but after half an hour I sat back, too disturbed to concentrate on either plane.

It was going dark, the fields were still lambent from the last rays of the sun, and the trees were Rorsarch blots on the horizon. I would go downstairs soon and make myself something to eat. Quite distinctly I heard footsteps on the stairs.

I was stunned by the sheer illogicality of what I was hearing. The front door was locked, and there was a policeman overlooking it. The back door was also securely locked, and although the *pigeonnier* was on one corner of the house and facing away from it, I was bound to have heard a car stopping at the front. Certainly the policeman would have seen anyone there. I couldn't move. The door opened and Rick Gillam stood there, smiling.

"Well, Miranda," he said, "we meet again." He was charming, insouciant, but Chantal had been right, there was something strange about him, a gleam in his eyes, a flicker at the corner of his mouth.

"How did you get in here?" I stood up. "The door was locked. Both doors. You have no right to break in."

He interrupted me, still smiling. "Have you forgotten I sold you this house? I kept a set of keys. I walked over the fields from . . . where I was . . ." he looked away, as if puzzled ". . . from where I was . . . and came in by the back door. So easy. Besides, you have the front overlooked – for your safety, is it?"

"You have a hell of a nerve barging your way in here." Terror made me furious. "This is my house."

"It was tempting, Miranda. Forgive me. I saw your light in the *pigeonnier*, so tempting . . ." He walked about the room like a house agent, cast a glance at the window. "Besides, I hope it will be my house soon." I opened my mouth to say something, but he went on. "You must realise by this time you're in the way here, poking your nose into everything, not what you came for at all."

My anger was now so intense that all fear had left me. "Oh, I'm sure you'd rather I went! But Chloë was my friend, and I can't bear to think about her unhappiness with you. I'm hearing . . ." I stopped because he had whirled round, his eyes cold, withering; but my terror was still giving me false courage. "Meantime, this is my property, so please go!" I even advanced a few steps, fists clenched.

"You can't be trying to frighten me, Miranda? He was smiling now, his voice level as he moved close to me. Before I realised what he was going to do he had put his hands over mine in a steel-like grip, his knee against my groin and thrown me on the bed behind us. I was winded for a second, but when I struggled to get up he struck me across the face, knocking me back again.

I was devoid of action or thought for another second. Rick Gillam, then, the charming husband of Chloë whom I had secretly fancied – yes, that was the word for it – was the same person as the stranger standing above me, who had assaulted me while still smiling.

I tried to sit up, but was thrown back again by him grasping my legs firmly and forcing them apart, in a businesslike manner. I felt a complete and utter blackness of the soul. He couldn't be going to do *that* to me, Miranda Stanstead, a believer in equality, respector of the other person's rights. He was tying my ankles to each corner of the iron bedstead. The stricture on them was agonising. I gave up struggling. I lay still while he tied my wrists in the same way to the top rail, biting my lip to stop myself from whimpering. The difficulty was in believing that it was actually happening, until I remembered Colette Jourdan telling me of Chloë's bruises, possibly on her wrists as well as her thighs. I was no longer surprised, only reduced to despair and an awful sense of inevitability.

Waves of nausea went through me, drenching me with sweat. When at last he straightened I looked up and met his eyes. He was still smiling.

"Sorry, Miranda," he said. "That's how it goes."

I turned my head away, unable to speak. You were warned, I castigated myself. Chris warned you, Ellen and Dr Pinard warned you, but you thought you *knew* Rick, had almost been in love with him, that you were as safe as houses . . . not this one. I waited, knowing what the next step would be . . .

But with the word 'rape' exploding in my mind, I mentally drew myself round myself for protection and screamed, scream upon scream. The last scream was choked halfway by him stuffing a handkerchief into my mouth. The swiftness and surprise of the action were too much for me. I lay waiting, spreadeagled, deathly cold, as if the blood had run out of my body. And out of my brain.

This isn't me, I thought, as I lay watching a strange woman who had been bound to a bed by a strange man. This is not Miranda Stanstead, widow of Ben, but making a new life for herself with someone called Chris Balfour – second choice, certainly, but none the worse for that. This is a strange woman humiliated by an even stranger man who had to be deranged. And then the schizoid feeling passed, I had slipped inside my skin again, and it *was* me, helpless, in a remote house in a quiet village with Rick Gillam – erstwhile friend and husband of dead Chloë – who had become warped, perhaps in childhood, and was now playing out his fantasies . . . no, the feeling of unreality was there again. It had to be a joke! I slowly met his eyes above me, watching me, strange, inward-looking eyes, and knew it was no joke.

Had other women felt like this in a similar position, I wondered, utterly humiliated, beyond fear, a sacrifice to evil? There had been young Guillemette, for instance, burned alive in nearby Lafont, betrayed by her lover who had turned his head away when she was tied to the stake. Did they hate being a woman, hate those men who searched for power in the subjugation of women? Did women in the same position long for death in preference? I kept looking at Rick, looking for the Rick I had known. I saw his eyes suddenly focus on me. He bent down and pulled the handkerchief out of my mouth.

I choked and coughed, keeping my eyes on his, and for a split second I saw not lust, as I had expected, but a lost, childlike expression. I had never looked so deeply into anyone's eyes before, nor seen such a look; and then, as swiftly, so that I doubted if I had seen it at all, it was replaced by a level gaze, an almost charming composure.

"Now that you're secured," he said, "perhaps I can have the pleasure of your conversation, Miranda. You like talking. But, remember, no more screaming. It grates on my nerves. Perhaps you've realised that it's pointless in any case. Your kindly policeman at the front is too wedded to his mobile to bother to get out of his car. You understand?"

"I understand." I turned my head away from that level gaze,

the slight smile, as if we were chatting together in some ordinary circumstance.

"I suffer from my nerves, you know," he said. *Now* you tell me, I thought, as if to keep myself sane. "Where has all that loving sympathy gone which you expressed so well in your letters?" There was a pleading tone in his voice. "Which brought you post-haste to comfort me in my affliction?"

I felt disgust and a kind of weariness which made me turn back to him. "I soon realised what you were really like, making Chloë's life a misery and then eventually—" It was as well that he broke in.

"You're a simpleton, Miranda, in spite of your academic pose. How can you believe anything you're told about Chloë by other simpletons – especially that moron, Luc Devreux. Oh, he ran to me and told me everything." He suddenly laughed, high-pitched. "Didn't you realise that's what he'd do? Didn't you?"

I didn't move, or speak.

"You know what you look like lying there?" His laughter chilled me to the bone. "An animal for sacrifice. Haven't you seen them roasting *sangliers* on a spit here? How does that appeal to a feminist like you?" Again that laugh, making my nerves screech. "Chloë was the same. Poetry, books on philosophy. 'You wouldn't understand, Rick. *You* can only sell houses!' Patronising bitch."

"Chloë wasn't like that," I said, wearily. "She was gentle, withdrawn, full of humanity." I felt his signet ring cut into my scalp as he struck me across the head. The blow was so hard that my eyes went out of focus for a second or two.

"Sticking together, eh? Typical of women like you. 'We know better than men like him!' Haven't you grasped it yet, you and all the other poor deluded souls, that you have only one purpose in life?" He was talking quickly now, not quite distinctly, I dared not look at him. "She talked rubbish about dignity, about how I humiliated her . . . as if she was fit for anything else! And that clever father of hers who went bankrupt, imagine, while I, who didn't even *have* a father, built up a thriving business by my own efforts. Well, let's be honest, with some help from Chloë's dad, although the poor sod wasn't aware of it. But no praise forth-coming for me, you may be sure."

I kept quiet while he went on and on, growing more and more indistinct, garbled, my head aching with the blow and with puzzling how the hell I was going to get out of this . . . knowing there was no way unless the policeman or – faint hope – Chris burst in . . . Almost idly, as I glanced at him, I saw that he was holding a whip. I watched as he raised his arm, and with a deft flick, unfurled the thong. It spun in the air.

"Pretty, eh?" He whirled it again like a circus master.

I came to my senses. "If you use that on me," I said, forcing the terror out of my voice, "you're out of your mind. I'm expecting my friend from London. He'll be here any minute."

"Is that so?" He smiled, evidently amused. "Well, well. If that's the case, why were you so afraid of me? And why didn't you say he was coming?"

"I just wanted to see how far you would go." I took a deep breath. "I'm warning you, if you use that I'll *know* you're out of your mind and that you killed—"

His arm rose, the leather thong spun in the air and then I felt its sharp bite on my arms and legs. I was wearing a shirt and a short denim skirt. There was plenty of bare flesh. He bent down and ripped the shirt open. This time the stinging pain on my breasts was not as bad as the humiliation, the sheer unfamiliarity of feeling such humiliation. I moved my head from side to side, my lips pressed tightly together to stop me screaming, howling, begging, knowing that was what he wanted.

"How do you like some of Chloë's medicine, Miranda?" I heard his voice through a kind of mist created by the abjectness he had forced on me. "That wasn't much . . . so far. What you're feeling is mostly mortification. Chloë grew to like it, you know. She screamed at me, just as you did at first, but she liked it. We had this love-hate relationship, you see. She hated herself but she admitted that it excited her." *I don't believe it, I don't believe it* . . . His voice rose. "You've no idea what we did together, with her screaming, encouraging me, 'More, Rick, more . . .' "

I heard the footsteps on the stairs first, and now my shouting drowned his voice: "You killed her! Her screaming was agony, not excitement! She hated you so much that she nearly died trying to get rid of the child you forced on her, raping her . . ."

The whip was raised, his face was a bursting purple, even his eyes were suffused with it when the door flew open . . .

The room was a welter of people, one or two of them uniformed, loud voices, Rick's one of them, shouting, once his laugh, and then it died down and there was quiet.

Someone was cutting the cords round my ankles and wrists. "*Comment va-t-elle?*" a French voice said, and Ellen Lerner was bending over me. She was rubbing my wrists gently, speaking just as gently.

"That was terrible for you, Miranda, terrible. Lie still. Matthieu's gone to get his bag out of the car. He'll make it easier for you."

"I'm cold," I said, and stopped speaking because I knew I was going to weep.

"I'll get something." She was back in a second or two with the duvet from my bed. It's soothing lightness and warmth helped.

I met her grey eyes, swimming with compassion, and I tried to reassure her. "At least he didn't . . . you know." I should have thought I could say most words, blasphemous or otherwise without flinching. Not this time.

"That's something at least," she said, and bending down gave me a hug. "Be thankful for small mercies." I laughed stupidly with her. The door opened and she straightened up. "Here's Matthieu."

He had cool doctor's hands, and he had some wonderful cooling salve which he soothed on the sore places on my body. "No weals so far," he said. "Once the heat goes out of your skin you won't be marked."

I wanted to say, 'Not outside', but knew I couldn't get my tongue round the words without weeping. I swallowed and smiled at the two of them.

"Look at her!" Ellen said. She shook her head at me, smiling also. "How about the bruise on her forehead, Matthieu?"

"He gave me a whack across the head as well." I was beginning to boast.

"Have you a headache?" Matthieu bent doctor's eyes on me.

"A little." A headache and a body-ache and a heartache. What had I done to deserve that assault? Not minding my own business? But it had been Chloë's. He had taken a pencil torch out of his breast pocket and was examining my eyes. His large nose was an inch from mine. Then he sat back and asked me to follow the direction of his forefinger.

"*C'est bon*," he said. "You are –" he turned to Ellen "*comment-dit-on en anglais, chérie – courageuse?*"

"A tough cookie." She nodded emphatically.

"I like it." His swift smile was charming to watch. "You are," he said, shaking his forefinger at me, "a tough cookie." I confirmed it by bursting into tears.

After a minute or two when I had managed to control myself, I asked, "What happened to . . . ?" I waved weakly because I couldn't bear to say his name.

"Shh!" He put his finger to his lips. "There will be no more worries from him. Just lie still and feel the sedative and the salve doing you good. Perhaps you already feel it?" His voice and eyes were doing their bit too.

"I would be more still if you would tell me," I said.

"You wish it?" I nodded. He sat down at the end of the bed and took one of my hands. "After our meeting with you, Ellen and I had been worried, especially as I knew the police were searching for Gillam. So, the next day, when Ellen had finished school and I my surgery we set off for your house. I knew, of course, the police had arranged a watch, but even so . . ."

"He was at the front. There is no place to park at the back." I couldn't manage long sentences. "Rick must have come over the fields . . ."

"*C'est ça.* It was unfortunate. However, Duval, the policeman, became worried this evening because you hadn't put on any lights downstairs when it got dark, and he reported this. He was told to get help from Lafont and break in. Meantime Ellen and I were *en route* from Cahors with a Cahors policeman for back-up,

187

and so we arrived just when Duval and his helpers were entering the house."

"That accounted for all the voices I heard. It's a pity they couldn't have stopped Rick before . . ." I felt I had a grouse.

"The police had been searching for him and the boy Devreux for two days without success. They were combing the Causse, but you know what that's like. But you need never worry about him again."

"They know he did it?"

"Yes, they had Devreux's confession, thanks to you . . ."

"And I have a letter saying he intended to follow her into the pool the night Luc saw them . . ."

"Better than ever, but on top of that Monsieur Gillam has confessed. He was babbling all the way downstairs, telling everyone he had drowned his wife. And the situation in which we found him with you . . . doesn't help him, eh?"

"He's mad, of course." I remembered that look in his eyes as he had bent to take the handkerchief out of my mouth, the look of a lost soul. A deep sorrow bit into me. I felt no malice towards him.

"How does one define madness?" Matthieu was saying. 'Sadism must eventually warp the psyche. The perpetrator is eventually the sufferer."

"Dr Pinard," I said, I knew my voice was shaking, "will you go downstairs and help Ellen with the hot drink I think she's making for me . . ." I had to stop.

He looked at me keenly. "Are you sure you're well enough to be left? I felt that you were the kind of person who wanted the truth."

"I am. And yes, I'm all right. I'll call you if I feel at all ill."

When he had gone I did what I had wanted to do since Rick had appeared, wept as if my heart would break, on and on. Once I heard the door gently open then close again. The soft footsteps could have been either Ellen's or her lover's. Strangely enough, the more I wept the less I felt the pain in my body, and my heart. Perhaps Rick Gillam had been right. It was mortification I had felt more than pain.

When at last I had finished I felt weak and cleansed. I could even tell myself it had been a valuable experience. It was a type of behaviour I had never come across before, and I hoped fervently I would never come across it again. And as experience is of no use unless one profits from it, I tried to change my feeling of outrage.

Now I knew at first hand, if I had ever doubted it, that there were men who were so warped in their thinking that this was the way they had chosen to bolster their self-image. And undoubtedly they got a kick out of it. Explanations that they were mad or that it was a kind of regression to basic man was too simplistic. There must have been hereditary factors in Rick Gillam's background which had contributed to his behaviour, culminating in the abuse and finally the murder of his wife. Now I believed in the power of evil which could manifest itself in so many different ways.

Matthieu Pinard had understood this, I felt. There had been real sorrow in his eyes. I was too raw inside yet to go the full hog, but it would come . . . if I became bitter and damaged the victory would be Rick's. All that thinking had tired me out. I decided to sleep on it and forego the hot drink. I went out like a light.

Twenty-Three

W hen I wakened I knew I was not alone. My heart gave a great leap of terror and then I knew. "It's you, Chris, isn't it?" I said.

"Yes, my darling." He bent and kissed me. He said with his cheek against mine, his voice rough, "I can't bear to think of what you've gone through."

"Who told you?"

"The two downstairs. Dr Pinard and the American girl, Ellen something. They said I was to go up and see if you were awake."

"What time is it?" He straightened to look at his watch, and then took my hand.

"Around ten."

"I'm still tired." I was too tired to ask him how or why he was here a day early. I slept again, this time healing, health-giving sleep, with Chris still holding my hand.

When I wakened the next time the *pigeonnier* was flooded with morning light and Dr Pinard had taken the place of Chris.

"Don't tell me I only dreamt Chris was here," I said.

He laughed. "I'm sorry if I am a disappointment to you. Yes, he arrived last night, in the flesh, very tired because he had driven non-stop from Rouen as far as I could gather. I packed him off to bed. I drove back to Cahors to – how do you say it – 'clock in' at home, and arrange with my partner to take over my duties then I came back. Ellen and Monsieur Balfour were here, of course. She does not go into morning classes at the *lycée* on Saturday, fortunately."

"It was good of her to stay on."

"She's a good girl, very good." He avoided my gaze. "Now, how are you feeling this morning?"

191

"Very rested. I still have a slight headache."

"*Alors*, perhaps I should arrange for you to go to the hospital at Lafont for a check-up."

"But they'll see the marks!"

"Do not be ashamed on Monsieur Gillam's behalf."

"No, it isn't that. Just that it's . . . ignominious."

He was shining the pencil torch in my eyes, and once again he asked me to follow his forefinger. "*Parfait.* Well, of course, you have had a shock. It would be surprising if you didn't have a feeling of malaise. Supposing we defer the decision, that is, if you promise to remain in bed?"

"Not this bed." I lowered my eyes, ashamed at my weakness.

"I understand. I'll ask Ellen when I go downstairs to help you to your own bedroom."

"And after that could I see Chris?"

"You think he will be a good tonic? Well, perhaps we should rescue him from the clutches of Ellen. She is making him the English breakfast at the moment. Fortunately she found some bacon in your cupboard."

"He likes it very crispy and with fried bread."

Matthieu Pinard shuddered. "*Les Anglais*," he said. "Now if I could just see . . . ?" He said that the weals were fading, as he hoped they would in time from my memory.

Chris came up when Ellen had installed me in my own room. The simple move made me feel myself again, and I was sitting up when he came in.

"Box and Cox," I said when he kissed me.

"What?"

"The three of you are whizzing around and up and down on my behalf."

"You sound like the old Miranda. Are you feeling better?"

"Yes, at least I've decided to be better. No bitter thoughts, etcetera. It was an unfortunate experience; it didn't kill me, it taught me a lot, but I shan't bite on it every day, I hope."

"Well said. Are you going to get up?"

"Is Dr Pinard there?"

"No, he's gone."

"Back to his wife, no doubt."

"Isn't Ellen the loved one?"

"She may be the loved one but he's married and his wife doesn't want to give him a divorce. I don't know the full story."

"Hard luck on them."

"Well, tell me about you. I gather you ate up the miles?"

"My trusty Rover did. Remember that last time you phoned me? I didn't like the sound of things. You were too airy altogether, and Gillam sounded like bad news. So I thought, what's the point of sleeping when I could be pushing on. It's surprising how easy it is to do without sleep when it's necessary. When I felt I was a danger to the public I pulled into the side for a kip. But I was too late."

"The thought was there."

"When I arrived I saw the cars round the house and felt sick."

"Don't castigate yourself. In any case, my honour was saved." I was being airy again, but it was better than weeping, which would have been easy to do. "Dr Pinard had had the same qualms as you and got here with Ellen and a policeman, so all was well."

"Not quite, and don't pretend." He knew me. "Pinard told me the state you were in when they burst into the room." His face went red. "I'd kill that bugger if I could get my hands on him."

The tears which were perilously close rushed into my eyes. I turned away.

"He's locked up by now," I said, trying to pull myself together. "Anyhow I've slept it off more or less."

Chris was sitting on the bed. He leant forward and put his arms round me, hugged me tightly. "Dr Pinard says you're a tough cookie. He seems to like the expression. He laughs when he says it."

"He's remarkably light-hearted for a man who's having an adulterous affair."

"Hey! Are your moral hackles rising?"

"Yes, since last night." My heart started to beat rapidly as images crowded in. "I've gone all vulnerable." I tried to laugh.

He was lying beside me and he stroked my face. "Stop the tough cookie act, eh? I'm going downstairs to keep Ellen company. Just lie quietly and rest." He kissed me as if I were fragile, which I was, smiled into my eyes and got up. He stood looking down at me and shook his head – a 'that's my Miranda' kind of shake – and I knew he was for me. He could see right through me.

I didn't sleep this time. I lay thinking how in fact it had turned out well. I was free of Rick and the menace which had emanated from him. Chris was here and that made everything all right. Also, I had been instrumental to a small degree in Rick being apprehended, and while I couldn't wallow in it, I knew it was just, and that Chloë's death had to be paid for.

Ellen brought me up lunch on a tray, scrambled eggs and coffee, and sat with me while I ate.

"I'll be interviewed by the police, Ellen?"

"Yes. They'll be brief, and understanding."

"I have something to show them, a letter Rick wrote. It will help to prove his guilt."

"Good. But he's confessed, you know. Dying to . . ."

I sighed. "It's . . . pitiful."

"Yea, pitiful. Anyhow, you have to concentrate on yourself for the time being. Though I guess you're pretty resilient, Matthieu thinks *formidable*." She grinned at me.

"I hope I'm not making you jealous?"

"There's only one woman who makes me feel that – Matthieu's wife. It was a miserable marriage before I came on the scene. She doesn't keep well . . ."

"Any children?"

"No, she can't."

"And you could?"

"Let's leave it, huh? See here, Miranda, if Rick Gillam is an example of someone born out of wedlock which I understand he is, I wouldn't wish that on any child." She must have seen my expression change. "Hey, talking about jealousy, that Chris is some guy. Are you two thinking of getting married?"

I smiled at her. "Not at the moment, and not for procreative reasons. He has two already from a previous marriage. Nice kids."

"But you might . . . later?"

"I don't give it a thought." But that was a lie.

Twenty-Four

After Ellen left, Chris said I was to stay upstairs and rest and he would go down and prepare a meal.

I didn't stay in bed. I got up and went to the bathroom where I washed myself gently all over with a soft flannel. I had promised him I wouldn't attempt a bath. The weals had faded and were no longer painful, and my headache had gone. Perhaps I *was* resilient. I certainly had been tested. I powdered myself liberally, gave my hair a good brushing and went back to the bedroom. Yes, I was quite steady. I wasn't going to make an invalid out of myself.

I dressed, pulling on fresh jeans and top, and sprayed some of my favourite perfume on my hair, spent a little time with a coral lipstick and then lay on top of the duvet for an hour or two. I was surprised how tired my little venture had made me.

"All the perfumes of Arabia," Chris said when he looked up and saw me in the doorway of the kitchen. "Is this wise?" He waved a stirring spoon at my clothes.

"I think so. I've got my sea-legs. We've a lot to do."

"Well, supposing you sit down there," he pulled out a chair for me at the table, "and we have a celebratory glass together."

"Suits me." I was happy because he was here.

"Dr Pinard telephoned to ask how you were. He offered to come tomorrow but I said I would phone him in the morning." He put a glass of wine on the table in front of me. "Cheers! The sparkle is back in your eyes again." He bent down and kissed me.

"I can hardly believe the whole thing. It's like a nightmare."

His eyes stayed on me, sympathising. "A horror film," he said. "My first sight of you when I came into that room was one of the worst experiences of my life, and that must have been only a fraction of how you were feeling. No one's meant to be demeaned like that. Especially you. You're not the type."

"It's difficult not to be when you're bound hand and foot. Don't let's talk about it, Chris. This is to be a happy, it's-all-over evening. What's that delicious smell?"

"I didn't cook it. Ellen left it, a chicken casserole. I've made a salad, and there's cheese and fruit to follow. I didn't do a thing."

"It's perfect. And you're both brilliant." I smiled at him. "When you've had a bad time, and it turns out all right like this . . . I could go down on my knees." He nodded and smiled back, then started laying the table, a baguette, butter, and followed it up with a salad which reeked strongly of garlic. "That's my perfume overpowered at least."

He was down on his knees at the oven, got to his feet and placed on the table a steaming casserole. "A capable girl, that Ellen. We got on together like a house on fire. But, then, we had something in common."

"What's that?"

"Stop fishing. She's full of admiration for your courage."

I shrugged. "Let's talk about you. Have you really got over your mugging?"

"Forgotten it. It was all fairly straightforward. Knocked down, stole wallet, made off."

"Did you get it back?"

"No."

"How much did you lose?"

"Around ninety, I think. I never count it, hoping I'll get a pleasant surprise."

"It was the thief who got that. What about the concussion?"

"No aftermath, except that I've fallen in love with you. Before that it was a regard – affectionate, of course." He dished up some steaming chicken, vegetables and gravy from the casserole on to two plates, put one before me. "We've both been in the wars, mine was nothing compared with yours, now we can go forward, as they say in financial reports." He refilled my glass. "*Serve-toi.*" He indicated the salad.

I discovered I was hungry. I've always liked the evening meal, and I set to with my usual gusto. The wine, a local Gaillac, with its flinty sharpness, toned down Ellen's rich casserole and Chris's pungent salad. I felt good, relieved, happy and thankful.

"Let's talk about the future," I said. "When are we due to be back in London?"

"Next weekend. I thought if we left here mid-week; Thursday, at the latest."

"I suppose we'd have to if we both start work on the following Monday. I was hoping we could go and see Adèle Bovier in Antibes, but it looks as if there won't be enough time."

"How is she?"

"In hospital. I'll telephone tomorrow and hope I can speak to her. I liked her so much and I'm afraid I might not see her again when I come back."

"You're coming back?"

"Yes, there's more to attend to."

"You'd come back to Meloir?"

"Let's talk about that later. Over coffee."

"We might have it in the garden. It's glorious outside. As soft as a peach . . ."

Chris carried out the coffee and we sat on a bench with our backs to the warm stone wall of the house. This is *France Profonde* to me, I thought: warm golden stone, evenings rackety with the noise of the cicadas, feeling the age of the place, not overlaid by sophistication as in urban England. France is in my bones.

In the gathering dusk we could still see the containing wall at the end of the garden, and the moleskin mass of the Causse beyond that. In the foreground, nearer us, was the *gariotte*, like a large beehive. Yes, it needs some sort of softening, I thought, perhaps clematis. I'll plant it next year, and then thought, perhaps I shan't be here next year . . .

"That's the famous *gariotte*?" Chris said.

"Yes, perhaps concealing an *aven*. The local doctor, René Bonnard, is interested in it too."

"What you have to do," Chris said, "is go and see the proper

197

authorities, the Mairie's office, perhaps, and ask them to investigate it."

"Supposing there is one, and supposing, just supposing, it led to a cave like Lascaux, what would happen, do you think?"

"The big guns would come into play. They would want to dig, but presumably you would have to give permission since it's your property, or perhaps permission is automatic. Then, if they discover something really important, they would want to buy . . . what do you think?"

"Or just compensate me? Maybe there's a law which would allow them to take over . . . in the interests of the State. I bet there's a law."

"Knowing the French there's bound to be a law."

"At least they're not obsequious like the Italians. Everything clear-cut. In a way, that's why I like them. We're accepted on their terms or not at all. This isn't a particularly friendly village, but it's typical – atypical, I should say."

I thought of the menacing quality I 'd felt from the time I had arrived. The power of evil. No longer, I hoped, feeling glad and yet feeling sorrow for Rick Gillam. Still, magnanimity could be overdone and result in smugness. "Never believe those stories of English people being absorbed into the community right away," I said. "You have to work at it, but it's worth having. What some people do when they come here is find other English people and make an expatriates' club."

"On your high horse, eh?" He was laughing at me, which was good. "You must be all right. To get back to the *aven*. There are imponderables here. It can only be decided if you notify the Mairie."

"Yes, I know. You might go for me, Chris?"

"Sure. And there are still other mysteries. Luc Devreux, for instance. Has he been found? And did you ever find out what happened to Gillam's dog?"

"Yes, he had it put down. Some of Chloë's hair was missing when she was found. I think I told you. Poor Leo wouldn't leave the pool and it got on Rick's nerves. Are you thinking the same as me?"

"That the dog tried to drag her out of the water by the hair?"

"Ellen and I thought that." Events and people were crowding in on me again. "Poor Adèle. We got on so well. She wasn't typical. Immediate friendship. Warm hearted."

"She was a Parisian, wasn't she?"

"Yes." I looked towards my stone wall again and could now see only a soft blankness beyond it, the mysterious Causse where the caves and the underground rivers were. I thought of the naked men who had danced there millions of years ago, the wall paintings coming to life in the flickering firelight, speared animals; the images filled my mind for a second, and then changed to the other image, the dominant one, Chloë's body floating in the pool . . . "Chloë . . ." I hardly realised I had spoken aloud.

"What did you say?" Chris was looking at me.

"She's still there . . . Chloë. When Rick met me at Lafont Station I thought she came out of the shadows towards me. She's still there." He put an arm round my shoulders.

"It'll go. You're safe from him now. He can't harm you."

"I know." I tried again, cancelling the bleakness. "Of course I know!" Now I was shrill.

"You're tired, darling," he said. "Shall we go in?"

"Yes, I'm tired." I allowed him to lead me indoors.

In bed together he held me in his arms, but that was all. He held me loosely, and gently, so as not to hurt, and soon I went to sleep, comforted and at peace.

The next day I stayed quietly about the house, reading, wandering around the garden, and preparing food, my favourite occupation. I was suffering from anticlimax, a peculiar sensation which made me feel fragile, and go about everything slowly. Matthieu telephoned and offered to come that evening, but I said my headache was gone and suggested we meet in Cahors for dinner before we left. He agreed.

Chris went to the Mairie at Lafont, and an appointment was made for an official to come and inspect the *gariotte* on Wednesday morning. "His eyes were out on stalks when I told him of your suspicions," he said. He also shopped for me in the supermarket and brought back essentials, and non-essentials like *foie gras*, wine and walnut oil for salad. He had been tempted as well by a basket of golden chanterelles which would go with his favourite crispy bacon.

When he came back I telephoned to Adèle's apartment in Antibes. Luckily I found her friend there, although he said she was still in hospital. He told me his name was Arnold Webster and he was visiting her daily.

"Got to keep her spirits up," he said. He sounded like an Army man. "She's having chemotherapy and she says I can help to choose her wig when the time comes. We've both decided that the only attitude to take up is an optimistic one. We laugh a lot together. I have always been able to make her laugh."

"Will you give her my love, please?" I asked him.

"I certainly shall. She has spoken of you with affection. She worried about you being safe."

"Please tell her I'm quite safe now, and that my friend is with me."

"Ah, good. We all need friends. Good luck to you both."

We went that evening to have dinner at *Le Repos*, and at the same time for me to say goodbye to the Carvels. They had scarcely been introduced to Chris when they burst out with the news.

"It's all round the village!" Chantal said. "Have you heard? Rick Gillam's been taken into custody . . . for Chloë's murder!"

"I know," I said. I was being very careful.

"Someone said there was a police car outside your house for a few nights . . ." Alain looked at me, eyebrows raised.

"Could we have two *Ricards*?" Chris said diplomatically, and then, "Will you both join us?"

"*Merci bien.*" Chantal looked pleased.

"Those friends of his at Cahors," Alain said, "they'll be surprised. They came to Chloë's funeral. Did you ever see them again, Miranda?"

"The Machins and the Lavanges? No, I haven't."

"Could you rustle up something for us?" Chris asked, "Miranda's been telling me how good your *boeuf bourguignan* is, but I don't expect . . .''

"As it happens I have a casserole already prepared." She looked gratified.

"You're lucky," Alain said, putting down the *Ricards* on the bar. And to me, "Were they afraid for your safety, Miranda? You and Rick Gillam were quite friendly, weren't you?"

"We knew them both, of course, but it was Chloë who was my friend," I said. "No, he didn't disturb me at all, the policeman. Hardly any need for him." I smiled brightly.

"To think of it, though," Chantal was more animated than usual. "I used to like him when he first came here, but there was something odd about him, didn't you say so, Alain, a peculiar gleam in his eye?"

He nodded judiciously. "Yes, I never felt really at ease with him. He was always a bit of a mystery, came to live here with an old aunt. He was clever, all right – got to Toulouse University, met Chloë there, I believe. Something odd about him, though," he stared at his glass thoughtfully, "as if he had a grudge against society."

Chantal suddenly giggled. "He certainly had a grudge against his wife." She sobered. "And Madame Devreux is worried about Luc . . . well, I'll go and put the finishing touches to my dishes." She looked at me. "You look a little peaky, Miranda."

"I've had a touch of flu. I was forced to stay in bed." I avoided Chris's eyes. He would tease me later.

The door with its half-lace curtain suddenly rattled and we all turned. It was René Bonnard, coming in, turning round to shut it carefully. If I had been accused by Chantal of looking pale, she would certainly say the same about him. And his eyes were haunted, all the twinkle gone.

"*Bonjour, tout le monde,*" he said. "Quiet tonight, Chantal. *Bonjour*, Miranda." He bowed to me.

I returned his greeting. "This is my friend, Chris Balfour. I believe I mentioned him to you. Dr Bonnard, Chris." The two men shook hands. "René is our local doctor."

"*Enchanté.*" René bowed. He turned to Alain. "When you're free, Alain, *un vin rouge, s'il vous plaît.*"

201

"Miranda has told me about your visit to Les Eyzies," Chris said. "I'm always sorry I didn't see Lascaux before it had to be closed down."

"Yes. Too many people." René spoke tersely. "Finds such as that have to be carefully guarded."

"Quite right."

Chantal reappeared from the kitchen and spoke to Chris and me. "I'm serving now." And to René, "Are you staying for dinner, Dr Bonnard?"

"I had thought so . . ." He looked distrait. "Forgive me, I'm interrupting. *Bon appetit.*"

"Would you care to join us?" Chris said. "I know Miranda wanted to say goodbye to you. It's a good opportunity, don't you agree, darling?" He smiled at me. I knew he was up to something.

"Well, if you insist . . . I was intending to have dinner." He looked from one to the other, uncertain.

"Come along, then," I said, and to Chantal, "My usual table?"

"Yes, at the window." She led the way, Alain following her. He pulled out my chair, opened my napkin with a flourish and placed it on my knees then looked enquiringly at Chris. "Wine, sir?"

"Thank you. Miranda always says your house wine is good. We'll have a bottle of each, white and red. That suit you?" he said to René who was sitting down tentatively.

"Please allow me—" He held up his hand.

"*Pas du tout.*" Chris looked as if he were enjoying himself. "And the menu?" he said to Alain.

"There isn't one." I smiled at Alain. "After the main course we leave it to Chantal, don't we?"

"*Comme d'habitude.*" '*Les Anglais!*' he would say to Chantal in the kitchen.

"So you're leaving soon?" René said when Alain had gone off.

"I'm sorry. I expect the news about Rick has disturbed you."

"Very much. But in any case I'm due back at the British Museum on Monday."

"And shall you come back here?"

"I don't know." I looked at Chris.

Alain arrived and uncorked the bottles, then offered Chris a glass of red. Chris sipped and nodded. "Excellent." When the wine had been poured he raised his glass to René. "I wish I'd had time to go to Pech Merle to see the cave paintings. Maybe another time. You'll know it well?"

"Of course. Along with many others. I only hope they're being more careful long-term, bearing in mind Lascaux. I should not like Pech Merle to have the same fate. Actually it's not the paintings as much as the actual caves I'm interested in, how they were discovered."

Chris said, looking at his glass, "It's amazing how those two boys at Lascaux came across the *aven* which led to such marvels . . ."

"Two boys and a dog," I said, face straight.

Alain arrived with a huge tureen of *potage* – it could only be called *potage*, I knew it of old, with seemingly half the produce of the vegetable stalls in Lafont in its composition, rich, satisfying, the equivalent of a day's nourishment. I was careful to serve myself a very small portion.

I watched René pouring half his glass of wine into it, a country custom. Perhaps he was the son of a small farmer and had shown more promise than usual at school and been encouraged to go on to Toulouse or Paris to study medicine. I was prone to ruminations of that kind. I realised he was looking directly at me. He was nervous. His little goatee beard was trembling.

"I feel I have to tell you something, Miranda." Now he was mumbling. "As you're going away. I haven't been sleeping since Rick was arrested."

"I know," I said. "It was dreadful. I was very upset too."

"I must 'come clean' as you English say." He looked at Chris. 'Monsieur, this is confidential."

"Chris and I share everything," I said. "You can speak safely in front of him."

"*Merci*. As you may know, Rick and I were . . . good friends. We shared many . . . confidences. I was his doctor. One evening, when we were dining here, I told him of my suspicion that there was . . . that there was . . . an *aven* in your garden."

"An *aven*! In my garden!" It was a consummate performance on my part. "You can't mean it! But where?"

"Concealed by the *gariotte*. Yes, I have to confess. I studied maps and I came to that conclusion." He was gaining confidence. "And I took a dreadful liberty. When you weren't there I tried to locate it. Rick and I looked together. There's no doubt there is what looks like an *aven* in there concealed by the brambles. They've probably grown over it again. Oh, yes, it's there . . ." He sat back and mopped his brow. He was white and trembling. Is there a doctor in the house? I thought.

"Well, Miranda isn't going to be upset that you and Monsieur Gillam had a poke around, are you?" Chris looked at me.

"Not at all. It was for my benefit, in a way."

"But that isn't the worst of it." René put another splash of wine into his soup. "Rick is astute, as you may know. He realised what a find this might be, and he was keen to buy the property back from you. I offered to help him, the understanding being that he would be the beneficiary financially, and I would get the acclaim. Abbé Breuil has been my mentor since I was a child. My dream has always been to discover a cave in this area. Think of it! I might even have become famous, written about in books, instead of a village doctor . . ."

"Well," I said, looking from him to Chris, "I don't know what to say. I understand your motives—"

Alain was at the table to clear away the plates. He gave up his role for a second. "Madame Devreux is in a state! She helps Chantal in the kitchen but she's had to go home. Sick with worry about Luc."

"I'm not surprised." Was he still hiding in the Causse, I wondered, if that was where Rick had come from? Or had he taken off somewhere else?

"It's the news about Rick that has upset her. She says anything could happen now . . ." He went off gloomily.

René looked at me. "He'll have run away. I know that lad. He has a hard time with his mother. I've warned her once or twice. She projects her bitterness about her husband onto Luc . . . can you forgive me, Miranda, for spying on your property, for

204

plotting? For even entering into such an arrangement with a . . ." he shook his head, biting his lip.

I patted his hand. "Nothing has happened. Let's say it was in the interests of science, shall we?"

"Oh, you're too kind!" He grasped my hand and kissed it. "I don't deserve your forgiveness. I'm so grateful. I realise now he was the wrong kind of person to have dealings with. There were so many small indications of his character which I chose to ignore – because of my obsession."

"We're all guilty of obsessions," Chris said smiling at him, "I have one about Miranda."

René returned his smile wanly. "You've both been most understanding. I've been foolish. As a doctor I should have known better . . ."

He didn't wait for coffee. He was evidently in a hurry to get away. He had to make an early start with his surgery, he said, he carried the chairs from his salon into the waiting room, there weren't enough to go round, you see . . . He shook hands with us both and said again to me that he hoped I would in time forgive him. "You've always been most kind, an asset to our village."

"Don't worry any more," I said. He was a natural victim. I didn't tell him that Chris had been to the Mairie.

We skipped coffee ourselves, said goodbye to the Carvels and walked home arm in arm through the soft night. It looked peaceful and welcoming now, but I wondered how long it would take me to forget that terrible evening when Rick had burst in on me in the *pigeonnier*. I would have to be in London and away from the scene of the crime, I thought. At least I had Chris.

I rang Ellen's number when we got in and luckily she was at home.

"I thought you might be seeing Matthieu," I said.

"No. Impossible." Her voice sounded bleak. "But we have a special date tomorrow evening, for dinner."

"Oh, what a pity! I was going to suggest we took you two out. Chris and I have to leave on Thursday morning."

"Well, in that case, join us."

"No, we shan't intrude. We'll have a drink with you and then disappear. It's just to say goodbye."

"I insist. Have dinner with us. It will make it easier."

I thought that was a strange word to use. "Are you sure?"

"Sure thing. Could you make it seven o'clock at the *Café Printemps*. It's after you go over the Pont Valentré on the riverbank. Do you know it?"

"No, but we'll find it. We have loads of maps. I'd hate to go away without seeing you."

"Me too. Seven o'clock, then. *Café Printemps*."

We made love when we went to bed. I dismissed the slight unease about Ellen. All would be revealed, as an old aunt of mine used to say. The loving started off with thankfulness on my part at Chris being there and ended in passion. He was equally passionate. It was the best healing therapy I could get.

Twenty-Five

The man from the Mairie came the following morning – the man from the Ministry, Chris called him. I saw what he meant when the official arrived, accompanied by another of seemingly lesser importance, for he took no part in the conversation, unless directly addressed. Some kind of inferior being, was the general impression given by Monsieur Duart, his chief. He spoke excellent English, but then I thought any *enarque* would. I'd had a boyfriend who was at the National School of Administration, the ENA, when I lived in Paris, and he'd had the same superior, almost arrogant air. I told him that I thought he must have been taught that too. At which he had looked down his nose at me.

Monsieur Duart had a clipboard with him, *naturellement*. "I think I have all the particulars here. Monsieur Balfour supplied them, your address, how long you have owned this house . . ." he was ticking off the items as he spoke ". . . the area covered by house and garden we have on file."

Naturellement. "A nice little property. It was sold to you by Monsieur Gillam of Cahors." Not a word about Rick having been taken into custody. That would be another department.

"May I offer you some coffee, Monsieur Duart?" I said. He looked disapproving.

"I never partake of refreshment while on duty." He looked at me as if I should have known that. I was tempted to say, 'Is it a crime?' but decided not to. I had learned years ago that the proper demeanour for an Englishwoman living in France is a tacit recognition of the superiority of the State. In England we like to query or question.

"In that case, shall we go into the garden first?"

"*Vous parlez très bien français.*" He looked kindly over his glasses at me as if to compensate for his refusal of 'refreshment'.

"*Suivez-moi, Messieurs,*" I said. He did, his minion and Chris bringing up the rear.

"*Quelle jolie vue,*" Monsieur Duart said when we emerged, "Ah, the mountains," he declaimed. "You are indeed fortunate, madame."

"Thank you," I said.

"And there is the *gariotte* Monsieur Balfour spoke about." He pointed. "Let us investigate." He strode across the grass, his little retinue following, as after the Sun King himself.

We gathered round the *gariotte*. "Michel," he said, "the torch, *s'il vous plaît.*" A large black rubber torch seemed to grow out of Michel's hand, and together they bent down and peered inside. I exchanged glances with Chris.

"*Des haies,*" Monsieur Duart pronounced;

"*Muriers,*" Michel muttered.

Monsieur Duart straightened. "It is impossible to make an examination of the *gariotte* in its present state. Would you have any objection to some of the bushes being cut away to enable me to make a preliminary surveillance?"

"Not at all," I said. "I have tried to clear it but I haven't had much success."

"One needs the proper equipment. Michel?" The young man nodded and went away. "*Une trés jolie vue,*" Monsieur Duart said again. "I live in Lafont. Well, of course, every Frenchman longs to live in the country, and yet they would not know what to do with it if they had it. And my wife likes to shop . . .' he pulled himself up, sighed. "Well, what woman doesn't?"

Me, for instance. Ben had loved shopping. I had told him he was like a child in Wonderland, longing for everything he saw.

Michel returned with a spade which was shining and looked lethal, also a large pair of shears, equally dazzling to the eyes. I could imagine Monsieur Duart inspecting them before they left. "*Bon,*" he now said. "*Au travail, Michel. Donnez-moi la torche électrique.*" Chris, always a quick thinker, had grabbed ours from the counter when we passed through the kitchen, and now, along with Monsieur Duart, they bent down and shone them into the interior of the *gariotte*. I, naturally curious, managed to position myself to one side of the opening where I had a fairly good view. Michel seemed to be in his element. He sliced through the tangle of brambles with his shears, then threw them aside, using his spade. They came away from the ground more easily than I had expected; in fact, it looked to me as if someone had wrenched them aside already. I think Michel had found the same thing, because he muttered to Monsieur Duart who raised his eyebrows in surprise. "*Curieux.*"

The tangle of bushes was cleared except for one clump. Now I could see a large hole in the earth. The *aven*? I felt Chris's hand tighten on my arm. He had seen it too.

"*Mon Dieu,*" Monsieur Duart breathed.

Michel bent to his task once more, and with one strong heave lifted the last clump of brambles to one side. He remained bent. There was a curious silence. The torches wavered, settled, sent a parallel beam towards something on the ground. I peered, then saw it, in a pool of light, a body.

The silence was broken by Monsieur Duart's voice, scarcely above a whisper, "What have we here?" Michel slowly straightened and turned to us. His face was a sickly white.

"*C'est un cadavre!*" He looked from one to the other, wiping his brow.

Monsieur nodded, speechless.

It was a body all right. I kept looking because I could not drag my eyes away. I was as rigid as it was, but with horror. I took in every detail, the knees pulled up to the trunk which was twisted, one arm outflung, the head back. I had to look at the face, the open, bulging eyes. On the neck there were two weals.

"It's Luc Devreux," I said. I put out my hand to Chris who was standing beside me. I felt his arm go round my shoulders.

"You know this . . . person?" Monsieur Duart's voice was still a whisper.

"Yes, he's . . . he was . . . a village lad. He gardened for me. He went missing . . ."

"I think Madame Stanstead should go into the house." Chris was terse. "It's been a great shock for her."

"Of course. I am remiss. A great shock for all of us." He muttered something to Michel, I recognised the word '*ecran*', and Michel went off, half running.

"We'll go in," Chris said. "Please join us when you've finished."

"*Merci.*" I saw Monsieur Duart was quite a young man, probably a few years younger than me. I was sure he hadn't been warned about this sort of thing in the ENA. His mouth was trembling.

"I'll make some coffee," I said. Chris and I walked towards the house. We sat down at the kitchen table and looked at each other.

"What a shock," Chris said. "And on top of everything else. Are you all right, Miranda?"

"Yes, but a bit punch drunk. You must be too. You don't think they'll accuse me of murder?" I laughed stupidly.

"Now you're being ridiculous."

"I'm being terrified!" I glared at him.

"Calm down. I can understand that all right. Have you any brandy here?"

"I've some illicit stuff in that cupboard above the sink. A farmer gave it to me. Makes it in his barn. But I don't want . . ."

"This is what it was meant for." He got up, found the bottle and poured me a tot. "Drink that. It seems strong enough. It would hardly come out of the bottle."

I took the glass. "It's like black treacle. Will you have some?"

"No, thanks. I'll make coffee while you're knocking that back." He got up and filled the kettle, looking out of the window as he did so. "They're putting a screen round the *gariotte*. Looks sinister. I'm glad we're leaving tomorrow."

One sip of brandy had set my throat on fire, but seemed to have remarkable restorative powers. "But won't it look suspicious? I mean us decamping?"

"No." He was pouring boiling water into the cafetière. "There will be fingerprints all over. They'll be Rick Gillam's."

"It's too awful to contemplate. Rick. You think he did it?"
"Yes."
"As well as Chloë?"
"Getting on to be a serial killer, if you include the dog."
I shuddered. "Did you see the marks on . . ."
"Luc's neck?" The door opened. Monsieur Duart stood there.
"All is accomplished, Madame." He had regained his voice, and most of his sang-froid.
"Come in," Chris said. "Have a cup of coffee."
"*Merci bien.* I don't usually, as you know, but the circumstances are, well, exceptional. And quite out of my jurisdiction, as you will appreciate. I have notified the police by mobile, and there will be someone here soon." He accepted a cup of coffee from Chris.
"What about your assistant?" I asked.
"He prefers to sit in the car, thank you. He is young and inexperienced. He is, shall we say, 'pulling himself together?' ". He looked for approval at me. I nodded.
After he had gone we still sat at the table. "We should have told him we're leaving tomorrow," I said to Chris.
"It's not his territory. Wait till the police arrives."
"And we have to be at Cahors at seven."
"Wait." He put his hand over mine. "Look, you go upstairs, have a bath and get ready. I'll deal with them if they come."
"Ask if we can go out tonight, and if we are free to leave tomorrow." I was trying not to be agitated.
"I'll take care of everything. Off you go." I went.
I heard the car drawing up as I lay soaking in my bath, and only felt relieved that I hadn't to face anyone. I made myself relax in the water, but another image was now there, Luc Devreux's face, his eyes. Once I'd seen a carp caught in a net. Its eyes had been the same, bulging, blood round the rims, mouth open. When I at last got out of the bath and looked out of my bedroom window, the car had gone. I dressed, made up my face and went downstairs. Chris greeted me, smiling.
"Who said you lead a quiet life in the country? You look gorgeous."

"Thanks. They've been?"

"Yes, Dr Pinard's name did the trick. It's all right if we leave tomorrow. He will vouch for us. Everything's under control."

"Is . . . Luc . . . still there?"

"Yes, various experts have to come this evening, but it will all be over by the time we get back from Cahors. Someone will come and see us tomorrow if necessary."

I went to the window and looked out. The screen was still round the *gariotte*. "You know the . . . whip . . . Rick used?"

"Yes?"

"I wouldn't be surprised if . . . it, I mean the thong, was used to . . . on Luc."

"I thought that too. Weals. Don't dwell on it." He looked at his watch. "It's six o'clock. Shall we start on our way? Take it easy?"

"All right." We were both being matter-of-fact. "I'm glad we're seeing them."

"Me too. Would you like to drive?"

"Yes, please." He knew that, unlike many people, driving soothed me. It was thoughtful. I was glad, all the same, that the car was parked at the front. I didn't want to see that screen again round the *gariotte*. My lovely garden with its view of the Pyrenees was ruined for me.

Twenty-Six

W e had difficulty in finding the address Ellen had given me, a small family restaurant tucked behind the Allés des Soupirs – appropriately named, I thought, considering her fraught affair with a married man.

"They believe in tucking themselves away," Chris said.

"It's called being incognito, but I suppose they've had to do it. Where I met them before, near the station, was permitted, I suppose, because it was a drop-in visit on his part."

Le Café Printemps was discreet-looking, small, but busy when we went in, with booths for some of the tables. Ellen hailed us from one. She looked pale. Not woebegone – she had too much character for that – but there was the same bleakness about her which I had detected in her voice when she telephoned me, and I imagined she had new lines about her mouth. But her welcome was warm.

"How are you, Miranda?" she asked when she had kissed us both. "I've worried about you."

"Ninety-nine per cent fit," I assured her. "Chris has been a good stand-in for Matthieu. I don't know what I should have done without him."

"He's quite a guy," she said, grinning at him. "If I hadn't known he was booked, I might have tried to steal him from you."

"But you are promised to another," I joked. Chris had gone to the bar for drinks.

"Not any more." Her mouth tightened, the lines reappeared. "Matthieu and I are splitting up. It's no damn good, Miranda. When it comes to the pinch he won't leave this wife of his. It's the worst kind of hold – illness. She suffers from rheumatoid arthritis. At first there were very occasional bouts, but it's taken a turn for the worse recently. Sometimes she's in a wheelchair." I looked at her, saw her eyes widen and swim in tears. "Damn, damn, damn," she said. "I told myself there was to be no more crying."

"You've told him?"

"Yes, I wrote him a long letter. I knew I couldn't go through with it face to face. This is a goodbye meal, four friends together."

"But we'll go at once! This is ridiculous."

"No, no!" She was fierce. "I told you when I called it would be easier if you were there. I'd cry and he'd comfort me and we would be back where we started. I'm going home. I've booked a flight for next week. Back to dear old Missouri. I think I've still time to get me a nice man and rear some kids . . ."

Chris came back with the drinks. "Have you told Ellen about the latest happening?" he said. He set them down in front of us.

"No." The tragedy of Luc Devreux's death had taken second place for a moment in my mind to Ellen's news.

"What's this?" she said, looking almost relieved that the subject had been changed.

"Luc's body was found in the *gariotte* in my garden. Strangled." I couldn't bring myself to say that it was possibly a whip thong that had been used.

"Rick Gillam! It must have been, the miserable bastard!" She put her hand to her mouth. "But how on earth . . . ?"

"My theory is," Chris said, "that Gillam had been hiding in the Causse with this lad, and he persuaded him, or pretended to persuade him, to go through Miranda's garden as a short-cut to his house." I looked at him. I hadn't thought of that.

"And it was a ruse." Ellen was absorbed. "He meant to kill him."

Chris nodded. "Could have been. He would get it out of the lad that he had spilled the beans to Miranda about having seen them both in the pool the night before Chloë was found. In any case, Gillam confessed that night he broke into Miranda's house. When he was apprehended."

214

My eyes met Ellen's, saw the sympathy there. "I think Chris is right," I said. "I wondered at first how he could have got Luc's body into the *gariotte*, but I see it now. He wouldn't have killed him until they had reached it. He might have made some excuse to stop, even to look inside it – yes, that would be better – and then he would throw the whip thong round his neck from behind and strangle him, then push his body under the brambles."

"My God!" Ellen's voice shook. "If you're right, he's really evil, that guy. Did *you* discover the body?" She looked from Chris to me.

"No," Chris said, "we were spared that, although we were looking on. We had asked an official from the Mairie to call that morning to investigate if the *gariotte* covered an *aven* as Miranda suspected. It was this man, along with his assistant, who found she had been right. We were with them. It was terrible."

Matthieu Pinard was suddenly there in the booth. He ignored us, going straight to Ellen. "It is impossible," he said. He had his hand on her arm, his voice low, entreating, "Ellen, you know you can't do this to me." His face was white, drawn, that of an older man. Ellen shook herself free.

"Don't be rude," she said. "Chris and Miranda are here." He turned and bowed, muttering something. "And sit down." She was treating him like a child in her classroom. "They have something to tell you." He stood stock still, breathing heavily, and then, in an obvious effort to behave normally, he sat down on the vacant chair.

"Is it about Luc Devreux?" he said, "Yes, I've heard. The wheels are set in motion already." He looked at me. "The police want you to lodge a complaint about Gillam's attack on you." And then, like a doctor, "I hope you're feeling better now."

"Yes, I'm all right, and I've decided not to lodge a complaint. He'll get his comeuppance more than ever now, without me. Do you think he's responsible for Luc Devreux too?"

"Assuredly. The fingerprint experts are busy now." He smiled bleakly, "Perhaps they'll say in the end he's mad rather than bad."

I decided to be honest. "Matthieu, Ellen asked us to join you, but I don't feel comfortable about that. Chris and I will have a drink with you and then we'll set off for Meloir. We're leaving tomorrow."

"Are you? *Je suis très, très desolé.*" His eyes went to Ellen again. "This is stupid, Ellen. You know we have to talk."

"No more talk." She held up her hand, "It's finished." She turned a ravaged face to Chris. "Could you get him a drink, please?"

"What would you like?" Chris asked him.

"*Rien.*" He waved his hand, looking utterly miserable. "Sorry, anything . . . *alors, un cognac, merci.*" He hardly looked at Chris. His eyes were still on Ellen. "This is so cruel."

"Well, you know the old saying," she made a poor attempt at flippancy, "you have to be cruel to be kind."

"But she'll get better again. It's just a setback." His voice was a rasp and he coughed to clear it. "And then you and I will be back where we were, and perhaps this time . . ."

"No," Ellen said, "it's taken me three years to be able to say that. And I don't know how many setbacks. Nor how many assurances from you that she was getting better." She looked up. "Here's your drink." Chris had come back.

"Have that, Matthieu," he said, "it will do you good."

"*Merci.*" He lifted the glass, put it down again and turned to me. "You shan't be sorry to leave Meloir?" He was making an effort to be normal. "You've had a terrible time since you arrived."

"Terrible," I smiled at him, "but yet sometimes the sheer beauty of the place takes me by the throat, can you understand? Oh, I'll be back in France, but . . ." I saw he had taken a sip of cognac while I spoke. "Of course, I may have to return to Meloir because of the *aven* . . . in the *gariotte*, remember? I've given my permission to the authorities to excavate, if necessary." I hadn't held his attention. His eyes had gone again to Ellen. I looked at Chris. "Have you finished?"

He nodded. "Ready when you are."

"Then we'll say goodbye for the present," I said.

Chris downed the last of his wine and stood up.

"Of course we'll keep in touch." I spoke to both of them. I stood up too. "Perhaps next time will be happier." I didn't see how it could, but there was no harm in saying it.

"Good luck," Chris said. I repeated it. I didn't kiss Ellen – I knew I would burst into tears – but we shook hands formally with both of them.

"And you and I must keep in touch," I said to Ellen.

"Wait!" She got to her feet hurriedly, gathering up her handbag and jacket. "I'm coming with you."

"Don't be silly," I said, trying to be light about it.

"We've hardly spoken!" Matthieu said. "Please Ellen . . ." He half rose.

"It's all in the letter." She was suddenly weeping. "Don't make it more difficult for me."

Matthieu went to her and took her in his arms. She was slight, and she seemed to disappear into them. The sight was infinitely touching. I thought: they're so suited. I met Chris's eyes, and we walked out of the booth. Everything was blurred for me.

We were standing dithering at the door when Ellen joined us. "Well, that's it," she said, "I've done it. I needed you." Her smile was a grimace. "But you've left him sitting there alone!" I said.

"It's usually the other way round. The times I've waited for him . . . well, it's over now. Come along."

We walked with her to her car. I kissed her this time. She was weeping. Her face was a river of tears.

"You do see it's the only way," she said.

"Let Chris and I drive you home. You can collect your car tomorrow."

"No, thanks. I've got to get used to this." She got in, rummaged for her keys in her handbag, inserted one in the lock. We watched, feeling useless. The face she turned to us was a pale blur in the dusk. She lowered the window and smiled. "You guys take care," she said, "and thanks for everything." She had started the engine as she spoke. She put the car into gear and drove away.

We didn't speak when we were in our own car. Chris was busy finding his way back over the Pont Valentré and then along the crowded Boulevard Gambetta. When the road was quieter he said, "We should have insisted on driving her home."

"No, she had to be alone." I couldn't rid myself of the image of her ruined face.

"I wonder if that poor guy is sitting in the restaurant getting stoned?"

"With all his moral rectitude? Not a chance."

"You sound disapproving."

"I don't know what I am. The situation was hopeless from the beginning. But it takes a heartless kind of man, or woman, to turn their back on someone who is ill, who needs them."

"They were both sensible enough to know that even their love couldn't cope with that kind of guilt."

"She was. What would you have done?"

"God knows. Ben, at least, made the way clear for me, dying . . ."

"Crude."

"It was worse. Cheap. But I think Ellen did the only sensible thing, clearing out. She couldn't fight it. Matthieu's wife had the Pope on her side."

We stopped halfway at a roadside café and had something to eat because we were both starving. Emotion seems to do that to you. I looked at Chris over the plastic tablecloth. "I'm lucky," I said, "with you."

"There are strings to me too. Sophie and Jon . . ."

"These aren't strings," I said, "they're an added enticement."

We drove home sadly, afraid to be happy in view of the monumental unhappiness we had witnessed.

This is a coda because the story stops here. There are imponderables in it, but then all stories have that.

Rick Gillam was convicted of two murders, his wife's and Luc's, and Ellen is still in Missouri.

She has taken a teaching post there and is being married soon to another teacher on the staff. I hope it's not on the rebound; she says not. She wrote, 'Mom always said, "Take a cat of your own kind", and there's a lot of truth in that. Greg and I have the same background. There was something exotic to me about Matthieu, and perhaps there was an added element of danger in flouting conventions, an added attraction. We write occasionally. He is still with his wife. Sometimes she is well, other times not. It's his problem.

'Greg is slower, a straight as a die kind of guy. We share a lot of interests: French (he's into the Cajun thing), taking the kids at school to summer camp. Perhaps the magic will come . . .' Rick Gillam had magic too, I remembered. Look where that got him.

After a few months I had a letter from Monsieur Duart, telling me that they had taken borings for twenty yards when they had come up against a solid mass of limestone which they estimated went as far as the river. There was little or no possibility of a tunnel opening into a cave, but the exploration had given them some valuable information about the terrain. I would be amply compensated for any damage to my property. There was a handwritten postscript signed 'Marvel Duart' saying that if I thought of selling he would be interested. I remembered him gazing at the mountains.

I think I'll sell. I'm expecting a baby soon. Sophie is thrilled at the thought of a sister (I know the sex already), and for a year or so Chris and I won't be doing much travelling.

I'm still at the British Museum and so is Chris. He is collaborating with me on my book, and we're hoping to publish it soon. There were a lot of stresses and interruptions to it while I was researching around Meloir, but I think in a strange way it has given the book an added depth.

We think St Cirque Lapopie might be an appropriate place to buy our next house. I got the idea for writing about Raymond and his cohorts on that long ago summer afternoon when I sat with Chloë gazing at the remains of the château.

We went back to the area around Meloir for some necessary detail before the proofs, and we went to the churchyard to see Ben's grave. I said I wanted his blessing for the coming baby, and Chris said, '*Bonne idée!*' We didn't go into the village. I couldn't face it. Too many memories. Chloë . . . that's how the story began. Sometimes in my dreams she still stretches out her arms to me, and it breaks my heart that I was too late to help her . . . and that Luc, that gentle soul, became embroiled in the tragedy.